Geoffrey Simmons, M. D., is a physician novelist specializing in internal medicine and exciting thrillers. He is the author of THE ADAM EXPERIMENT and THE Z-PAPERS.

THE Z-PAPERS

"A fresh, original and wholly authentic novel of medical detection . . . truly an astonishing achievement."
  —Gerald Browne, *author of* 11 HARROWHOUSE

"The M. D. author knows his stuff."
                                —KIRKUS REVIEWS

THE ADAM EXPERIMENT

"Realistic medical details add an extra dimension!"
                                —Houston CHRONICLE

"Exciting! . . . does a better job than Crichton."
                                —Baton Rouge SUNDAY ADVOCATE

Berkley books by Geoffrey Simmons

THE ADAM EXPERIMENT
PANDEMIC

PANDEMIC

GEOFFREY SIMMONS

BERKLEY BOOKS, NEW YORK

This Berkley book contains the complete
text of the original hardcover edition.
It has been completely reset in a type face
designed for easy reading, and was printed
from new film.

PANDEMIC

A Berkley Book / published by arrangement with
Arbor House Publishing Company

PRINTING HISTORY
Arbor House edition / September 1980
Berkley edition / October 1981

ISBN: 0-425-05062-9

A BERKLEY BOOK ® TM 757,375
Berkley Books are published by Berkley Publishing Corporation,
200 Madison Avenue, New York, New York 10016.
PRINTED IN THE UNITED STATES OF AMERICA

To Cathy

"Microbes will have the last word."
— LOUIS PASTEUR

CHAPTER ONE

By 4:00 A.M., the Mathesson household was alive with activity. The noise and lighted windows made it seem like early evening, but the surrounding neighborhood was silent and dark, enveloped in a shroud of heavy fog that the streetlights barely penetrated. Working outside in the driveway, Gordon Mathesson, a burly man with salty gray hair, was forcing some extra blankets into an already cramped compartment inside their recreational vehicle. His wife, a thin woman with her hair up in a bun, had been doing some last-minute cleaning in the kitchen, and now she opened the screen door and called to him.

"Did you take the potato chips?" she asked. Her voice echoed through the neighborhood and set off barking in the distance.

"Potato chips?" Gordon Mathesson muttered, struggling with a stack of loose tent poles to make room for the blankets. "I can't get these damn blankets in here and she's all hot and bothered about potato chips. Who's going to care about potato chips if they're freezin' their asses off?" Each time he pushed one pole aside, another came tumbling out on his head.

"What's that, honey?" she called out again, hearing a few muffled words. "I can't find them anywhere. I thought maybe you already took them out to the van. You know how much the kids like them." By now several dogs were barking.

"No, damn it, I don't have them," he answered as he finally got the blankets inside the compartment and closed the door. His voice had a slight crack to it and as he turned, he felt a sharp pain shoot up from his shoulder blades to the base of his neck. It only lasted a second or two, but it had been painful enough to bring him to a surprised halt. The pain left as quickly as it had come, however, and assuming that it must have been some type of muscular spasm, he went on with his last-minute checks.

"That's strange," came his wife's voice again. "I thought I put them on the table with everything else. Are you sure they're not already out there?"

"No, Harriet, I haven't seen them. None of the food's been loaded yet. If they're all that important, we'll buy more on the road." The exaggerated patience in his voice was not lost on Harriet Mathesson. She watched him for a moment from the screen door as he continued packing the van, then she shook her head and turned back to her own chores.

The large white van was the type that dealers placed in the "medium price range"—four times the cost of an average automobile but barely half the price of the top-of-the-line model. Inside, it had most of the conveniences but few of the luxuries: a toilet and shower, but no bathtub; a gas stove with two burners instead of four and no oven; and a dining table tucked away under one of the two beds that doubled as padded benches during the daytime. They had owned it for ten years, and when the kids were smaller it had been perfect. Now quarters were cramped.

Gordon Mathesson had hoped to be on the road by

five or five-thirty at the latest. He wanted to beat the morning rush-hour traffic going into central Los Angeles but his plans were only wishful thinking. The Mathesson family had never gotten off on time for anything in the past and he suspected this morning would be no different. When he went inside to join his family for breakfast he found them running true to form.

Jamey, their blondish, often mischievous seven-year-old, couldn't find his air gun, couldn't decide which fishing rod he preferred, dallied at the breakfast table as if he were already full, and then, with his excitement over the trip, suddenly developed the runs. Now, time was lost just waiting for the boy's stomach to calm down.

The middle child was a ten-year-old by the name of Lynda, a curly-haired brunette who'd been suffering from a cold for the past two days and now dragged at everything she did. Through a hacking cough and runny eyes she slowly dressed and at breakfast spent more time blowing her nose than eating her toast. Had she been running a fever, Harriet Mathesson might have vetoed the trip, but the thermometer barely measured ninety-eight degrees and she checked the girl's temperature twice to be sure. With prodding she slowly made her way to the van.

Marcey, at sixteen, was the oldest child and to her this trip was little better than punishment. She didn't want to go and had made her feelings clear from the first day the Mathessons had begun making vacation plans. There was too much she would be missing at home —parties, friends, and, in particular, a cute football player who had just begun to notice her. Two days ago he had called for a date and Marcey had regretfully told him that she and her family were "going off to some stupid place in the woods." Now, at breakfast, she made one last effort, arguing that vacations were for relaxing and that she would be more relaxed at home.

She was old enough to make her own decisions, she insisted, but her father silenced her by threatening to "drag her by the ears" if she didn't come willingly. Visibly upset, she grudgingly left the table to finish packing her clothes, hoping all the while that something unusual might happen and prevent the trip.

Her wish didn't come true and finally Gordon Mathesson backed the cumbersome van out of his driveway, a good hour later than he had hoped, and started north through Long Beach en route to Yosemite National Park. When he reached the Interstate, the lanes were already crowded—just what he had wanted to avoid. He had wanted to be deep in the San Fernando Valley by this time and headed in the direction opposite the flow of commuters. Instead, he was stuck in the middle of heavy, slow-moving traffic and despising every minute of it.

Although he rarely displayed his temper around the children, this morning it was readily apparent. Jamey's jumping about in the back and Lynda's coughing only added to his irritation, and the first time that Marcey complained about coming along he responded with an outburst of profanity that shocked his family into silence. Not another word was spoken for several minutes afterward. They silently stared out of their respective windows, and none of them noticed when Gordon suddenly winced with another lightning-quick pain in his back.

When they reached the outskirts of Los Angeles, the sun was coming up and the skies above looked clear.

"I bet it'll be a nice day in Yosemite too," Harriet finally remarked, hoping to get her husband into a pleasant mood.

"That's if we ever get there," he snapped, glaring at a Cadillac that had just cut him off and slowed to a snail's pace directly in front of them. "Com' on, you son of a bitch! If you can afford to drive a Caddy, you can afford to keep up with traffic," he yelled, but his voice tapered off in hoarseness.

"You're not getting sick, are you?" Harriet asked, reaching across to feel his forehead and finding her hand quickly pushed away.

"Just these goddamn fumes," he muttered.

"Are you sure?" she asked. This wasn't like him.

"Of course, I'm sure!"

As they traveled north, more and more cars converged on the Interstate. Soon, all four lanes going north were filled to capacity, moving at less than ten miles an hour in a stop-and-go pace that only intensified Gordon Mathesson's outbursts.

During the first half hour of their trip, his wife ascribed his irritability to his fatigue from the long hours he'd been working to get ready for this vacation and to his recent depression over his job. But once the sun was well above the horizon and lit up the interior of their cab, she noticed some red spots on his face. "You know, if I didn't know better, I'd think you were getting the measles." Her tone was light, reflecting little of the concern she really felt.

"Measles?" He laughed. "I must have had them three times as a kid. Old Doc Conally said it could never happen again."

"Then it must be something else. There's definitely a rash, and you're not acting like yourself. I've never seen you so irritable, Gordon . . . I think we'd best go back home and have you looked at. We can go on this trip another time. We can even leave tomorrow if there's nothing to worry about."

Marcey was all ears during this exchange, but her sudden hope that they might be going home quickly faded.

"No chance! There's no way I'll sit through this traffic all over again. We're in it and we'll stay until we're out. There'll be doctors up there. *If* I need one."

Harriet Mathesson stared at her husband for several minutes. There was no question that something was wrong. It wasn't just the rash or his behavior that bothered her. His color was poor and there were dark bags under his eyes. He was drenched in sweat when everyone else appeared comfortable. She'd never seen him look so badly before.

As the van approached the downtown area and cars began cutting across three and four lanes at a time to make their exits, he began to have trouble navigating. He would drift out of the lane and then swerve back, jam on his brakes when he didn't need to and on several occasions he cut people off as they were turning. He seemed to be squinting now, his wife noticed, and after a very close call with another recreational vehicle she resumed her pleas.

"I think we should stop and go back," she said, not wanting to scare the children and yet alarmed enough to express herself firmly. "You have to see a doctor."

"It can wait," he said, looking straight ahead. "I'm just getting a cold, probably Lynda's."

"I don't think so," she said. "Rashes don't happen with colds, and the way you're driving you're going to get us into an accident. She thought of her sister's home in Pasadena. "Why don't you stop at Ann's house? It's almost on the way."

Mr. Mathesson, still squinting at the crowded road ahead, said nothing.

"I can't believe you're being like this, Gordon. Whenever one of the kids is sick, you race them off to the pediatrician."

He remained silent, not even cursing at the other drivers now, but his driving continued to be erratic, even after they had passed through the downtown area and traffic had lessened. The increased room and speed only gave him more room to swerve. He had trouble staying in his lane and when he skirted the embankment, Mrs. Mathesson began to get frightened.

"You've got to listen to me!" she cried out, but her husband's eyes remained glued to the windshield and he gave no sign of having heard her.

"Honey, you don't realize how sick you are," she

said, trying to calm herself. One way or another she had to get him to listen. "Can't you see that you're going to get us into an accident? Please let me drive. Just pull over and you can go into the back and lie down."

"Daddy, let mommy drive," Marcey urged from behind.

"I'm . . . not . . . sick," he said, the words coming haltingly. He turned toward his wife and started to add something, but his mouth wouldn't open. Suddenly his eyes rolled back into his head and he slumped forward. An instant later, the van went out of control as the weight of his body drew the steering wheel sharply to one side. The children screamed as they were thrown across the back of the van, and Harriet grabbed desperately for the steering wheel, acting purely on impulse. Outside, cars and trucks were backing off, horns blaring, as the van wildly traversed four lanes and then veered back again, when Mrs. Mathesson tried to move her husband away from the wheel.

"Marcey, pull daddy back from the steering wheel!" she called out. The teenager struggled forward and tried pulling her father's shoulders back. Working together, they were able to free the steering wheel, but it was impossible to get him out of the seat.

With more room to move, she tried reaching the brakes while keeping the van on the highway, but her husband's legs were in the way. Instead she grabbed the emergency brake and pulled with all her strength. The van came to a screeching halt two hundred yards down the Interstate. By then her husband was waking, but he remained groggy and disoriented. After the children helped her pull him into the back, she quickly got into the driver's seat and headed for the next exit.

She wanted to get her husband home as quickly as possible, but as she circled back over a cloverleaf into the southbound lanes she found herself deep in rush-hour traffic. She took the Hollywood Freeway, hoping to skirt the downtown congestion, but found the jam-up there just as bad. Her nerves were frayed. She knew that this was a time she had to maintain control, but she wasn't sure she could. In the back, Gordon had begun retching in deep, almost convulsive heaves.

"Momma, he needs a doctor!" Marcey called out, anxiously searching for a bowl or a towel.

"I know, I know!" Harriet said, her eyes searching the road ahead for an answer. A moment later she spotted the blue and white *H* sign indicating that there was a hospital somewhere off the next exit.

The hospital turned out to be the University of Southern California—Los Angeles County Medical Center, a mammoth, eighteen-story building that stood on a hill and dominated most of the east side of downtown. She was reluctant to take him to a county hospital—too many gruesome stories—but she didn't know what else to do. The Los Angeles area was foreign to her and it was obvious that her husband needed prompt medical attention.

Following a series of signs, she found herself in a maze of narrow streets with all kinds of confusing signs . . . the Women's Hospital . . . the Contagious Disease Unit . . . the Children's Division . . . the Nurses' Dormitory, the Psychiatric Unit—there it was, the Main Emergency Room. She began looking for the emergency room doors, but she had to drive up a winding hill and back down again before she found the ambulance loading docks.

"You can't park here," a neatly uniformed black orderly called out and pointed toward a distant parking lot.

"I can't leave," she responded, studying the available slots. She had to squeeze in somewhere.

The orderly came over to her van to direct her to the visitor's lot, but she interrupted him mid-sentence.

"I can't go there . . . my husband's too sick . . . I need someone to look at him right away." Her voice trembled but she was not about to leave.

"Is it a heart attack?" the orderly asked, peering through her window toward the back. "Is he having chest pains, trouble breathing?"

"No, I don't know what it is. He had a rash . . ." She began to describe the sequence of events but stopped when she heard the commotion in the back of the van. Behind her, Gordon was having another seizure. The children were struggling to hold him down, but his arms and legs began jerking back and forth, his back arched upward and blood began spewing from his bitten tongue. "Oh, my God! We've got to stop this!" she screamed out.

"Calm down, ma'am," the orderly said, and hurried to the other side of the van. As he opened the door, he called to a nearby nurse. "Bring a tongue blade. Looks like we've got an epileptic in here."

Once inside, he helped the children subdue their father, but it was difficult. A few seconds later, the nurse had joined them and helped shove a tongue blade into his mouth. Outside, a stretcher was raced to them, and running behind was an intern carrying his black bag.

At the moment the younger physician stepped inside, the seizure stopped and Gordon Mathesson lay limply on the floor. Then as the physician started his examination, his eyes found what was now a purplish rash that covered most of the man's face and both arms. "Stand back!" he ordered the others in the van, moving away himself even as he spoke and then turning to Harriet to ask how long her husband had been ill.

"Just today as far as I know. Just this morning," she answered. She quickly related how irritable he'd been, how she had noticed the red spots and how erratic his driving had become. "What is it? What do you think he's got?" she asked, desperate for an answer.

"I don't know for sure yet, but I think you'd better take him directly to the Contagious Disease Unit just to be on the safe side."

"Can't you take care of him here?" she asked, reluctant to move. She remembered seeing a sign for that unit, but it seemed like miles away.

"We can't take care of his problem here. Listen to me, they're just down the hill. It'll take you five seconds to get there. We'll call and tell them you're coming. And don't let anyone go near him unless they're protected."

"Protected how? From what?"

"They'll be wearing gowns and masks . . . they'll tell you when you get there. You'd better get started before he has another seizure," the intern urged her. He escorted her around to the driver's side and then ran off to phone the Contagious Disease Unit.

As the medical personnel climbed out of the van and closed the door, the original orderly came around to the driver's side to reassure her and give her directions.

"I don't think I can drive another foot," she cried, fumbling to fit the key in the ignition.

"Of course you can. You have to." He explained how she merely needed to retrace her steps and follow the signs.

As she backed out, she kept repeating the instructions in her mind. The distance was only three blocks, but the short trip seemed to take forever. Her fear heightened her awareness of the sounds from her husband. Every labored breath seemed like his last. Any twitch seemed like another seizure. If something happened on the way, they'd be helpless. Why hadn't the nurse come with them? She knew she had to remain calm for everyone's sake, but she couldn't. Somehow, she managed to find her way, however, and as she drove up to the five-story building at the foot of the hill, three gowned, gloved and masked people were waiting with a stretcher.

CHAPTER TWO

As the Mathesson van was pulling up in front of the Contagious Disease Unit, which was actually two floors of the pediatric building, the chief of the department, Dr. Michael Ogden, parked his burgundy BMW in an adjoining lot and went inside through a private entrance. He was tense and in a hurry.

Under normal circumstances, his daily routine would take him first to the admitting area to check the book on all admissions to his unit, then to his office to drop off his briefcase and grab a white coat, and lastly to the cafeteria for a breakfast conference to discuss all of the new cases with the interns and residents on the unit. There were twelve trainees altogether, and he used the breakfast conferences to both supervise their patient-care plans and do some teaching. This morning, however, he had to forego those responsibilities and let Dr. Lester Paige, his assistant chief, take charge. Although his second in command was quite competent, Ogden felt a bit remiss in not going himself. He had always been the compulsive type, a textbook Type-A personality, and at the back of his mind was always the worry—an irrational worry, he realized—that something might go wrong if he did not personally supervise every case.

Instead, the thirty-five-year-old physician was scheduled to demonstrate his research project to a group of scientists from Atlanta who were partly responsible for allocating federal research grants. Ogden's request this year was sizeable, a fraction over a half million dollars, and his previous grant was only two weeks from termination. He didn't think they would turn him down. In fact, he was sure they wouldn't, but there was a chance that they might try trimming it back and that was something he could not afford now. He actually needed more and was asking the minimum necessary to continue his work.

The scientist in charge of the four-man group from Atlanta was Dr. Sidney Bellows, director of the Center for Disease Control. Bellows was an old mentor of Ogden's, but that relationship carried very little weight in the business at hand. The old man was just as demanding of his ex-students as he was of strangers, maybe more so at times, and it would only be detrimental if Bellows and the others felt that Ogden expected any special favors. In essence, the experiment had to come off without a hitch. It had to be clear, precise, accurate and reproducible. Ogden knew that he could meet the requirements. He just had to prove it, right now, while the four of them watched.

The scientists had flown in the night before from San Francisco and were slated to return to Atlanta on a noon flight. "Ample time," Bellows had said when Ogden complained about the brevity of their stay. "We've already reviewed your data, studied the slides, and we only want to see the tumorophillic stage."

To Ogden, however, the five hours didn't seem ample at all. He'd spent five years on the project, and two months in preparation just for the demonstration. The least they could have done, he thought, was come in the afternoon before and spend the evening together over dinner, but—typically Bellows—this trip was entirely business. Ogden did not want to try to make it seem like anything else.

When Ogden arrived at his office, the door was locked. It would be another hour before his secretary would arrive. He let himself in and stuffed his briefcase in a corner next to the filing cabinets, then donned a long white coat whose right cuff was fraying. He started to take another, but found the pocket inkstained and spotted with blood. Despite all of the extensive advanced preparations, he'd forgotten to tend to the most obvious, and it was too late to go home to get another white coat. He quickly snipped the loose threads with a scissors and then stepped into his private bathroom to check his tie and hair. The face in the mirror was not the same one he had seen when he worked with Bellows. His hairline had receded (much more obvious to him than to his associates), there were gray streaks in his black hair and a few wrinkles of age beneath tired looking blue eyes. Inside he still felt like a twenty-five-year-old, but the external casing was, no use denying it, someone older. He quickly brushed his hair back and hurried out. It was five minutes to seven and he was expected in the laboratory at exactly seven.

Dr. Ogden was the youngest head of any department in the County Hospital, but his credentials were considerably more impressive than most and he'd earned the position by achievement rather than seniority. By the age of twenty-three he had earned simultaneous doctorate degrees in microbiology and medicine from Harvard Medical School. After taking specialty training in infectious diseases there, he had joined the World Health Organization in Geneva, participating in their "fire fighting crews" (medical teams that took off on a moment's notice to fight epidemics anywhere in the world) and then done research at the Center for Disease Control for the next three years. His special area of study was in altering the nucleoprotein within the nucleus of bacterial cells to curtail the spread of certain diseases.

Outwardly, Ogden was a very serious person, not likely to joke, and usually quiet—except when teaching. During those times, he loved to talk. He could spend hours discussing an esoteric point if others were willing to listen, and they usually were. There was a quiet self-assurance about him that promoted confidence in patients as well as colleagues, but left no doubt that he was the chief. Like the captain of a ship, he took command. Very little ever escaped his attention, and anything that went wrong was immediately corrected if humanly possible. In his department, incompetence was not tolerated and indolence was unheard of. When residents elected to take a rotation on Contagious Disease, or C. D. as they called it, they knew that the hours would be easy but the chief's expectations extremely high. Every case had to be thoroughly investigated before any treatment was initiated.

Ogden's hardnosed exterior, however, contrasted sharply with the inner person, a sensitive man who had been widowed by a car accident two months after his only son was born. That was seven years ago, but to him it was yesterday. Karen had died a long and painful death with multiple fractures, a collapsed lung and kidney failure from shock, and she remained awake almost to the end. Most people thought that he was divorced, like so many other professional men, and he left it at that. To discuss his past would be to relive it. Instead, he dedicated himself to his work, and his son, Peter. There were many evenings when he would come home to have dinner with Peter, and then drive back to the hospital after the boy went to sleep. There were women, of course, but he always maintained an emotional distance from them. He'd had his love and lost it and didn't want to take a chance that it might happen again.

The infectious disease research laboratory was situated in a separate building across a parking lot. When he arrived, he was told that the four scientists were already inside the experimental area. He'd hoped to give them an introductory synopsis, but instead quickly changed into clothes that resembled surgical garb, loose-fitting green pants that tied at the waist and a pullover V-necked shirt. He moved to a second room where he scrubbed his hands in a large metal sink . . . Betadine, alcohol, then Betadine again. Before leaving he put on a white nylon suit that covered him entirely except for a Plexiglas face mask and an air filter beneath it.

Dr. Tom Ling, his research associate, was waiting for him in the preparation room.

"I see everyone's inside already," Ogden observed.

"Picked them up at their hotel an hour ago. Started them on the quick tour but Dr. Bellows insisted on going inside. He said you'd be on time. I guess he knows you from before."

Ogden smiled beneath his mask. "I hope it's a good show. Are the stars ready?" he asked, referring to a species of bacteria called *Bacteroides*.

"They're all labeled. I double-checked them last night," Ling answered as he crossed the room and opened a large metal incubator whose outside was marked with the three radiation-warning triangles. He carefully removed a test tube rack that held a lead tube in its center and carried it back toward Ogden. "My count indicates that two million bugs have picked up the radioactive marker. That should be enough, don't you think?"

Ogden nodded. Two million was twice the number of bacteria they normally used, but, of course, this was hardly one of their normal experiments and they had best increase the count to be safe.

Ogden took the rack from Ling and the two men started toward the amphitheater. As they entered, the electric doors parted and revealed a group of white-uniformed technicians working around an anesthetized Dalmatian that was lying on its side on an operating table. Standing behind them and closely watching everything that transpired were four men in nylon suits and masks.

Ogden addressed the tallest, certain that he must be Bellows. "I hope this isn't too early for you." Bellows was stooped in the same way he had always been when watching a procedure, gawking almost, with his hands clasped behind his back.

"No, not at all," Bellows responded with his distinct Boston accent. "But I must confess that this is one of the reasons I never became a surgeon. They seem to enjoy these ridiculous hours." He turned toward the other three scientists and introduced them to Ogden. Kleinfeldt, Christopher, Ruben . . . the names were familiar, almost a Who's Who of microbiology, but in the all-encompassing white suits these men could have been anyone.

Ogden acknowledged the introductions and then checked the dog to be sure it was properly anesthetized. The vital-sign sheet indicated that the animal's blood pressure, pulse and temperature were all stable.

"Those are the dog's X-rays," Ogden said, pointing toward a row of viewing boxes. He set the test tube rack down and a technician flipped on the bright lights behind the panels. "As you can see, we've created three tumors of the fibroblastic type. The first was in his lungs, but it has metastasized to two other spots." Ogden walked to the viewing boxes and pointed first to the apex of the dog's right lung, where a small coin-sized lesion sat, and then to the neck and brain films where a smaller tumor could be seen. "Obviously malignant," he said, adding, "and unquestionably terminal."

"Terminal unless treated by your protocol, correct?" Bellows inserted.

"Yes, but I should point out that this is a tumor that we've designed. In a sense, everything about it is man-made and its behavior may be considerably different than human tumors."

"Understood, but it's still a cancer and it'll be interesting to see what happens," Kleinfeldt said through his mask.

Ogden returned to the center of the room and pointed out an X-ray machine with a large, gridded screen suspended over the dog's body. "With this we'll be able to watch the dog's internal organs." He flipped a switch and an oversized television screen lit up on the opposite wall. On it, the dog's outline framed the pulsating, moving organs within. "This is where my suicide squad will go," Ogden said as he stepped to the large screen and marked in grease pencil the spots where the tumor had been shown on X-ray.

"Suicide squad?" Dr. Ruben asked.

"To locate and attack the tumor is one thing, but to leave the bugs inside their host without killing them would probably be just as dangerous as leaving the malignancy alone. So my bugs, unfortunately, have to die after they've penetrated their target."

According to Ogden's theory, the *Bacteroides* species, unlike other bacteria, could only survive in tissues with low oxygen levels such as these tumors maintained, and would therefore seek out the tumors in preference over other tissues of the dog's body. It was a natural affinity and one that Ogden expected to capitalize on. Once these organisms had situated themselves inside the malignant growths, they would form abscesses that would kill the tumor cells. Then the dog would be treated with antibiotics. It was a simple theory and thus far had been borne out experimentally.

After answering a few technical questions, Ogden took a 20-cc syringe and drew up a cloudy, yellowish fluid from the shielded metal test tube. After changing needles on the syringe, he injected the radioactive material into an intravenous line that had been placed in the dog's hind leg.

"If you look at the screen, you can see the radioactive tracer entering the dog's leg." Ogden emptied the contents of the syringe into the intravenous tubing and flushed it through with another fluid. On the screen, they could see a gray haze flowing through a major vein in the dog's leg and entering his pelvic area.

Over the next half hour, the scientists watched the tracer slowly move up through the dog's major veins to the right side of his heart. From there it shot out into the lungs in a broad mist and recirculated back to the left side of the heart, leaving a small spot where Ogden had marked the first tumor. After the tracer reaccumulated in the left side of the heart, it shot out again, this time outlining all of the major arteries, organs and extremities. The radioactive tracer then regrouped and worked its way back to the right side of the heart again, repeating itself eighty times a minute. With each pass more and more radioactive bacteria stayed behind at the three tumor sites until finally they were the only places in the dog's body that were radioactive. "Just as your protocol says," Bellows remarked.

Kleinfeldt asked if the bacteria themselves killed the tumor cells.

"No, only the inflammation created by the abscess. The bacteria don't affect the cancer cells directly. Of course, the infection will be bad enough, but with this kind of treatment the dog's future is considerably less bleak."

"Until you autopsy him, anyway," Bellows said.

The hospital intercom sounded out over the cafeteria, cutting through the noise in the crowded room. "Dr. Yates, come to admitting, stat! Dr. Yates, report to admitting, stat!"

The breakfast conference had just begun, and Dr. Joanna Yates, a tall resident with closely cropped dark hair, had just lit up a cigarette to go with her morning coffee. "Damn!" she muttered as she stubbed out the cigarette in an ashtray. Turning toward the bearded intern next to her, Dr. James, she said, "You'd better come along too. Who knows what they've brought in. I may need some help."

At the far end of the long table was Ogden's assistant chief, Lester Paige, distinguished from the white-coated residents and interns by his three-piece suit and the Phi Beta Kappa key that dangled from its gold tie chain. He had been discussing a newly admitted case of hepatitis with them and running through a list of possible causes when the page had sounded. As Yates and James got up to leave he gave them a sympathetic look and told them he would review the new cases with them later.

In the corridor, Joanna Yates complained about her luck. "Every damn time *we* come on duty there's an emergency right off the bat. Just one day I'd like to get our scut work over with first." The intern smiled behind his straggly mustache. The two doctors were on call for admitting for a period of twenty-four hours every six days. It was hardly taxing, but there was always a lot of scut work—the painstaking follow-up on previously admitted patients—that had to be done in the wards in the morning and Joanna liked to get it out of the way first. If they could, the day seemed more organized. She'd have less on her mind and be able to concentrate on new admissions. Despite her wishes, however, it rarely happened.

"What is it?" she asked the ward clerk seated behind the admitting desk. Her voice was gruff, but everyone who worked there knew that the woman doctor was always grumpy in the mornings.

The clerk's answer was quick and to the point. "The Main Emergency Room called two seconds before the patient arrived. We didn't even have time to page you until now. They said it was a case of possible meningitis and that he had a seizure up there. No meds were given."

The isolation room being used was only a few paces

away. Standing outside the door was a large open-faced cabinet where Yates and James grabbed gowns, gloves and masks—requirements for work around meningitis—before entering. Inside they found two aides and a nurse transferring the new patient from the stretcher onto a bed.

"Do you have any history?" Yates asked the nurse as she grabbed a trailing leg and helped move it onto the mattress.

"No, except . . ." The nurse repeated the same story relayed by the clerk and then added, "His wife's out in a recreational vehicle. I told her to come into the waiting room with her kids . . . the woman's panic-stricken."

"No doubt," Yates said, her tone sympathetic now. She moved to the head of the bed and began examining the semicomatose man. He seemed to be breathing on his own. She felt for a pulse in his neck . . . it was rapid but strong. When she touched his arm, he tried to pull away but didn't have enough strength. "Do we know his name yet?" Yates asked without looking up.

"Martinson, I think," came the nurse's hurried answer as she wrapped a blood pressure cuff around the man's left arm. "I didn't have time to get any details."

"Mr. Martinson!" Yates said loudly into the man's ear, but his eyes remained closed and his body motionless. She repeated the name twice, but there was no response.

"Blood pressure's 90 over 50, pulse is 120 and regular. Borderline shock," the nurse reported as she and the aides undressed him so that they could take a rectal temperature.

"He must be postictal," James said, suggesting that the patient's confusion was due to the seizure.

"I'm not so sure," Yates answered. She had already noticed the spots on his face, but as she watched the others undress him she was surprised to see the huge purplish splotches across his chest and abdomen. "Jesus," she blurted out. She tried to bend his neck forward, but found it to be stiff as a rod. "That's not just a case of meningitis, that's meningococcal meningitis." Suddenly there was an urgency to her actions. "Better get me five million units of penicillin stat, and push it . . . get me a spinal tray and an extra needle . . . and a stat CBC . . . tell the lab that we might have . . . no, that we definitely have a case of meningitis, and I want the results on his spinal fluid as fast as they can get them out."

The examining room was already equipped with spinal trays, and after handing one to Dr. James the nurse hurried off to get the penicillin. En route, she tossed her gown, gloves and mask into a special enclosed hamper and then scrubbed her hands. To return to the room, she would have to re-gown and re-glove.

The two aides and Dr. James helped roll the patient on his side and then into a ball, with knees brought up and neck flexed as far forward as possible. In this manner the vertebrae in his back would be spread farther apart and the needle could enter the spinal canal more easily.

"Hold him tight," Yates warned as she prepped a small area over the lower spine with an orange antiseptic solution. "I'm not going to bother deadening it. I doubt he can feel much of anything."

Yates placed her fingertips on two adjacent vertebrae, aimed between them and pushed the needle deep into muscle, but she hit bone instead of the spinal canal. She pulled back, reaimed and probed for a second time, but only found bone again. "Damn it, damn it, damn it." Time was critical here and she had missed twice, which was quite unlike her. Reconfirming her landmarks and telling James and the aides to ball him up a bit more, she aimed for the third time and slowly worked the needle inward until she felt the characteristic pop. A moment later, a yellowish fluid exuded from the needle's external tip.

"This stuff's solid pus." She sounded surprised, but

other than the intensity of the color it was exactly what she expected. "He must have had this for days."

"I don't think so," one of the aides said. "I heard his wife say that he just got sick today."

"She must be wrong," James said. "That fluid is way too thick."

Yates measured the pressure of the exuding fluid with a tall, thin tube that was marked in millimeters, noting that the fluid stopped rising at the upper limits of normal. She then collected three test tubes of fluid for the lab. "Those purple spots are called purpura," she told the others as the fluid slowly dripped into her glass containers. "Typical for meningococcal meningitis."

Meanwhile, the nurse returned and started an intravenous line in the patient's forearm. It was awkward with him lying on one side, but she freed one arm, tied a tourniquet around it, waited for a distal vein to bulge and then slipped a small-gauge needle into the blue pipe. After taping it in place, she injected the penicillin into the plastic line and washed it through.

"The textbook says that you have to give penicillin the instant they hit the door," James said. "I was just reading about this exact disease two nights ago." The two aides kept their eyes on the fluid that was being collected from the center of the patient's back.

"I hope he's not allergic to pen," Yates remarked with sudden distress. In her haste to treat this life-threatening illness, she'd forgotten to check on drug allergies.

"He's not. I already asked his wife," the nurse replied eagerly. It was her job to double-check, and when she had passed the waiting room on her way back she had asked his wife. "He was given penicillin for a cold last year and didn't have any problems with it."

After they collected the tubes, each about half full, they rolled the patient onto his back and the nurse rechecked his vital signs. "His blood pressure's down to 80 over 50 and his pulse is 140." she reported, and lifted his scrotum to insert a rectal thermometer.

"You'd better run those IV fluids in as quickly as possible. His pressure's way too low. I hope it's fluids, but it might be from sepsis." Yates picked up the isolation room stethoscope and listened to the man's heart and lungs.

"Temp's 105.6."

"Tell the floor to get a cooling mattress ready and get me a stat chest X-ray, sinus films, chemistry profile, a urinalysis. Make that the intensive care unit. I doubt they'll be able to handle him on the ward. Not like this."

Yates continued her physical exam. She checked both ears and found fluid behind the right eardrum—possibly the origin of the infection before it had spread to the brain. His throat was inflamed and there were a few swollen glands in his neck, but, oddly, everything else checked out normal.

Since Dr. James was responsible for writing up the history and physical, he repeated each step of her exam, moving in tandem, and afterwards the two physicians carefully removed their protective clothing, disposed of it in special hampers, scrubbed and went to the waiting room to speak to Mrs. Mathesson.

"Think we should call Dr. Ogden?" James asked on the way. During the daytime it was standard procedure.

"No. He's got more important things to do today. There's a group of bigwigs from the East here to see his research. Anyway, I don't think he'd have much to add. All that patient needs is some penicillin—and some prayers that it's in time."

Harriet Mathesson was sitting in the waiting room with her three children. The television was on, but none of them were watching. As the two doctors came in, she got up quickly. "How is he? Is he all right?" Her voice trembled with anxiety.

"You're Mrs. Martinson?" Yates asked.

"Mathesson, yes."

Yates asked her to be seated and sat down across from her. "I'm sorry to tell you, but it looks like your husband has meningitis." Her words came out more bluntly than she had intended.

The woman was stunned. "Spinal meningitis!"

"Well . . . yes, but we don't call it spinal meningitis. Meningitis means that there's an infection of the meninges, the tissue that covers the brain. He seems to have a rare kind caused by a bacteria with a similar name, called meningococcus."

"Where did he get it?" Mrs. Mathesson asked, her voice almost a whisper. Her children sat quietly beside her and listened.

"That's hard to say. We often don't find the source. Some people just carry this bug around—bug is what we call bacteria around here. Sometimes they carry it for long periods of time and never get ill. Other people seem to be more susceptible and come down with meningitis almost immediately."

"He's going to be all right, isn't he? We got him here as fast as we could. He was fine just a few hours ago."

This was the second time Joanna Yates had heard about the illness's short duration. Although she doubted the woman's account, she didn't argue. Instead, she inquired about each of his symptoms, noting his earlier irritability, his past medical history, a social history, a family history, allergies, and a general review of all organ systems. Throughout, Dr. James kept notes recording that for the most part Gordon Mathesson's health to date had been good.

"Will this leave him . . ." Harriet Mathesson hesitated. "Crippled . . . I mean, disabled in some way?"

Assuming that Mathesson survived, the aftereffects might indeed be serious, but Yates, in an effort to make up for her earlier bluntness, simply said that it was too early to tell.

"What about my children? What about me? Is there any danger? Lynda has had a pretty bad cold." She put her hand on the head of her middle child and Yates stepped over to take a quick look at the girl.

"A cold is probably all it is," Yates said after feeling the girl's neck. "She looks like she just has a virus. Meningococcal infections rarely start off like a cold. In fact, I've never seen one, but we'll culture everyone's throat and put you all on antibiotics just to be safe. I'm sure Dr. Walters of the Health Department will be contacting you."

James left the room and returned quickly with four throat swabs. While he was taking cultures from the backs of their throats, Yates wrote out a prescription for rifampin, an antibiotic.

"He is going to make it, isn't he?" Mrs. Mathesson asked again, her voice a trembling appeal for reassurance.

Yates didn't know how to answer. If treated too late the disease always had disastrous consequences, and there was a possibility that they had gotten to her husband too late. Trying to steer Mrs. Mathesson between greater alarm and false hope, she fell back on the standard answer. "It's too early to know." She smiled tightly and left the room.

CHAPTER THREE

Murray Clagston was the orderly who first met the Mathesson van outside of the main emergency room and helped subdue the seizing patient before the intern had transferred the case to the Contagious Disease Unit. At the time it was change of shift, and rather than stopping to wash his hands as he customarily did, he headed for the time clocks, punched out and then hurried off to his car in the employees' parking lot. Today was his son's eighth birthday and he wanted to get home to catch the boy before he left for school.

Before getting into his car, he checked the trunk. The gift-wrapped package was still there, a big blue and green striped box that contained a radio-controlled, twin-engine airplane. The present had cost him a hundred dollars—a three-day fishing trip—but he was very proud of it. The boy had been infatuated with model airplanes ever since he could point or talk, and this present was bound to be the highlight of his day. He couldn't wait to see his expression.

Clagston's old Chevy sputtered out onto the Golden State Freeway, leaving a haze of smoky exhaust behind as he headed south against the heavy flow of rush-hour traffic. Fifteen minutes later, having pushed the speed limit the whole way, he pulled up in front of his small white stucco house in Compton, a residential neighborhood where many of the houses were identically small, old, and discolored. Like the others, his lacked a garage, but there was an asphalt driveway that abutted the back door.

His wife was still in her bathrobe and clearing breakfast dishes from the table as he came in. His son Jossie was just coming out of his room with two schoolbooks in hand and a shy smile on his freshly washed face. He'd heard his father's car pull up and was expecting something.

"Hey, how's my big man today?" Clagston asked, walking toward his son with his arms outstretched to hug him. "Should we sing you a round of happy birthday?"

The boy seemed embarrassed as his father lifted him up into the air and held him there until he'd finished singing the four-line verse. Laughing, he set him down and added, "I've got something special for you in the trunk."

Mrs. Clagston was about to tell her husband that the boy was already late for school, but thought better of it. Today was special and she liked to see Jossie happy. Excited, he quickly pushed through the back door and raced to the car. "Whatever it is that you got, he can't play with it until after school, you know," she said, turning toward her husband.

"After he sees it, he may not want to go to school."

Together they watched from the doorway as Jossie flipped open the trunk and began tearing the paper away as he lifted the package out.

"Hey, bring it back in here first," Clagston called out, but he was too late. The boy had already seen the side panel of the box and knew what was inside.

"Can I fly it now, dad?" the youngster asked as he

left the paper on the ground and carried the present up the driveway. "Just ten minutes, please?"

Clagston stepped out into the driveway and showed him that the airplane had to be assembled first. "We'll put it together the minute you get home. I'll be up. You can count on it." He hugged the boy again.

"You heard your daddy," Mrs. Clagston said as she joined them in the driveway and handed the boy his schoolbooks. "He'll be here when you get back. Now, run along."

"Yes, ma'am," came a downtrodden response.

Only after his son was out of sight did Clagston go back inside to clean up and change clothes, something he should have done first. Mathesson's bacteria were on his hands and face, and now they had spread to his son.

Mary Mitchell, the registered nurse who had followed Clagston into the Mathesson van, had conscientiously washed her hands before going off duty, but her closer proximity to Mathesson's mouth as he was seizing had left invisible droplets of saliva and sputum on her uniform, each teeming with the same malignant organisms.

After punching out at the nurses' time clock, she headed down the hospital's main corridor toward a side entrance at the other end of the building that would eventually lead her to the interns' dormitory. Defiantly, she unpinned her nurse's cap and let her long, blondish curls tumble to her shoulders. Getting off the graveyard shift at County's main emergency room was like being set free from prison. She had worked eight and a half hours without a break. Practically every examining room was jammed with sick patients, all calling for attention, some screaming from pain. As one would leave, there was always another to take his place. The rooms were never empty. In a way, the main emergency room was like a massive information booth sending patients off in every direction: neurology, general medicine, general surgery, neurosurgery, orthopedics, urology, eye, chest medicine, cardiology, drunk tank, E.N.T., minor trauma and sometimes the morgue. Each specialty service had its own admitting team in the gigantic institution and the physicians on emergency duty were only responsible for stabilizing the patient, if possible, and then getting him or her off to the appropriate floor as quickly as possible. Those whose lives were in imminent danger were covered with a red blanket and raced upstairs. Those who were certain to survive for a while yet merely received white sheets and had to wait until someone had time to take them upstairs.

Altogether there were four nurses, six aides and six doctors on Mary's shift, manning one of the busiest emergency rooms in the country. Obstetrics and gynecology, pediatrics and psychiatry had their own emergency rooms, and there was a walk-in clinic for those less ill, such as insomniacs, hypochondriacs, and those with other mild ailments. Her area, however, was for the very seriously ill and it was nice to leave the stresses behind.

The rest of the day was hers, after one very important stop. There was an intern anxiously waiting her arrival in the next building. The meeting was a planned rendezvous of sorts, squeezed in between his reporting for work and her going home to sleep—something that added a little excitement to the days for both of them. It was a stop that she'd made on many mornings after work, although not always at the same room number. Dr. Cunningham was this month's beau. They'd met at an interns' dance a week before, spent that night together and then every morning after her shift.

After traversing the hallway, which was the equivalent of a city block, she reached the side door, climbed a cascade of concrete steps and seconds later was passing the interns' swimming pool where a lone swimmer was taking his morning laps. As he reached her end and flipped over to return, she caught a glimpse of his tanned face and tight bathing suit. He wasn't anyone she recognized, but the sight of his bare broad shoulders and muscular arms heightened her anticipation of her rendezvous with Cunningham.

As she waited for the elevator to come, two interns exited a nearby stairwell, stopped what they were saying and smiled in her direction. Both knew her from the emergency room as well as the dorm, and both knew her reputation.

"I wonder who the lucky guy is today?" one of them whispered as the outside door closed behind them.

Although she couldn't hear the words, she guessed them by their facial expressions. It didn't matter, however. She enjoyed what she was doing and found nothing wrong with it.

Upstairs, Cunningham was finishing his shower. He dried off, wrapped a bath towel around his waist and shaved quickly. He had only twenty minutes before he'd have to report to the medicine floor, but he'd cut it this close before. A good lay was worth being late if it came down to it, but with Mary there was never any foreplay. She usually showed up as excited about sex as he was.

Two soft knocks, a delay, and then a third softer knock was her sign. The door opened in front of her, but no one was there. Perplexed, she stepped inside. The door closed behind her and two hands instantly came from behind to caress her breasts.

"I thought you'd never make it," he whispered, unfastening the buttons of her uniform and kissing her neck from behind.

Giggling, she pulled away and turned around. Her uniform was parted down to her panty hose. Her breasts hung freely without a brassiere, bouncing as she moved. "Can't you at least say good morning or ask me about the night?" she said teasingly as she pulled her uniform back together.

"Good morning." Cunningham laughed and reached for the last button. "We'll talk afterwards."

"I think we should talk first. We never talk. I just come over and we jump into bed." She sat back on the edge of the bed and crossed her legs.

Cunningham glanced at his clock radio. It was a quarter to eight. "You never wanted to talk before. I've only got fifteen minutes," he said, standing over her and lowering the shoulders of her uniform to her waist. She didn't resist.

"Fifteen minutes. That's a lot. They say that the actual act of love takes fifteen seconds."

"If you keep talking like this, we won't even have that much time," he said, leaning down to kiss her. He slowly pushed her back on the mattress, and as he finished undressing her she reached up and in one motion undid his towel and pulled his eager body on top of her.

The contaminated uniform lay at their side, having already spread the bacteria.

"Impressive, very impressive," Bellows said to Ogden as they walked down the hallway toward the lab's autopsy room. The older scientist stood half a head taller than his younger colleague.

"Well, it's not all done. We've got a long way to go yet." Ogden's response was characteristically circumspect, but he was very pleased that someone of Bellows's stature had complimented him.

"What's your next step?"

"We need to try it out on a naturally occurring tumor. That won't be easy, but I've left word with several veterinarians in town. If they come up with any dogs with cancer, they'll ask the owners if we can experiment on them. I doubt anyone would object."

"You never know. Some folks treat their animals like members of the family. We do in my house, or at least we used to when the kids lived at home." For a fleeting instant, there was a hint of sadness in his voice.

"I know, but I'm sure we'll find a few out there with

the kind of tumor we can work with. We can't do this with all tumors, especially not the ones that have a good blood supply.''

Bellows nodded and then slowed to allow the other three scientists to get ahead of them. ''I don't know if I should tell you this, but I'm sure you'll learn about it soon, anyway.'' Bellows's voice was purposefully soft and it immediately alarmed Ogden. ''You remember Bill Mossberger, don't you?''

''Sure. We were research fellows together.''

''He's doing the exact same experiment that you are. It's been under wraps until now. To keep it from the competition, I'm sure. The theory's the same, but he's using Clostridia bacteria instead.''

''You're kidding.'' Ogden was stunned. He had presented the theory behind the experiment to Mossberger years ago in an effort to convince Mossberger, whose research experience was then in advance of his own, to conduct the experiment with him. But then Mossberger had gone to work for a pharmaceutical company, and the last news Ogden had heard was that he was trying to develop a new antibiotic. Suddenly, he felt betrayed.

''He's applying for the same grant you are, but you have the inside track as far as I can tell. At least, for the grant. You've been doing it longer, and as long as your experiment works he probably can't outbid you. It's too bad he's not doing something more different. Your protocols are mirror images of each other.''

Ogden thanked Bellows for the information and then walked on silently. He had thought that he was alone in this research. The fact that someone else might be thinking along the same lines wasn't all that surprising, he admitted, although he couldn't help resenting Mossberger's use of ''his'' theory. Nonetheless, he reminded himself, the fact that their protocols had worked out to be so similar was pure luck—either that or a sign that they were both on the right track. It remained to be seen whether Mossberger was closer to a breakthrough in his choice of Clostridia bacteria.

Meanwhile, the dog had been sacrificed. Dr. Ling had given it a large intravenous dose of barbiturates, and once it was taken off the respirator the Dalmatian died in minutes. It was a clean and painless death, a fact of experimental life that Ogden never liked, but accepted as necessary. Dogs were expendable, humans weren't. If the killing eventually saved lives, it was always worth it.

The four scientists lined up along a metal table with a drain in the center as Ogden and Ling gloved for the autopsy. Ling was to do most of the work with Ogden assisting, and as he deftly sawed through the dog's sternum and extended the incision from the base of the dog's throat to the top of the pubic bone, the others watched carefully. The dog's body was still warm and most of the organs bled when they were cut. Once Ling removed the lungs—two spongy, pyramid shaped organs—Ogden pointed out the same tumors that they'd seen on the monitor earlier.

"The reason the tumor is so hemorrhagic is due to the bacteria. This organism causes local damage and bleeding."

Ling proceeded to dissect out another tumor located in the dog's neck and took a few additional lymph glands that lay in close proximity. After removing the other organs, he turned to the skull, unroofing it with a noisy electric saw. Beneath the frontal lobe of the brain was an additional tumor that was similar in appearance to the previous ones.

"Just to be sure, we'll check for any unnoticed tumors," Ogden said, turning toward a wooden counter and setting the organs out. He didn't expect to find any, but it was imperative that the experiment be conducted thoroughly in every aspect—especially now that he had competition from Mossberger. He first dissected through the heart chambers, then the kidneys, and finally the spleen. Everything seemed normal until he reached the liver. He cut through the beefy red organ and then suddenly stopped about halfway through. In view of everyone was another nodule that by all external appearances seemed malignant. *God, I can't believe this*, he thought and almost said, *It's not possible*.

"Looks like you found another cancer," Dr. Christopher remarked, leaning forward for a better look.

"It may just be a benign adenoma," Ogden said, almost stumbling over his words. "I think it would have lit up the screen otherwise. We'll have to wait for the microscopic sections to be sure." He had done this experiment a dozen times and never missed a metastatic tumor before. Despite its appearance, it had to be something else. Everything depended on its being something else.

Trying to sound confident, but realizing that some of the scientists might be having some doubts, he proceeded to carefully dissect the dog's adrenals, gonads and intestinal tract. No other nodules could be found and as he handed the tissues to Dr. Ling to do the microscopic sections, he breathed an exhausted sigh. It would be an hour before they would be ready for viewing, perhaps the longest hour of his life.

The laboratory reports on Gordon Mathesson were back in Dr. Yates's hands by 8:30 A.M. and they were confirmatory. Her patient definitely had meningitis as evidenced by the high white count in his spinal fluid—normal being zero to less than ten cells—and the organism responsible appeared to be Neisseria meningitis or meningococcus. The latter result was shown with special staining, so-called Gram's stain, that showed numerous small pinkish spherules, or cocci, in pairs and often seen within the bodies of white cells. In addition, his white count on the Complete Blood Count (CBC) was extremely high, further indicating that his infection was severe.

•　　•　　•

Patient: Mathesson, Gordon, age 43
PF Number: 345-87-046
Complete Blood Count
Drawn: 0735

	Result	Normal Value
Hemoglobin	15.1	14–16 gm/100ml
Hematocrit	45%	42–47 ml/100ml
Red Cell Count	5.0	4.8–5.4 mil/cu mm
White Cell Count	19,000	5–10,000 cu mm
Neutrophils	84%	36–66%
Bands	10%	5–11%
Eosinophils	1%	3%
Basophils	1%	0.5%
Lymphocytes	4%	24–44%
Monocytes	0%	0–4%
MCV	86	82–92
MCH	29	27–31
MCHC	34	32–36

Red cell morphology: slight anisocytosis, occasional helmet cell

Patient: Mathesson, Gordon, age 43
PF Number: 345-87-046
Spinal Fluid Analysis
Drawn: 0735

	Result	Normal Value
Description	yellow, cloudy	clear
Amount received	7.5cc	variable
Cell count		
Total white cells	4500	less than ten
Percent neutrophils	99%	0%
Percent mononuclears	1%	100%
Total red cells	12	0
Protein	132	15–45 mgm/100ml
Sugar	10	45–80 mg/100ml

Gram stain: Many Gram negative diplococci, intracellular and extracellular consistent with the *Neisseria* species, probably meningococcus

● ● ●

Other routine meningitis screening tests done on the Mathesson blood included a check on his electrolytes (salts), in particular sodium and potassium which were normal; kidney function, which suggested that he was slightly dehydrated; liver tests, which though in the normal range were high and consistent with sepsis; blood sugar, which was elevated but assumed to have been raised by the glucose in his intravenous fluids; and his albumin and globulin (proteins), which were also normal. Before being transferred to the floor from admitting, portable X-rays of his chest and sinuses were taken to see if the infection could have started there, but they were normal.

As Dr. Yates reviewed the results she was glad that she'd started the penicillin so promptly. The meningococcus organism was known to be acutely sensitive to the antibiotic—it always had been, in contrast to other organisms like *Hemophilus* and *Pneumococcus* which also cause meningitis. During the past year, there had been several reports of increasing resistance among these organisms. Fortunately, however, they could all be distinguished on Gram stain, and she and James went down to the laboratory to reassure themselves that the report was accurate.

In the interim, Gordon Mathesson was moved into a four-man room on the third floor. Like him, the other three were comatose, two on respirators with a diagnosis of encephalitis and one breathing on his own despite a large brain abscess caused by a fungus. Precautions there were tight. Each patient had his own nurse, each bed had a complete monitoring system for heart rate and blood pressure, and each quadrant of the room was separated by a glass partition. No one could come in or out without wearing protective clothing and visitors could only see their relatives through small windows along one wall.

Once Gordon Mathesson was shifted to a bed, small

electrodes were attached to his chest so that the heart-beat could be visually displayed on a scope overhead. His intravenous line was fed through an electronic drop counter and a Foley catheter, a long skinny red tube, was inserted through his urethra into his bladder so that urine output could be monitored on a hour-to-hour basis. As the Foley was forced through the flaccid penis, usually an uncomfortable insertion, he didn't budge.

It was almost an hour before Harriet Mathesson and her children were allowed to see him. Standing outside the window and viewing him inside was more than she could handle. Tears filled her eyes. She kept thinking he was going to die and then chided herself for being so pessimistic. She was trying to put up a brave front, a more confident, more controlled one, at least for the children's sake. They were obviously frightened in spite of her reassurances that while their father was seriously ill she was sure that he would get well in time, that he was too strong willed not to.

This was the first time in her life that she had felt so helpless. It was also the first time that she had ever thought of losing him. They had made out wills a year ago, but only at their lawyer's behest. Their parents and grandparents had lived into their eighties and nineties, and until now there had been no reason not to expect the same for themselves. Her mind moved to insurance policies, house payments, Gordon's job, the kids' college funds, the possibility of her working . . . but she was unskilled and had always left their financial worries up to him. Now she didn't know what to do . . . except wait and hope.

CHAPTER FOUR

At nine o'clock that same morning, Dr. Hilary Walters, an investigator with the U.S. Public Health Department, drove into the rolling hills of the Truesdale Estate, a wealthy residential section of Beverly Hills. There was a cool breeze coming through her car window as her dark eyes looked out at passing house numbers. She looked businesslike in a gray linen suit and mauve silk blouse, her chestnut hair pinned back in a chignon. In her dashboard tape player was an educational tape from the National Institute of Health, a speech by the director of the Atlanta Center for Disease Control, Dr. Sidney Bellows. ". . . The face of pneumonia has changed. In previous decades, the disease would kill its victims in a matter of hours despite antibiotics. Now, most of the victims survive, but this disease—and many others—are becoming resistant to drugs. In 1949, it took three hundred thousand units of penicillin to treat gonorrhea. Today it requires four point eight *million*, and ten percent of the time it fails. . . ."

As she followed the winding road uphill, every house looked more palatial than the ones below it, some with statues, some with fountains, all with beautifully waxed cars arrayed in the driveways. She was there on what some people might consider a very touchy subject. To her it was serious business. In the Department she was known as a very determined woman.

". . . In 1972, the Shigella strain that caused a severe dysentery outbreak in Mexico suddenly became resistant to ampicillin, and a similar pattern soon followed with typhoid fever . . ."

According to the confidential files downtown, a fifteen-year-old male prostitute from Hollywood Boulevard had been treated for gonorrhea of the rectum, and among the people he named as contacts was Michael Finn, a movie star who lived near the top of these hills. Finn's screen image was the epitome of masculinity—suave, macho, with a resemblance to Clark Gable—but the prostitute had given an unmistakable description of the man's car and home. Although it was common for these youths to name celebrities, this tip seemed more legitimate than most, and Hilary felt that it had to be checked out. She knew that Finn would refuse to see her if she telephoned, so she was going to drop in without notice. The prospect of confronting Michael Finn couldn't help but bring out a smile on her face.

"The streptococcus in Japan has developed a resistance to tetracycline, erythromycin and chloramphenicol in eighty percent of cases, and the pneumococcus in South Africa is resistant to these three plus penicillin."

Gonorrhea had been rampant in the Hollywood district, geometrically expanding among heterosexuals and homosexuals alike, and now with an epidemic at hand, the U.S. Public Health Department had assigned her staff to help local officials.

"In the 1960s only five percent of our bacteria cultures showed some resistance to an antibiotic. In the 1970s, the number reached forty percent in several metropolitan laboratories. The prospect for the 1980s looks worse with the indiscriminate use of drugs in animal feed, crowded city conditions and the easy adaptability of microorganisms."

In a way Walters felt like a policeman. The poor and
disadvantaged were easy to catch, find and treat, but the
rich and influential kept their genital afflictions hidden.
Private physicians cooperatively concealed the diseases
behind euphemistic diagnoses: gonorrhea was recorded
as bladder infection, syphilis as a viral rash—both
nonreportable. They would lose business if they didn't
concede to their patients' wishes. Her job, on the other
hand, depended not on concealment but on contacting
and alerting infectious disease carriers so that they could
be treated.

"Some organisms mutate and change their cell walls,
or alter their metabolites, or secrete a substance that
destroys the antibiotic before it can harm them."

She had been with the Department for only six
months, having spent the preceding year at the N.I.H.
in Bethesda. She had originally trained as a family
practitioner but then had gone on to earn her master's
degree in public health. Her father was a general
practitioner in Amherst, Massachusetts, as was his
father before him, but she preferred the detective aspect
of medicine over private practice. Superficially, she
seemed frail, standing five-five at one hundred-and-five
pounds, but when working she presented a tough
exterior that was difficult to thwart.

Finn's home was located at the end of a cul-de-sac. It
was an immense Spanish villa with a circular driveway
that was lined with palm trees and two shiny, new Mercedes. She drove her old Saab through an unlocked gate
and parked at the front door. A tanned hulk of a man,
well over six feet and wearing a T-shirt and Levi's, answered the doorbell with an annoyed look on his face.

"Look, I'm sorry—" he began, apparently taking her
for a fan.

"I'm here to see Mr. Finn," she cut him off, wondering whether this was Finn's bodyguard or his
boyfriend.

"I'm sure you are, but I'm sorry—"

"I'm from the Health Department. The law requires

you to let me speak to him." She opened her purse to show her ID.

The man stared at the card for a moment and then asked her to wait, closing the door behind him.

It was several minutes before he opened the door again. "Mr. Finn says that his health is quite fine and for you to call his secretary for any information you need." He started to close the door.

"I wouldn't if I were you," she said, sticking her foot into the doorway. He began to push the door against her shoe. "Your health might be in jeopardy also. I'll have to see both of you."

"My health? From what?" He relaxed his pressure on the door a little.

She got her foot back out, leather crinkled but toes intact.

"From what?" he asked again.

"Do you drink milk?" she asked. If the answer were anything less than two quarts a day, she'd be surprised.

"At least a gallon." He proudly flexed the biceps in his right arm.

"That's what I was afraid of." Walters sounded serious, but was desperately trying not to laugh. "And you feel all right?"

"Yes . . . I think so." He became concerned.

"And you buy it around here, I suspect?"

"A store at the bottom of the hill."

"That's what I thought. Let me see your tongue." She took out a small flashlight from her purse and, standing on her tiptoes, shone the light into the man's mouth. "Uh, huh . . . judging by that, I think I'd best see Mr. Finn now instead of waiting."

"What did you see?" he asked, obviously worried.

"I'd better discuss this with your boss first."

Alarmed, the man let her in and started feeling the glands in his neck as he walked toward the back of the house. After passing through three different rooms, all of which had already been described to her by the prostitute, they found Finn eating breakfast on a back balcony. He was wearing a satin bathrobe and reading a newspaper. Walters stepped through the open doorway and sat down across from him. He looked at her in surprise.

"Don't bother getting up," she said, pulling her chair in closer and momentarily eying the huge breakfast before the man. Off to her side and beyond a railing was an immense panoramic view of the city of Los Angeles. As usual, there was a brown haze.

"Larry, I thought I told you to get rid of her," Finn said, glaring at his bodyguard.

"She said that I was sick too."

"Oh, hell, you're not any more sick than I am," the celebrity sharply replied and returned his attention to Walters. "Now, what is the real reason?"

"Do you know Ronnie James?" she asked.

Finn hesitated for a moment. He was visibly taken aback, but quickly regained his composure and waved the guard to leave.

"A blond, blue-eyed boy about fifteen?" she prompted him. "He hangs around Hollywood Boulevard at night?"

"No, I don't think so. Was he in one of my films?" Finn's manner was offhand—too offhand.

"He has gonorrhea."

Finn set his coffee cup down unsteadily and stared at her, momentarily speechless.

She glanced over the railing and changed the subject to give him a chance to assimilate the news and drop his act. "You're above the smog here, aren't you? Imagine, I spend all day down in that mess, but it doesn't look so bad when you're down there."

"Certainly you didn't come up here to discuss the inversion layer and you might also take some lessons in etiquette. I don't know this boy you speak of, never heard of him, and I think you're wasting your time."

"He says that he had sex with you five nights ago. That you picked him up on the Strip and brought him back here where he spent the night.''

Finn forced a laugh. "Not my type and certainly not my style.''

"He says that you drove a blue Mercedes.''

"The city's full of Mercedes.''

"That you have an Oriental rug in the main entryway and several antique Chinese cabinets.''

"My house has been pictured in a dozen magazines.''

"He says that you use perfumed soap in the bathroom off your bedroom.''

"That's enough!" Finn's patience had been pushed too far.

"We need to have you checked by one of our doctors and I need to know the names of any contacts you've had since that night.''

Finn's face was beet red. He glared across the table and his voice was strained with anger as he said, "Ms. Walters, you can either leave on your own or I can call Larry to assist you.''

"I'll leave on my own, thanks," Walters quickly replied and stood. She had never expected him to admit to a homosexual contact, especially one with VD, but at least he'd been informed and would probably get medical attention somewhere. Perhaps, she hoped, he would even notify his contacts. Mission accomplished, as well as could be expected.

Larry met her in the hallway and opened the door.

"Don't worry about drinking that milk," she said, smiling. "That is, unless you have a lactose intolerance. Then, it'll give you diarrhea.'' As she stepped outside, the door slammed closed behind her.

On the way back down the hill, her pocket beeper sounded. First came a loud annoying buzz and then a woman's voice. The operator told her to call her office immediately. Five minutes later, she reached Sunset Boulevard and used a pay phone at the first service station. Her secretary told her that the bacteriology laboratory at U.S.C. was reporting a presumptive case of meningococcus meningitis, and that she was to drop everything and report to Dr. Michael Ogden immediately.

After taking the group of scientists on a tour of the Contagious Disease Unit and introducing them to most of his staff, Mike Ogden directed the team back to a conference room next to his laboratory. Originally he had planned to give them only a brief review of his earlier experiments, but with the possibility that something might have gone wrong with his demonstration he felt compelled to show them a number of their previous successes.

No one had said a word about the liver nodule—scientists don't like to talk about failed experiments—but it made for an uneasy silence as they walked through the halls and he suspected that it was in the back of everyone's mind. It certainly was in his. If he had not been so thorough in his dissection, so confident when making sure that the liver was so thinly sliced, the tumor might not have been found and his work would have been considered a success. And yet the uppermost thought in his mind was that if that nodule truly was an unexpected malignancy that the bacterial suicide squad had missed, it was only right that he know now before proceeding into more complicated testing.

The answer lay in the autopsy slides, and he knew that it could mean the difference of thousands of dollars in his grant. It might also mean that Mossberger would get the grant entirely and eventually be credited with finding a cure for cancer, something he had dreamed about for himself.

The men sat along both sides of a long oak table with Ogden next to a slide projector. While Dr. Ling was finishing up the work on the autopsy slides, he showed the group data from earlier work, projecting a complicated table with graphs on the screen. "My feeling a few years ago was that malignant tumors must have certain markers or characteristics that set them aside from normal body tissues, and we at first tried creating antibodies to them, much as the body would do to fight off a bacterial illness. We injected a variety of homogenates made from tumor cells into guinea pigs, dogs and monkeys, but after several attempts that approach didn't seem to work. Or at least we couldn't find the right key. On the few occasions that we did develop a serum, the serum's antibodies merely stuck to the surface of the malignant cells and never caused them any damage. In fact, sometimes this artificial coating made them resistant to other modes of therapy."

Ogden advanced the slides and took a quick drink from his coffee cup. "Next we moved to radioisotopes. We hooked up radioactive particles to the antibodies, hoping that they'd carry these mini H-bombs, if you will, around on a microscopic level to each of the tumor cells. On paper the theory looked good, but the antibodies were not as effective with their hitchhikers on board and unfortunately they caused more harm to normal tissues en route to the tumors."

He changed the slides again. "As an alternative approach, we decided to make use of an old law of nature with a little twist. Every species of animal has a natural enemy and this is as true on the microscopic level as it is in jungles or forests. We know that certain viruses will attack certain bacteria and kill them instantly. Well, viruses at this stage of the game are too difficult to work with, but bacteria are not. Instead of allowing them to merely attack man, we can program them to make insulin and other hormones and we're in the process of developing farms of bacteria to make a multiplicity of drugs. Why not teach them to hunt and seek—actually hunt, seek and destroy? It sounds science fictionish, I admit, but as we were trying to establish a genetic code we fell upon a natural code that could be easily substituted. There are certain species of bacteria, such as *Clostridium, Peptostreptococci, Peptococci, Veillonella, Treponema* and *Bacteroides*, whose oxygen requirements are similar to those of cancer cells. These bacteria can only survive within these malignant tumors and not in the rest of the body. Like magnets, they attract each other.''

Ogden began flipping through several slides showing the work that they had done with each of these groups. "We needed an organism that would be promptly detrimental to the tumor cells and not immediately harmful to the host. There were only two that caused a significant infection, *Clostridium* and *Bacteroides*, and only the latter could be tolerated.'' He stopped for a second, wondering how Mossberger could have used the first organism. It seemed impossible . . . "From that point on it was simple. We merely needed to find the proper number of organisms necessary to infect the animal, then to figure out how to trace them, how long to leave them so that the tumor would be destroyed and how to kill them with our antibiotics once their work was done.'' After showing the data from each of these experiments, he showed a series of pictures of healthy dogs that had been treated and dying dogs that had not.

As he finished discussing the last slide, the conference room door opened and Dr. Ling entered, pushing a small cabinet on wheels with a projecting microscope situated on top. Stacked beside the projector were a dozen stained slides from the dog's autopsy.

"Well, we might as well see what today has brought,'' Ogden remarked, resigned to face his mistake if it were there. He began with the sections that had been made through the lung tumor. "As you can see, the bacteria have filled the small blood vessels and are making their way into the tumor itself. If this slide were made two or three days later, as were those slides I showed you a few minutes ago, you would be seeing dying cells and the formation of an abscess. And if checked again a week after antibiotics, you'd see some scar tissue and mostly normal tissue, but no tumor cells.''

Ogden shifted to the lymph gland in the dog's neck and then to the brain tumor. Each of them showed the same bacterial invasion and early signs of destruction.

The last set of slides were from the liver nodule and with some trepidation he placed the first glass slide on the projecting stage. This must be how a man feels climbing the steps to the gallows, he thought. Once the tissue was in focus, he walked to the screen to get a better look. There were no bacteria to be seen. The suicide squad had missed it. The blood vessels were clean, but as he studied the cells closely, he realized that the nodule was not a malignancy at all. It was entirely benign. It had looked like a malignancy when he did the autopsy, but microscopically it was not. There wasn't any need for his bacteria to have attacked it.

"These cells are normal," he said, his voice betraying the relief he felt. He flipped to another slide to be sure. He tried to calm himself. He was supposed to be confident.

"Did you expect anything else?" Bellows asked with a smile.

"To be honest, I was a little worried. The experiment has always worked before, but there was a little room to be concerned today."

The remaining slides of the liver nodule merely confirmed that the cell type within was normal. Had it not been early morning, Ogden might have offered to buy the group a round of drinks. Suddenly, he felt like celebrating.

Hilary Walters drove directly to the Medical Center, parked quickly and started toward the Contagious Disease Unit. Her first stop was their bacteriology laboratory. When she was cleared through security outside the lab, the chief technician let her in and steered her toward one of six microscopes. "I left the slide on the stage," he said. "I knew it wouldn't be too long before someone from your department showed up. No one's going to wait too long with this bug."

"I agree. What do you know about the case?" She

positioned the glass rectangle on top of the microscope's stage and fiddled with the background lighting to improve her focus.

"Not much more than the guy just arrived . . . maybe an hour ago at the most, and the white count on his spinal fluid was forty-five hundred with ninety-nine percent polys. Obviously bacterial, to my mind. You can see the proof in front of you."

Walters listened, but didn't reply. The fact that there were ninety-nine percent polys was extremely significant. If this were viral and of less concern, the percent of polys would be small, but with bacterial infections, it is the opposite. She studied the magnified fields on the slide. Every circular area that she viewed was glutted with these polys, a pinkish staining white cell with a distinct nucleus and each filled with tiny red spherules that were clumped in pairs.

"I don't blame you for calling," she said, her eyes still at the lenses. "I'd be surprised if this doesn't turn out to be a meningococcus case."

"I called thinking you might want to get a jump on the culture." The technician laid a Xerox copy of the other laboratory results next to her. "The cultures will take another twenty-four hours, but I'm sure they'll show what we already suspect."

"I'm sure it will too." As she spoke, she experienced a sudden feeling of alarm. This was a highly contagious disease that could easily spread to close family contacts and friends and was potentially fatal to everyone who contracted it.

After spending a few more minutes reviewing the test results, she picked up a wall phone and called her office. The moment her secretary answered she said, "Cancel the rest of my appointments. I've got a meningitis case here at U.S.C."

The woman on the other end understood—meningitis always took a high priority—but she didn't know what to tell the school board. "You know that you had a meeting at three today?"

Walters hesitated. She had completely forgotten. "They've been calling all week, but it'll just have to wait. I'm sure they'll understand. Just put it off a day or two, but don't tell them it's meningitis. That always upsets people. Pick another disease. Tell them I'll send over my recommendations for next year's immunization program later. It's all made out. You can handle it, I'm sure."

The "You can handle it," momentarily surprised her secretary. She had often heard the words from Hilary's predecessor, who used the pretense of an emergency to escape to the golf course, but this was the first time she'd heard it from Hilary. She knew that in Hilary's case the excuse was legitimate and was almost sorry that it was. Hilary was conscientious—too conscientious, she thought, and in her six months in L.A. seemed almost to have avoided developing any social life. But all she said to Hilary was that, yes, she would handle the school board.

After hanging up, Hilary proceeded to the third floor to find Dr. Yates, who was seated at the nursing station enveloped in cigarette smoke and rewriting some of the intravenous fluid orders. "This must be what you're after," Yates remarked, and handed her the metal folder. She had only seen Hilary once before, at a meeting, but women investigators were such a rarity that she remembered her well. "Your department must have a hotline into our parking lot or lab. Sometimes we hardly get these cases into bed before someone pops up here."

"Bothered?" Hilary asked with a smile. She automatically opened the chart to the nursing notes.

"No, just amazed. It's too bad all government services aren't this prompt."

"Got to keep up with those germs, you know. Can't let them get out and terrorize our city." Hilary was looking down at the empty sheet. Other than Yates's orders and some admission vital signs, the chart was empty. "There's nothing here," she said, closing the metal flaps.

"That's one of the prices you pay for being so quick." Yates told her the history and physical. When she got to the laboratory values, Hilary interrupted.

"I've already seen them."

"I thought you might have. You haven't seen the patient yet though, have you? Come on."

Hilary smiled and followed Yates back into the intensive care unit, where she examined Gordon Mathesson herself after putting on a protective gown, mask and gloves. It was obviously a bad case, possibly the worst that she had ever seen, and she was glad that she had decided to cancel her day.

"On penicillin?"

The resident nodded.

"What does Dr. Ogden think?"

"He hasn't seen him yet."

"How come?" Mike Ogden was known for getting personally involved in his department's cases.

"He's showing off his research project to a group from the Center for Disease Control. The word we got was that he didn't want to be disturbed today, so I discussed the case with Dr. Paige. I doubt there's much we can do at this stage."

"I guess," Hilary said, but she was curious. This wasn't like the chief, and she wondered what was distracting him. She asked Yates, but the resident didn't know, and after pondering a few possibilities aloud the two left to speak to Harriet Mathesson, who was seated in the waiting room.

After introducing herself and sitting down next to the patient's wife, Hilary said, "I need to know any and all contacts your husband might have had in the last twenty-four to forty-eight hours."

"I don't know. Just family and work, I suppose," Mrs. Mathesson's manner was distracted, Hilary noted, and her thin face was pale and drawn. She appeared to be in semi-shock.

"There are four children?" Hilary asked, pulling out a notepad.

"No, three."

"Their names?"

"Lynda, Marcey and Jamey."

"Any other relatives visit your husband in the past two days or stay with you?"

"No."

"Any neighbors spend time?"

"No . . ." She hesitated as if her answer might be wrong. "Oh, yes, Jim came over. Jim Thackery. He lives across the street. The two of them went out for a beer the night before last. They often do."

"What bar did they go to?"

"I never ask. It's his private night out. You'll have to ask them."

Hilary wrote the man's name down and got his address. "Anyone else come to your house? Is anyone sick at home?"

"No one came, but Lynda's had a pretty bad cold this week."

Joanna Yates spoke up. "I already checked the girl. In fact we took cultures from everyone's throat and they've all been given rifampin," she said, referring to the standard antibiotic protection given to meningitis contacts.

"What about his job? What kind of work does he do?" Hilary asked.

"He's an inspector with Customs at L.A. International Airport."

Hilary's expression changed dramatically. Mathesson could have exposed hundred of travelers.

"Does he work in the office?" she asked, hoping.

"No, up front checking suitcases for the most part," the woman answered, not aware of the significance of her statement.

"He didn't happen to take the last few days off before leaving, did he?"

"No, not Gordon. He always works up to the last minute. No need in spending a vacation sitting at home, he always said." She began to cry.

CHAPTER FIVE

"Your work shows a lot of promise," Dr. Bellows said to Mike Ogden as they followed Kleinfeldt, Christopher and Ruben out to Dr. Ling's car to leave for the airport.

Ogden, still beaming from the experiment's success, said, "Well, we're a long way from any practical applications. A lot of things could go wrong . . . but it does look encouraging."

"Encouraging!" Bellows chortled as he turned from the car to face Ogden. "You do yourself a disservice, Mike. It might just be a major breakthrough, the kind that textbooks are written about, but if I were you I'd try to come up with something that's just one step beyond and I'd do it rather quickly. Something that's clearly different than Mossberger's experiment."

"How much more do you think I need?"

"Anything that would indicate that you're further along than he is. We all know that you started this project before he did, but the grant committee looks at results. Black and white figures match up with green numbers. If he's more efficient, more cost conscious, even if the wording in his grant reads more clearly and everything else is the same, he could win the vote. I don't mean to alarm you—"

"You have, nonetheless."

"I only offer this in fair warning. I probably shouldn't." Bellows climbed into the front seat.

Before the car drove off, Ogden thanked him. He didn't like what he was hearing, however. Deep within there was a bitterness toward Mossberger for stealing his work, but he rationalized that at least there was a little time to knock out something new. "A cure for cancer is at stake" kept racing through his mind. His name in textbooks, potential fame and fortune were at his fingertips and yet someone's shoe—a friend's shoe—was mashing down on his outstretched hand. He knew that he had to get to work right away. Somehow he had to get rid of his ward responsibilities for a while, but he'd also have to spend less time at home, less time with Peter. The latter was the most difficult pill to swallow. He had promised himself and his son that he'd have more free time as soon as Bellows's group left. Instead, he now found himself with less.

Coming up with a valuable piece of research in such a short time would be difficult, and the most logical choice was to simply proceed in the direction his experiment was already headed and move on to a naturally occurring tumor right now. He had planned this as a next step anyway and there was no harm in hurrying it along. He headed toward his office to retelephone the veterinarians on his list, but when he arrived he found that one of the vets had already called him, leaving a message that he had a cocker spaniel with cancer and that its owners were agreeable to experimentation. To Mike Ogden this was a godsend and he phoned to make arrangements. He wanted the dog in his laboratory the same day if possible.

Meanwhile, Dr. Hilary Walters was entering the first passenger terminal at Los Angeles International Airport. The drive there had only taken her twenty minutes, but she'd spent another thirty trying to find a parking place. Usually, delays like this were extremely annoying to her, but she was preoccupied with several tentative plans of attack. She needed some means to track down all possible exposures, which might include calling Atlanta for additional investigators, and yet there was a chance that there were no bona fide contacts. She doubted it—there had to be—but being new, she did not want to sound like an alarmist. Intimate contacts down here were definitely out, but not close ones. No one knew how this disease spread. A handshake, an uncovered cough, a sneeze, or even handling a sick person's clothing were all possible sources of contagion and any of these could have happend at Customs. The problem was that she didn't know if Mathesson had given it to others or contracted it from an ill passenger—or both. No telling how long she would be working with the meningitis case, so to be safe herself she had started taking rifampin tablets.

After making her way into the crowded lobby, she scanned an almost uncountable number of signs indicating the airport's services and international carriers before she saw one for the Customs office. She worked her way across the main lobby and followed the signs until she found the right corridor, an inconspicuous, narrow hallway with a tiny cubicle office at the end.

Sitting inside was a man in his sixties, wearing the gray slacks, gray shirt and black tie of a Customs official. His name tag said Inspector Van Horn and he was hurriedly shuffling through some papers on his desk as if he were about to leave and needed to take them with him. "Can I help you?" he asked without looking up. "Desk's closed. If it's Lost and Found you want, they're in the next hall over."

"No, they're not who I'm looking for. I have some questions I'd like to ask you." She pulled out her ID card and held it in front of his eyes, which were still intent on the papers he was shuffling through.

"Health Department? Dr. Walters?" He kept his head down as he read every word: her height, weight, ID number, office address and date of issuance. Finally, he set his papers aside and asked her to sit. "I'm sorry. People are always jumping on us about their lost luggage. They see the uniform and right away they think we had something to do with the baggage handling in Istanbul or Frankfurt."

Hilary smiled.

"What can I do for you? Another outbreak of something abroad, I suppose. One that we should be watching for here. It's not the pet turtles again? I never saw such a fuss. What was that disease? Salamander?"

"Salmonella," she corrected him. "No, I'm here about one of your inspectors, Gordon Mathesson."

Van Horn nodded.

"He's been hospitalized with a very serious type of meningitis and I need some information about possible contacts. Things like where he might have gotten it, who he might have given it to."

"Contacts?" Van Horn knew the routine and was already wary. "I'm sure you saw that crowd out there. It's a madhouse like that every day. People are always bringing diseases back from somewhere. Unless they crawl through here with orange and green spots all over their bodies, we can't be responsible—"

"No one says you are. I merely need to be sure that people haven't contracted or spread the disease while passing through."

"I can't believe that he caught it here—or gave it to anyone, for that matter. We never catch anything more than a cold around here, and even that's rare."

"That's just the point. We think it spreads just like a cold does, but this isn't a disease to be fooled around with."

"I should show you our sick leave record." Van Horn reached into a bottom drawer. "We have the lowest record of absentees in the country. My men are never off from work. I really doubt he got it here."

Hilary couldn't help getting impatient with the man. She did not care about his health records or even his

opinions. She needed specific information, and quickly.
"Perhaps you're right," she said sharply, "but being an
investigator I have to check out everything. You can understand that, *can't you*?"

"Sure, but you won't find the cause here. How bad is
Gordon anyway?"

"Serious, very serious. He may even die. The index
case—that's what we call the first case—often does. It's
usually discovered too late, even though Mrs.
Mathesson got her husband to the hospital so quickly.
It'll be several days before we know the outcome for
sure."

Hilary went on to explain how the disease usually
spreads among families or troops in Army barracks and.
how some people are immune and others highly susceptible. "There's no way to predict who's going to get it
and who won't, except by checking throat cultures. I'll
need to swab your throat and anyone else's who's been
around him recently."

"That ought to be about eight men here, but I don't
think I can tell you much about the passengers who've
passed through here." Concerned now, Van Horn
reached into another drawer and pulled out a thick
packet of papers. "These are the flight manifests," he
explained, handing them across to her. "There might be
as many as three thousand names in there. That's
everyone who's come through our port in the last couple
of days . . . or do you need more?"

She told him that two days was enough.

"By now most of those people have scattered across
the country. They come through our inspection lines in
a random fashion. Unless there's trouble we don't have
any way of knowing who checked them through. Sometimes we just wave them on and don't bother looking. It
takes too long. Other times we search everything."

"I know," she answered, recalling a European trip
she had gone on with her ex-fiancé, Dr. David Kerr. The
purpose of the trip was to patch up their faltering
relationship of two years. Instead, Hilary had finally

recognized that David really was just as self-centered as he seemed, that his arrogance was no mere pose. She had ended their affair then and there and they had cut their trip short, returning emotionally exhausted and anxious to be away from each other—only to have a suddenly zealous Customs inspector in New York detain them with a search so thorough as to include emptying the entire contents of a tube of toothpaste. The memory and the associations still rankled.

Hilary determinedly shook off these thoughts and skimmed through the sizeable pad of single-spaced, computer typed sheets of flight manifests. The task of sorting these people out seemed impossible even if she got additional investigators, and she wondered if it might not be more prudent to just wait for the second case. It was tempting, and that way she could concentrate on the Mathessons and their contacts. And yet, the time lost in waiting had distinct dangers. That second case might not be one person, but ten or a hundred.

Looking across the desk at Van Horn, she asked, "Did you see or hear about any prolonged interactions with anyone? Was anyone ill, or just didn't look right? I need something to go on."

After a moment's reflection, Van Horn grinned. "Yes, there was one kind of funny incident, but I don't think there's a connection."

"Tell me anyway."

"Some ten-year-old, probably in a hurry to get to the front line, grabbed the wrong Samsonite suitcase. It all happened so quickly that we didn't spot the commotion in time. As it turned out, that case belonged to a courier for the Russian consulate—do you believe it?—and boy, was he mad. Gordon was just starting to open the case, or trying to. The thing was locked, and that Russian grabbed it away like the queen's jewels were inside, then chewed Gordon out in English and Russian both. No harm done, I'm sure, but even if it was top secret stuff it was still just an honest mistake. These foreign diplomats are all prima donnas. But like I said, he didn't *look* sick. Diplomatic immunity, you know?'' He laughed.

Hilary smiled back, but wondered why the courier would be so touchy if his case was locked. Prima donna or not, the Russian's angry outburst reminded her of the irritability Mrs. Mathesson had noted in her normally mild-mannered husband just before he was stricken. It was a tenuous connection at best, but it was all she had. ''Do you have his name?'' she asked.

Van Horn reached across the desk and skimmed down the list of names on a BOAC flight. Two thirds of the way down he pointed to a name—Szlenko.

''Any others? A conversation, an argument? If there's anything that comes to mind, tell me about it.''

''You're probably going to have to speak to the other inspectors. The only cases that I hear about back here are potential violations.'' Van Horn hesitated as another incident came to mind. ''Now there was a drug case, at least, a suspected drug case . . . this grubby kid who looked a little like Rasputin . . . God, was he filthy. He had long, black scraggly hair with a beard that must have had crumbs from three days' food in it. He resented all of our paperwork and was really impatient. I guess his attitude bugged Gordon. We didn't have any drug alerts out that day, but this kid just looked the type. He said that he'd just come back from missionary work in Africa, but there's no church who'd send anyone looking like him. Anyway, Gordon made him unpack his backpack and even searched his clothes in the back room. He must have spent a good half hour. Later on, Gordon said that the kid hadn't bathed in a month. He had trouble handling it. I guess if that's the kind of contact you're looking for, I wouldn't be at all surprised if he was carrying a half dozen illnesses.''

''Did he find any drugs?''

''Not a damn thing. Too bad. They would have given him a bath at the jail. He's probably rich. They get out of hock with a phone call to dad. Some of these traveling beggars have more money than I'll ever see.

Poor's a fad this year, you know . . ."

"His name?"

"Gordon can tell you. He should have it in his records. Maybe I can track it down for you. I think he was on the same BOAC flight as the Russian."

After taking a culture from Van Horn's throat, Hilary proceeded to the inspection stations to interview the other inspectors. Most of them recalled the incident with the Russian and a few recalled the unkempt youth, but they came up with only three other potential cases. One was an older woman returning from Greece. She came off the airplane in a wheelchair with an accompanying nurse. Supposedly, she had sustained some type of injury while visiting the Acropolis and required hospitalization. Later, she had complications that extended her stay. The inspector who related the story thought that it might have been pneumonia, but he wasn't sure.

Another case was an Asian businessman who came through the lines "coughing his insides out." The man couldn't seem to be able to stop and didn't always cover his mouth, and at lunch later, Mathesson had told some of the others that he hoped it wasn't tuberculosis.

The third prospect was the most intriguing. The information was sketchy, but garnering what she could from the inspectors, she pieced together that a high school drama teacher had taken a group of her students to England to see Stratford-on-Avon. While there, two of the group became ill and had to remain behind in a London hospital. The diagnosis was meningitis.

Hilary was elated. It was hard to believe that she could have found the source so easily, and it was too strong a lead not to pursue immediately. Everything else was pushed aside.

Dr. Paige saw Ogden leaving his office for the laboratory.

"How'd it go?" he asked as he hurried to catch up.

Lester Paige was stockier than Ogden, "Harvardishlooking'' as the nurses liked to say, his only eccentricity the crumpled-up science fiction magazine he often carried folded in his back pocket. The only things that changed from day to day were the colors of the stripes in his tie and the title on the magazine: *Analog, Omni, Asimov* . . .

Les Paige was the only one at the hospital who knew that Ogden was not divorced but widowed, and also the only person other than Tom Ling with whom Ogden had discussed his experiment in any detail.

"How'd it go, Mike?" he asked again as he walked alongside.

"Pretty good," Ogden said, his tone indicating something else.

"You don't say? Did something go wrong? I was hoping for a little more exuberance."

"The experiment went off pretty much as we planned, except for an unexpected nodule that turned out to be benign, but there's another problem. One I didn't expect." Ogden went on to explain about Mossberger's work.

"That s.o.b.!" Paige said.

"Les, do you think you can hold down the fort for another week or two? Until I get this one last piece of work done?"

"Sure." Paige was pleased to do the favor. "Actually three's not that much to do. Your residents this year are all pretty sharp. I doubt they need much more than a pat on the back most of the time."

"I'm sure you have a lot more to offer than that. It's just that I need every second I can get for the next week or two." Ogden leaned against the door to push it open. His mind had slipped off to his work again.

"You might want to know about the meningitis case we got in before you take off. It looks like meningococcal."

Ogden stopped halfway through the door. "How bad?"

"Comatose, probably won't make it, or if he does he'll have a serious neurological deficit. Don't worry, we don't need you. Yates already started him on penicillin and he's in the unit. Just thought you might want to know."

"I do. Thanks. Maybe I'll come back and take a look at him later."

"Don't bother. I'll call you. Leave this place to me. We're all counting on you to swing this grant. Get that work done." Paige started back toward the wards, happy that Ogden seemed relieved and yet wondering how much deeper he would now bury himself in his research. The scars of Karen's death seemed to have healed over, but Ogden had not only ignored Les's suggestions that it was time to come out of his self-imposed isolation but had seemed to withdraw even further from life and from his son. The fact that a cure for cancer was at stake was a pretty good excuse, Les knew—and one he envied more than he liked to admit—but that wasn't the only explanation behind Ogden's obsessive work habits.

His thoughts were interrupted by the hospital intercom informing him that Dr. Yates wanted him in admitting. When he arrived, Joanna Yates seemed worried and she spoke softly so as not to be heard by others. "I think the oldest Mathesson girl might be coming down with meningitis also. They've only been here three hours, maybe less, and she seemed fine when I checked her earlier, but now she's got a headache and a temp of a hundred. I hate to make a mountain out of a molehill, but I wonder if we shouldn't tap her to be on the safe side. If I tell the mother, she'll panic again, I know."

"What would you do if I wasn't here? If you were out in private practice and had this problem?"

"Tap her," Yates said.

"Then do it, but I'm really surprised that the disease could have spread to other family members so quickly."

"Her mother says that the girl gets tension headaches fairly easily, and she certainly has good reason to be tense today."

"Maybe, but she also has a fever, and if there's no

other obvious cause I'd still like to go ahead and tap
her. The procedure's harmless. She won't like it, but it's
harmless.''

The two physicians carefully gowned and gloved outside the examination room and then went in through the
airlock.

"Marcey, this is Dr. Paige, one of my bosses. I'd like
him to examine you also.''

The girl tried to smile, but her upper lip quivered. She
was sitting on the edge of the table wearing an
examination gown.

"Do you still have a headache, Marcey?" Dr. Paige
asked as he picked up an otoscope, examining first her
right ear and then her left. Both tympanic membranes
were semilucent and readily reflected the instrument's
tiny light.

"Yes," came a muted answer which he had to ask her
to repeat.

"And where is it?''

The girl pointed to the back of her neck and moved
her hand to show how the pain radiated upward to the
top of her head and over both eyes.

"Your ears or throat bothering you?" Paige continued, picking up a flashlight and taking a tongue blade
from a glass jar to look inside her mouth. She shook her
head, as he slid the wooden stick between her teeth and
pressed her tongue down. She gagged, but he didn't
move. Both tonsils appeared normal and there were no
other foci of inflammation that could cause a fever.

"Any cough or runny nose?''

"No.''

Paige turned toward Yates, who was quietly waiting
to hear his opinion. "It doesn't sound like the temperature's from a respiratory source to me.''

Yates agreed.

"Any stomach cramps, diarrhea, vomiting, rash or
any bladder symptoms like burning when you urinate?"
he continued, seeking a possible explanation that would
obviate the spinal tap.

"No," she whispered.

Paige bent the girl's neck forward, and although there wasn't any resistance she complained that the maneuver hurt her. To him this suggested meningitis, but his face remained expressionless.

After apologizing for the discomfort, he proceeded to untie her gown. As the garment fell to her waist, her face and neck reddened with embarrassment. Her breasts were early in their development, mere buds, and this was the first time that a man had seen them. Paige proceeded, undaunted, sliding a cold stethoscope along both sides of her chest in the back, below both collar-bones and between her breasts to listen to her heart tones. Everything seemed normal. He then moved to examining her abdomen. Both the liver and spleen were normal in size and nontender. Listening with his stethoscope again, he found that her bowel sounds were active and of normal pitch, and as he palpated with his hands he could discern none of the muscle wall rigidity that would be apparent with an underlying infection. After checking her knee reflexes with a rubber hammer and several other joints for swelling, he asked her to stand undressed and then studied every inch of her body for the early spots of meningococcal disease. His search included the area between the folds of her buttocks, behind her ears and beneath her fingernails, but the only lesions he found were a few flat warts on her hands and some acne on her face.

The remaining part of the exam was the pelvic. After deliberating on how to approach the subject, he asked, simply, "Is there any chance of venereal disease?"

"No way!" came a prompt answer which he believed.

"I don't think we have a choice." He turned toward Yates. "A headache with a fever, no other source and a father with meningitis. I think you have to tap her."

The girl remained motionless and quiet as Yates explained the procedure. "It'll hurt just a little. Something like a bee sting when I inject the novocaine. Like a dentist deadening a tooth. Afterwards you shouldn't feel a thing. We need a little fluid to be sure that you don't have the same illness your dad has. Do you understand, Marcey?''

Marcey nodded as tears crept into her eyes. She had always been afraid of doctors and especially needles.

Despite the girl's concerns, however, the procedure went quickly. Yates had the nurse roll Marcey into a tight ball on her side, deadening a small area at the base of her spine and quickly inserted the long needle straight into the spinal canal. Marcey flinched for a moment as the needle popped into the channel and complained that a pain shot down her leg, but then held still as clear fluid dripped into the first test tube.

"It looks crystal clear," Yates remarked to Paige, who was watching from behind. After collecting the customary three tubes and checking some pressure readings, she pulled the needle out. "That's it. It's all over," the resident announced, and complimented the girl for being so cooperative.

As the nurse was putting a bandage on the needle site, Dr. Paige held the last tube up to the light and compared it with a white sheet of paper. At first it looked normal to him too, but as he jiggled the fluid he thought he saw some turbidity. He wasn't sure, but there was a suggestion that something might be wrong with it. After asking Marcey to lie on her stomach for a half hour to minimize the post-tap headaches that most patients get, he and Yates decided to make rounds on Yates's patients while they waited for the lab's analysis.

On the way out, they stopped by the waiting room to tell Harriet Mathesson that the procedure had gone well and Marcey was fine. When she asked about the results, Paige could only shake his head apologetically and tell her she'd have to wait.

Once Yates and Paige arrived on the third floor, they picked up Dr. James, who had been doing his morning scut work, and the three physicians went to visit Guadelupe Hernandez, a nine-year-old girl who had been admitted during the previous week with typhoid fever. The youngster had been ill with high fevers and bloody diarrhea since the day her family had illegally entered the country. Being aliens and afraid they would be sent back, they delayed seeking medical attention and resorted instead to folk medicine remedies that only made her condition worsen. From a few loose stools with a streak of blood, her symptoms had changed dramatically to frank blood mixed with mucus, occurring at least twenty times a day and eventually making her so weak that she could barely walk or speak. When she arrived at the unit, she was severely dehydrated. Her skin puckered when pinched and only slowly fell back into place. The inside of her mouth was parched, her eyeballs were soft and sunken, and the only sound that she made was an occasional pathetic whimper whenever her stomach cramps returned.

The diagnosis of typhoid fever was suspected from the beginning. Firstly, she was Mexican, an ethnic group often afflicted with the disease; the bloody diarrhea was a typical symptom; and lastly, she had a few reddish spots on her chest that were consistent with the disease. Antibiotics and intravenous fluids were started immediately while they waited for cultures on her stool and blood, but the abdominal cramps worsened until late one night when they suddenly stopped. X-ray revealed that her colon had dilated drastically to a diameter that was four times normal. And then it perforated, like a toy balloon. This was always a dreaded complication that carried an extremely high mortality rate. She was rushed off to surgery, where a large segment of bowel was removed along with the equivalent of a pint of pus.

The illuminated warning sign outside the girl's door read "ENTERIC PRECAUTIONS."

The three physicians gowned and gloved, then checked the taped seals on each other's suits for integrity. Inside they found an emaciated little Chicano girl lying quietly in bed, tubes and sensor wires taped to her.

"Her condition's worse," Yates whispered as she picked up the temperature chart and showed Paige the unrelenting fever and low blood pressure readings. The pattern had been downhill for several days.

As Paige checked her over, the other two physicians watched from the bedside. "The wound's healing, at least," he remarked, probing the reddened edge. Normally, the pressure of his touch would have hurt, but the girl didn't move. She merely stared up at him with half-open eyes. *"Dolor?"* he asked. His Spanish vocabulary was limited, but everyone at County knew the word for pain. Again there was no response. Finally, he asked Yates if she had been doing any talking.

"Only a few cries since surgery."

"Does the family know how serious her condition is? That she might—" He stopped himself and looked at the girl's open eyes. He doubted that she understood, or could even hear him, but he couldn't take the chance.

"They've been told, but they're insisting that God will pull her through. They've been here praying every day."

"That may be the only hope she has." Paige sighed as he went out through the airlock and tossed his gloves in the wastebasket. He scrubbed in the sink. He had seen so many prayers go unanswered in this part of the hospital. . . .

Another case that belonged to Yates's service was Harry Campbell, an alcoholic with tuberculosis. The seventy-eight-year-old transient had been there for several days, constantly coughing, severely short of breath, and hallucinating from the D. T.s. Previously, he had been hospitalized at Rancho Los Amigos, a convalescent hospital in south Los Angeles, but he walked off the hospital grounds one day, went on a drinking binge and never returned, despite the smoldering abscesses in his lungs and worsening symptoms.

Three months later, Campbell was found lying in the hallway of an old tenement building, and when he was brought to County Hospital he was admitted to the

Drunk Tank, unshaven, thick with dirt, reeking from the cheap wine and urine that soaked his clothes and covered with roving lice. After being disinfected and scrubbed down, a routine chest X-ray picked up the signs of tuberculosis and he was immediately transferred over to the Contagious Disease Unit, where a further workup by Yates and Jones showed that the tuberculosis organism had spread to practically every organ system in his body. In essence, he was a living petri dish for the *tubercle bacillus*, with abscesses now in his brain, heart, kidneys and intestines, as well as several enlarging pus pockets in both lungs.

As the three physicians and a nurse entered Campbell's room, the old alcoholic was twisting about in his bed, fighting to free himself from the restraints around his wrists, ankles and across his chest. Intermittently, he'd stop to speak to some imagined presence in the room or to scream out in horror. Tremors wracked his body from one end to the other.

"Before we catheterized him, he drank his own urine from the urinal. Now he's pulled the catheter out twice and his IV three times," the nurse complained, obviously annoyed. "We can't keep him still. Last night his screaming kept the whole floor awake. He's impossible to care for."

"Mr. Campbell, hold still!" Paige cried at the drunk as he grabbed at the man's hand and tried to remove it from the restraints. A second later he jerked his hand back, gouged by the man's dirty fingernails. Then, as Yates and James tried to help him get the patient back into the center of his bed, he tried to spit, but the saliva only drooled down his chin and pooled on his chest.

"Lovely!" Yates remarked, adding, "I don't know why we're even bothering. We found his old records. The stack of charts is over a foot thick. There's at least twelve admissions for drunkenness, he's refused rehabilitation innumerable times and he's come back with cirrhosis and GI bleeding twice. Now he's got tuberculosis, an old-fashioned way to make his exit.

There's no way this man will ever take the medications for a year on his own, and God knows who'll he'll spread the infection to. Society would be better off without him.''

''I know how you feel,'' Paige answered quietly, stepping back and staring at the fidgeting figure of skin and bones. He understood the futility. Dozens like him had come through the unit over the years and few ever got on the wagon. The cost in time and money was enormous, but letting him die was tantamount to murder. He might feel like letting these hopeless cases die, but as acting chief he couldn't even say it. And he would certainly never do it. ''Just do what you can,'' he responded. ''Maybe the disease will get him despite your efforts.''

''He'll just come back if we cure him,'' Yates answered.

''At least it won't be on your rotation here, if that's any consolation,'' Paige said as he headed toward the door.

Their third stop was the intensive care unit, where Gordon Mathesson lay semicomatose. He'd woken up some, responding to simple commands like ''move your toes'' or ''turn your head,'' but for the most part he'd lain asleep. When Paige tried calling his name, his eyes remained closed and the only sounds they heard were an occasional sigh and the constant blipping from the overhead heart monitor. His fever had resisted all of their efforts to lower it and the continuing low blood pressure made the outlook bleak.

''Now, here's a man who's done nothing wrong,'' Yates continued in the same vein she'd struck in Campbell's room. ''The typical upstanding citizen, hard-working breadwinner, a family man, all that stuff and he might not make it. And meanwhile that drunk down the hall may walk out of here. It doesn't make sense.''

''No one ever said it was supposed to,'' Paige responded. He tried bending Mathesson's neck forward, but it wouldn't flex. ''I think you'd better tap him again in eight hours . . . make sure that things are going the right way.''

The suggestion was directed to Yates, but James wrote it down on his scut list. Spinal taps done after admission were considered scut work, and therefore his to do.

By the time they had washed their hands and removed the protective garments, Marcey Mathesson's spinal tap results had returned. They were positive.

Patient: Mathesson, Marcey, age 16
PF Number: 345–87–047
Spinal Fluid Analysis
Drawn: 1043

	Result	Normal Value
Description:	slightly turbid	clear
Amount received	6 cc	variable
Cell count		
Total white count	72	less than ten
Percent neutrophils	98%	0%
Percent mononuclears	2%	100%
Total red cells	3	0
Protein	56	15–45 mgm/100ml
Sugar	35	45–80 mgm/100ml

Gram stain: Rare Gram negative intracellular diplococci consistent with meningococcus

The elevated white cell count was considerably lower than her father's, but it combined with the positive Gram stain for the presence of bacterial organisms to give conclusive proof of meningitis. Suddenly there was concern for the other members of the family.

CHAPTER SIX

Hilary Walters had been working hard at the L.A. International Airport. Her most likely suspect was the drama teacher whose ailing students had been left behind in England with meningitis. Earlier, en route to the airport, she'd imagined organizing some monstrous investigation, possibly drawing in several additional investigators and tracking down hundreds of passengers, but now it appeared that she'd been handed the solution on a silver platter. It was still too easy to believe.

Unfortunately, other details were sketchy. None of the customs inspectors knew the lady's name, and when Van Horn broke into Mathesson's locker they found that only the long-haired youth's name, Gerald Katzenbach, was recorded. Just in case, she jotted it down, but she doubted she'd need it.

The best description of the teacher that she could get was of a woman of medium height, maybe five-three or -four, who had frizzy red hair and was in her fifties but trying to look younger with heavy makeup. The inspector remembered her especially well because of the large boil on the side of her nose and her loud voice.

"Maybe from New York," the inspector added. When she asked if the group might have gone onto a connecting flight, he said that he doubted it. He had overheard one of the boys remark on how nice it would be to get home to his own bed in the next half hour.

Vague, but enough information to work with. In past searches she'd worked with less. After collecting a handful of dimes, she thumbed through the telephone directory and began calling every high school within a half hour's drive. Altogether there were nine, and on her second to last call an administrative clerk verified that their school had a red-haired drama teacher by the name of Trumbell and that she'd just returned from Europe with a group of her students. Unsure what to do, he refused to give the woman's home phone number, but added that it was easily found in the white pages. Hilary quickly dialed the number she found in the book, explained that she had to ask some routine questions about the students who had become ill in England, and a few moments later she was on her way to the teacher's home.

On her way across town, her satisfaction on hearing of this lead gave way to doubts. If the inspector had been mistaken and the students had been hospitalized with something other than meningitis, then she was back to square one. And if he was correct, there was the possibility that these students had spread the disease to other passengers on the plane, just as they'd given it to Mathesson. Even if she was on the right path, it might be about to divide into dozens more avenues of investigation, and there could be a lot of work ahead—and a need for extra help.

When she arrived at Miss Trumbell's home, the teacher was frantic with worry. "It's all my fault, isn't it?" she said in an accent that was unmistakably New York. Miss Trumbell fit the inspector's description perfectly, down to the large boil on her nose. Not knowing whether the woman was a carrier of meningococcus, Hilary kept her distance, choosing to sit in a chair rather than next to her on the couch.

"Those kids are worse, aren't they? I just knew it. All this because I had some silly notion . . ." The woman rambled on without allowing Hilary a chance to say a word. "I thought that they'd appreciate Shakespeare so much more this way. Oh, if I just hadn't taken those little children away from their homes. It must have been the cold air . . . it was much chillier there than here, you know . . . none of them brought the right clothing. Who would have thought it would be that cold this time of the year?"

"You can't blame yourself for their illness," Hilary finally interjected, finding the woman's flair for the dramatic evident. Every other word was emphasized, as if she were reading an overrehearsed script.

"And who else should I blame?" She stared over at Hilary for a second, waiting for her to read her line now. "I know they're worse. I felt it. You're here to tell me that, aren't you?"

"No, I'm only here to ask you some questions. I don't have any more information on their health than you have. Not yet, anyway."

"What kind of questions?" She looked worried.

Hilary considered explaining the series of events that had brought her here, but changed her mind. Any more information might scare her. Instead, she said, "We always investigate illnesses that our citizens contract abroad. I'm only here on a routine check."

"Routine?"

"Yes."

Miss Trumbell seemed to relax somewhat.

"I've been so worried. I had to tell their parents the minute we got in and they've all called me several times since. I think the girl's father is going to fly to London tonight."

"What did the doctors there tell you she had? Do you

remember the name of the illness? Weren't they worried about everyone else?'' Hilary had decided that she had wasted enough time.

"How'd she get sick? I don't know. We all went to a nice English pub together and then to Trafalgar Square. The statue was crawling with pigeons. Disgusting animals. The ground was covered with droppings. Everyone had it on their shoes. I can't see why anyone lets those birds stay there. Anyway, we were going over to Madame Tussaud's Wax Museum when Jill said she had a headache and that she wanted to go back to the hotel instead. She took a taxi while we went ahead, but while we were there Larry got sick too. He turned white and his forehead felt like he had a fever. It must have been those dreadful pigeons. Pigeons carry a lot of diseases, you know. Anyway, I took him back to the hotel as well. A tiny room, not like we expected. The bedspread was stained, the curtains torn, and the bathroom so small you couldn't sit to do you-know-what. Not without cramping your legs anyway. Breakfast was expensive too—''

"What happened to the two students?''

"Oh, yes, sorry. Well, they both looked awfully pale, and Jill had a fever. I didn't have a thermometer, but my hands are very sensitive. I'd say it was around a hundred and one. Anyway, I took them both to a hospital nearby . . . I don't remember the name, but I wrote it down." She stopped talking long enough to search her purse for a small sheet of paper she handed to Hilary. Dr. Crabtree of Hammersmith Hospital, it read. "They were in there for an eternity, poor kids. And this doctor,'' the teacher added, pausing to point out the physician's name, ''came out and told me that they had meningitis. Scared the you-know-what out of me. I'd been with them for days and had no idea they had such a dreadful illness. He said they'd have to stay behind for observation. He didn't give them any medication though.''

"Are you sure?" Hilary asked. That was a key point, *if* she was correct.

"Of course, I'm sure. He said he wouldn't. That bothered me a lot. I know a little about medicine. You read about it all in the magazines these days. They looked so sick, so miserable, poor things. I'm sure their parents blame me. I called them the minute I got back to the hotel."

"Are you sure they didn't get any medicine?" Hilary repeated. The diagnosis couldn't be meningococcal meningitis if that were true.

"Absolutely! Well, maybe some aspirin for their headaches, but that was it."

"Did they do a spinal tap? Stick a needle in their backs?"

"Indeed they did."

Hilary asked to use the teacher's phone. After charging the call to her office, she had the long distance operator connect her with Hammersmith Hospital, but she was told that Dr. Crabtree had gone home for the night. She requested his backup, and after checking the charts he confirmed that the two Americans did have meningitis, adding, however, that theirs was the viral type.

"Not meningococcal?"

"Just a minor virus. Just enough to give them a headache that'll last a couple of days. We should be sending them home soon."

Hilary's promising lead had fizzled. After taking a culture of Miss Trumbell's throat and, just to be thorough, another of the sore on her nose, she thanked her and left. There were still several paths to follow, but not one of them stood out as a likely source.

The cocker spaniel was twelve years old, with graying hairs along the edge of his floppy ears and speckled through his muzzle. He was also extremely thin from his illness and distinctly unfriendly. Each time Mike Ogden bent down to pet him, the dog bared his yellowed teeth and started to growl.

"He won't bite. He never has. He's just a cranky old man," Mr. O'Malley reassured him, but Ogden decided to keep his distance for the time being. The elderly owner was a short, stooped man, quite similar in appearance to his dog, with graying along his ears and through his mustache. Even Mrs. O'Malley resembled the dog, and all three tended to walk with the same limp.

"Dr. Peters explained what we plan to do here, didn't he?" Ogden asked as he returned to the other side of his desk and asked the O'Malleys to sit across from him. He knew that whatever he said it had to be convincing. He couldn't afford not to be. He needed that dog for his work.

"He said that you might be able to help Clarence," Mr. O'Malley said hopefully.

Lying on the desk in front of Ogden were copies of the dog's X-rays, slides from the excisional biopsy that the veterinarian had done and a stack of blood tests. Superficially, it looked like the chart of a human patient, even to the name: Clarence O'Malley.

"Dr. Peters tells me that your dog has cancer," Ogden said matter-of-factly, but seeing the change in their expressions he realized that he might have said the wrong word. The O'Malleys didn't seem to want Clarence to know.

"This . . . sickness has spread throughout his intestines and into his liver and lungs. It's . . ." Ogden hesitated. He wanted to say fatal, but was afraid that was also something they didn't want Clarence to hear.

"We know," Mrs. O'Malley said bravely. "Dr. Peters has already told us."

"And you know that this is only experimental. I can't promise you that it will work, although I fully expect it to. His disease is much more extensive than I expected."

"All we want to be sure of is that you won't hurt him," Mr. O'Malley inserted. "We're all getting old and we'd like to spend our remaining time together, but we don't want to hurt him."

"I can understand, but there might be a little . . ." Ogden stopped for an instant. He could see their immediate alarm. He didn't want to lie, but he didn't want to scare them off either. "Discomfort," he said, substituting a kinder word for pain. "But we have medications we can give him that will keep him comfortable." Ogden then went on to explain the experiment as clearly and simply as he could to make sure the O'Malleys understood the procedure.

The couple wasn't sure. "Maybe we'll think about it," Mr. O'Malley said and started to rise.

Ogden couldn't let them leave. "We've done this on lots of dogs," he quickly said. "None of them have suffered." He left out the fact that they had all been sacrificed for autopsies.

"I don't know." Mr. O'Malley was the hesitant one.

"Suppose we let you come and visit him every day here. If you think that we've done too much or he's suffering, we'll stop. It's his only chance."

Mrs. O'Malley seemed to want to do it. "Let's give it a try," she said to her husband, putting her hand on his.

While the old man thought it over, Ogden's mind was racing through every argument he could think of to convince them. It might be good for humanity . . . the dog might live another twelve years, Clarence might be written up in the medical journals. He even considered telling them that his own work depended on this dog, but didn't have to. Mr. O'Malley agreed, repeating that he'd be by to see the dog every day.

When the couple finally left, Ogden excitedly moved the dog over to his laboratory. He felt as though he'd lied to the O'Malleys, but he'd only bent the truth a little. He knew that he'd have to be sure that the dog wasn't suffering, but that was something he always avoided. The dog had to be a cure, he told himself, not a fatality. Ogden's whole life seemed to depend on it.

In the interim, across the parking lot, Dr. Paige was reexamining the Mathesson family. They'd been checked by both Yates and James already, but with two family members afflicted, he wanted to be sure.

Harriet and Jamey Mathesson checked out as normal, but Paige was bothered by Lynda's "cold." She had the typical symptoms of a runny nose and cough, without the meningitis symptoms of a headache and stiff neck, but there was always the chance that she had an early case.

Under normal circumstances, he might prescribe aspirin and rest, but this time he ordered a CBC blood test so that he could get an idea of whether she should have a spinal tap also. If the white cell count was elevated, it would mean that she had a bacterial infection and he'd have to proceed. If depressed, it meant a cold.

The CBC was ordered stat and over the next ten minutes that it took to get an answer everyone remained tense.

Patient: Mathesson, Lynda, age 10
PF Number: 345–87–049
Complete Blood Count
Drawn: 1101

	Result	Normal Values
Hemoglobin	14	14–16 gm/100ml
Hematocrit	44%	42–47 ml/100ml
Red Cell Count	4.8	4.8–5.4 mil./cu mm
White Cell Count	3,300	5–10,000 cu mm
Neutrophils	40%	36–66%
Bands	2%	5–11%
Eosinophils	2%	3%
Basophils	1%	0.5%
Lymphocytes	50%	24–44%

Monocytes	5%	0–4%
MCV	86	82–92
MCH	29	27–31
MCHC	34	32–36

Red Cell Morphology: slight anisocytosis

Much to everyone's relief, the results—a low white count—confirmed that she had a typical cold.

At noon that same day, an emergency call came into the Glendale Fire Station.

"I think she's trying to kill herself upstairs!" The woman on the phone sounded frantic. "I'm sure I smell gas. I tried knocking on her door, but no one answered . . . I know she's there . . . someone's got to come!"

A paramedic van was dispatched within seconds, and five minutes later two firemen with gas masks and several medical cases were pounding on the apartment door. The hallway reeked of gas. When no one responded, they put on their masks and butted their shoulders against the door until it gave way. The living room was deserted, but lying in the bedroom was a woman, her skin bluish, apparently not breathing. As the first man in rushed to open the windows, his partner quickly pulled back the woman's covers to feel for some sign of a femoral pulse at the groin and then at the carotid in the neck. Neither was palpable.

"Looks bad," the paramedic by the bed said to his colleague, who was struggling with a stuck window. "We'd better get her hooked up to see if she's even alive." He quickly unpacked an oxygen tank and connected it to a black bag to pump air into the girl's lungs. As he squeezed, her chest barely moved. He was surprised at how stiff her body was. Her color was unusual, too—more blotchy than most gas suffocation victims he had seen.

Meanwhile, the first paramedic removed the EKG electrodes from another case, ripped the nightgown from the girl's upper torso and attached the leads to prescribed areas to pick up any heartbeats. Once the machine was switched on, however, the scope showed a flat line. He quickly rechecked his lead placement to be sure, but they were all correct and functioning.

"Just what I thought, damn it. Dead as a doorknob." The second paramedic stopped his efforts with the oxygen and called County Hospital. When he got through to the receiving physician and reported that they had a flat EKG line, they were given permission to cease cardio-pulmonary resuscitation and to call the police instead.

While they waited for a squad car, both men looked around the apartment for a suicide note, being careful now not to disturb anything. They found nothing. Maybe it was an accident—the oven was on but the pilot light was out—and when the police arrived the investigating officer came to the same conclusion. The door and windows had been locked from the inside. After the coroner's office was called and a few photographs taken, the body was transferred to the morgue. No one noticed the intensity of the blue spots compared to the rest of her body or that her neck was disproportionately stiffer than her other joints, and no one at the scene washed their hands after handling the body.

CHAPTER SEVEN

It was close to one o'clock by the time Hilary returned to L.A. International Airport after stopping for a few minutes at a hamburger stand and telephoning Atlanta to report the meningitis case. The response on the other end was noncommittal. Dr. Raynor, her immediate supervisor, was not impressed with the occurrence of an isolated case. He discounted Mathesson's connection to the airport, which she considered a potential disaster. Raynor had seen meningitis before. He urged her to stay on top of it and keep him informed. His reaction made her feel like an alarmist, but it also made her more determined to head off any further spread of the disease.

The next likely suspect on her list was the elderly lady who had passed through Customs in a wheelchair. Supposedly, the woman had been hospitalized in Greece and there was a remote chance that her postoperative complication was due to meningococcal disease. Unlikely, but she couldn't exclude it. All of the other suspects were even less likely carriers.

When she found Inspector Van Horn's office empty,

she made her way to the inspection area where a Lufthansa flight was disembarking. Three hundred and twenty tired and irritable Germans were queueing up to six inspection tables, some being waved through, some having their luggage searched, all complaining about bureaucratic delays.

Hilary spotted Van Horn working in Mathesson's spot. The chief inspector had a woman's nightcase open and was closely examining the contents when he saw Hilary approaching. Her timing was poor. He was too busy to deal with her now and his face reflected his annoyance.

"I've come back to find out about that lady in the wheelchair," she announced, oblivious to Van Horn's problems.

"You sure are persistent, aren't you?" Van Horn went on working. He pointed to a second case and asked the woman to open it.

"I have to be. Car salesmen, tax collectors and me."

"We've already told you all that we know. Why don't you come back later today if you need to talk to me?"

"I don't have time and your men didn't give me enough to go on. There must be a thousand old women in wheelchairs in this town. Maybe ten thousand."

"I'm really not in the mood to count women in wheelchairs. Nor am I in a mood to discuss this now." Van Horn quickly ran his fingers through several layers of expensive clothes, checked the inside pockets of the suitcase, then waved the woman on. The next passenger was a business executive type whom he decided not to inspect. As the man left, he turned toward Hilary. "You know this is an extremely busy place and I don't think I can help you any more than I have. In fact, I really doubt you'll find any answers here. You're wasting your time."

"I'm not so sure," Hilary answered as she stepped away. She couldn't agree with him, not yet anyway, not until she'd exhausted all of her leads. As she headed

back toward the main lobby, she suddenly got an idea.
Walking fifty yards ahead was a nurse pushing a
wheelchair. Hilary quickened her pace and made her
way to the first aid station at the far end of the terminal.
When she asked the nurse on duty about the woman
from Greece, she recalled helping her. A chauffeur had
come to the station and asked her to assist him, but the
nurse had been surprised to see that the woman appeared to be in good health. They hurried her through
Customs as if she were a VIP and then off to a white
Continental whose license plates read F-L-I-P.

"Flip?" The letters didn't ring a bell, but she called
the Department of Motor Vehicles and learned that the
car belonged to Congressional Representative Charles
Fitzhugh, whose nickname was Flip. She recalled from
newspaper articles that he'd been given the appellation
when he was a gymnast in high school and it had stuck,
having even been used on campaign posters.

Fitzhugh's home address was in Marina Del Rey, a
mammoth complex of modern apartment buildings and
condominiums around a small bay that was glutted with
expensive yachts. His residence was a three-story
townhouse and Hilary was greeted at the door by a ser-
vant.

The woman she was seeking turned out to be the
congressman's mother, and when Hilary was announced she found her engrossed in a TV soap opera,
her hands busily knitting a sweater and her right leg
propped up on a pillow. Hilary estimated her age to be
eight-five.

"Health Department?" the woman said when she
heard the introduction. "About my illness in Greece?
It's about time somebody looked into it. Did my boy
Chuckey call you?"

"No, ma'am. This is more of a routine check . . ."
Hilary started to explain why she'd come, but the
woman's attention had reverted to the television screen
and Hilary had to wait for a commercial to divert the

woman's attention. She explained that a customs official had gotten sick and she was checking all travelers who were near him.

"Well, I'm sure he didn't get it from me, if *that's* what you think." The woman's eyes kept darting back and forth between Hilary and the TV set.

"I'm merely checking." Hilary started to ask about her ailment when a man's voice from behind interrupted her.

"Checking what?" The congressman entered the room. He was short and heavy, with slicked-back hair and a large cigar in his mouth. "Did you clear this through my office first? Whatever it is?"

Hilary introduced herself and explained that she didn't have time to go through customary channels.

"We can't just have people dropping in here, you know," he said gruffly. He sat down next to his mother and started twirling the cigar between his fingers. "You look like a reporter to me. Suppose you tell me what this is about."

The congressman's apparent irritation bothered her, but she tried to remain pleasant—too much was at stake—and carefully went through the details on the Mathesson case.

"Certainly my mother hasn't got the same thing," he sarcastically remarked when she finished.

"Nothing's certain. Some people can carry this bacteria for long periods of time. Every lead has to be checked out and I need to know more about your mother's illness."

By happenstance, another commercial came on and he asked his mother to relate what had happened.

"I always take a cruise at this time of the year," she began with a nostalgic grin, and then proceeded to describe unrelated trips until the show resumed.

Obviously irritated, Fitzhugh rose from his chair and slammed off the switch. "You've got all year to catch up. Tell this doctor what she has to know."

"Well, I was climbing up to the Acropolis. They said I was too old, but I've climbed the temples in the Yucatan and the stairs in the Vatican." She hesitated when she saw her son's annoyance and then returned to the point. "I slipped somehow. My leg went out from under me and I broke my hip. Years ago, I could have fallen twice as hard and not even bruised myself. Anyway, they carried me off to some local hospital, if that's what they call it. The food was lousy and the bed hurt my back. I didn't even get my luggage off the ship before it set sail."

"Mother, I'll tell the story," Fitzhugh interrupted. "She needed surgery and they said it was too dangerous to fly her home for it. I shouldn't have allowed it when I got there, but they went ahead and sure enough she got an infection in the incision. Afterward she got a blood clot and then pneumonia. It was one thing after another. Whatever the risks were in moving her couldn't have added up to all that she eventually went through."

"And they didn't have a television in my room," the woman added. Hilary smiled, but Fitzhugh's impatient expression remained.

"You wouldn't have understood it anyway," he remarked.

"Do you know what kind of pneumonia she had?" Hilary asked.

"Pneumonia's pneumonia, isn't it?"

"Not quite. There are several different types of bacteria that can cause it."

"All I know is that hers was the resistant type. They had to change her antibiotics several times."

"No one happened to mention meningococcus to you? Or did someone near her have meningitis?"

"No, I don't think so, but it was hard to know what was going on."

After taking a precautionary culture from the woman's throat, Hilary thanked them both and quickly departed, hoping that the next interview might be more helpful.

Progress in the research laboratory went slowly despite Ogden's eagerness to get started. Hungry for additional subjects to work on, he called half the veterinarians in the city but came up empty-handed. He even tried some of the dog pounds, but not unexpectedly, the attendants there had no way of determining if any of their animals actually had internal tumors. For the moment, it looked like he was stuck with Clarence, an uninterested and uncooperative subject. The dog resisted being put in a pen, growled whenever Ogden or Ling came near, refused to eat and kept tipping over his water dish. It was as if he had already decided to die and was now determined to do so.

"Nothing like a friendly patient. One who respects his doctors." Ogden leaned over the top of the pen as Clarence bared his teeth again.

"It's probably meanness that's kept him alive," Ling said as he pushed a new bowl of water toward the growling dog.

"Well, we'll have to make him feel at home somehow."

"Put some nails in his bed. Maybe that'll do it." Ling laughed.

"When we're done, that's probably what he'll think we did."

Their first step was to reassess the extent of the dog's cancer. They needed to know how many metastases there were, where they were and how extensive, but the routine screening tests were inconclusive.

They decided to administer a radioactive tracer into his bloodstream. The compound was designed to accumulate in any tumor cells; then, with a special camera and counter, they could pinpoint the locations. This was followed by another tracer that was specific for liver and lungs, and altogether they eventually picked up five different cancer sites.

Initially, they tried doing their tests with the dog awake, but when Ling almost got his index finger bitten, they were forced to sedate him.

The last set of diagnostic tests were the X-rays. Every part of the dog's body was examined, beginning with his bones, then his skull and lastly the internal organs. The kidneys, heart and lungs were easy, but when they got to the stomach and colon they had their hands full. The sleepy dog couldn't retain the chalky white enema and it took Ling and Ogden several trying and unpleasant attempts to get the barium substance to flow backwards through the loops of bowel so that they could finally get an accurate picture. When they were done, they had found the original tumor site. Situated halfway up the ascending colon was a large cancerous mass that had totally encircled the narrow bowel lumen and was threatening to close it off entirely. Judging by its size, Ogden estimated that it had been growing there for at least a year.

Once the two researchers were done with the nuclear imaging and radiographies, they took the referring veterinarian's slides and projected them upon a white wall. The first tissue was from liver, the basic pattern similar to the one they had shown Bellows, but here the tumor mass was clearly cancerous and it had obviously spread through the bloodstream from the colon malignancy.

At the magnification used, the abnormal cells were the size of grapefruits, pink with dark blue centers that varied in shape and size—the hallmark of cancer. Some had two and three centers, whereas the normal number was one. Many were dividing—reproducing—in clear contrast to normal tissue where few divisions would be found. Many were bizarre shapes, some twice normal size. Some of the tumor cells were eating away at nearby blood vessels or nerves, while others were already slipping into small capillaries and about to spread to other parts of the body through the bloodstream. There was no question that these cells were malignant and highly aggressive. If gone untreated, it was unlikely the dog would survive more than a month, dying of liver failure or bowel obstruction, and the disease probably accounted for his bad temperament. Ogden suspected that he was in pain and had no other way of telling them.

As it turned out, this dog was not the ideal subject, especially when Ogden's entire project hinged on his cure. There were more metastases than they wanted and the first tumor in the colon was much larger than any they had treated before.

"If we abscess that colon mass, it'll probably kill him," Ogden said when they finished reviewing the slides.

"We could cut it out, debulk him," Ling suggested, referring to the method commonly used in humans wherein large tumors are surgically removed so that physicians can chemically treat the smaller, distant metastases.

"It's not in our protocol," Ogden answered pensively. He was hesitant to jeopardize the integrity of the grant proposal by deviating from his experimental plan at this late date.

"Neither is letting the dog die," Ling argued. "If debulking him leads to your being able to demonstrate a cure, no one's going to criticize you."

"No one can say what they'll do, but I think we have to do it your way or not at all." Ogden knew that he didn't have a choice. In financial terms neither he nor the hospital could afford for him to fail. "Let's get started."

An hour later, while the two physicians were suturing two loops of bowel together, they were interrupted by Ogden's secretary speaking over the intercom.

"I'm sorry to interrupt, Dr. Ogden, but I've got Dr.

Joseph from the coroner's office on the line. He says it can't wait.''

"Patch him through," Ogden replied, annoyed and not wanting to break scrub for a call from the morgue. Lying in a sterile silver pan next to the dog's body was an apple-sized mass that had been strangling a segment of bowel.

"Mike?" came a familiar voice through a ceiling speaker.

"Tom, I'm in the middle of some surgery. What's the problem—you find another live one in your cold storage?" Five months before there had actually been an instance of a man waking up in one of Tom Joseph's refrigerated vaults.

"I've got a case here that I think you'd be interested in seeing."

"What's that?" Ogden answered, doubting that he'd go today. If it was dead, it would hold.

"It looks like meningococcal meningitis. They just brought the body in. I haven't done the autopsy yet and I thought you might want to have a look."

"It's not from my unit, is it?" Ogden asked, remembering now what Paige had told him about the new meningitis patient.

"No, why? Have you got one too?"

"That's what I was told. Can it wait? I'm right in the middle of something."

There was a silence for a moment. In the past, whenever the coroner called Ogden had responded immediately. Now, Joseph felt as though he was imposing. "I suppose we can put it off for a few hours, but we've already laid the body out and I was just about to pick up the scalpel when I thought of you."

"Go ahead, Mike," Ling urged him. "There's just a few more sutures left to put in. I'm sure I can handle it alone and there won't be much to do until the dog wakes up."

Reluctantly, Ogden agreed to go. Before leaving,

however, he called the bacteriology laboratory to check on the Mathesson culture and learned that there were two cases of meningitis in the house, not one as he had thought. If the diagnoses were correct, the morgue case might be a third. If so, it was imperative that he check it out now.

The County Morgue was located within the same medical complex, a minute's walk from the Contagious Disease Unit. When Ogden arrived, he went down to the basement and entered a long, tiled room that contained six shiny metal tables. Toward the back was a glassed-in and biologically isolated room where Dr. Joseph and an obese assistant were standing over the nude girl's body. The two men looked a bit like surgeons in their face masks, surgical caps and plastic gloves, but they also wore rubber aprons, and none of their operating tools were sterile. After putting on the same protective garb, Ogden joined them.

"She's got these lesions all over her," Joseph said, pointing to bruise-like marks over her right breast, next to her navel and along the inside of her left thigh. "They look like purpura to me."

"You sure some guy didn't just kick the you-know-what out of her?" Ogden asked, hoping that it wasn't another meningococcal case, and plenty worried that it was. The spots were all too round and symmetrical, too similar to be caused by trauma.

"He'd have to have kicked her in some very funny ways," Joseph said, spreading the girl's stiffened legs apart and showing Ogden another spot, as well as one behind her right ear and two more in her scalp. "Although we sure get some funny cases around here sometimes."

"I'll say," Ogden answered, taking a closer look.

Joseph picked up a scalpel from a drawer full of knives and deftly sliced the girl's body from the edge of her voice box to the top of her pubic bone. Gaseous loops of bowel oozed up through the incision. They, too, as well as several other organs inside, were covered with the tiny blue lesions.

"I have to agree it looks like meningococcus," Ogden admitted. He was beginning to feel the continuity of his research work being threatened by this outbreak of cases, and he offered an alternative diagnosis. "It still might be a leukemia case. I've seen them do this."

"I doubt it," Joseph answered, perplexed by Ogden's resistance. He expected him to be excited. Specialists of his sort were always excited about the unusual or rare cases, despite their sometimes tragic consequences.

"We'll have to wait for the cultures. Do you know anything about her? Her name?"

"Look down there at the toe." Joseph took out a bone cutter that resembled a poultry shears and began cutting her ribs away from their attachment to the sternum.

The name tag read Tina Hudson.

"Half the time, Mike, I don't know their names until I read about them in the newspaper. Unless it's a celebrity like Sal Mineo. But then I wasn't on duty that day." There was disappointment in his voice.

"Missed getting his autograph?" Ogden teased.

Once the longitudinal incision in her chest was pried apart, Joseph began removing the girl's inner organs and placing them on top of a butcher's table for further inspection. Every tissue had the purpuric spots, and when he finally dug out her adrenal glands he found them grossly hemorrhagic. "This is what killed her so quickly." He pointer to the two tiny organs that were responsible for releasing cortisone. Without them, she lost her blood pressure.

Ogden agreed, although meningitis would have killed her within a short time also.

After taking several cultures from the diseased organs, the coroner moved to the girl's head, making a circular incision along the back of her skull and then peeling the scalp forward over her face to expose the bone beneath. Using an electric saw, he made a halo-shaped cut and lifted the cap of bone away. Inside, the brain tissue was covered with a yellow pus that was as thick as molasses.

"Voilà! There you have it. Meningitis," Joseph remarked as he scooped a small amount out and put it in a test tube for culture.

"Better notify the Health Department, and let me know right away if you come up with any more." Ogden was disrobing, and he appeared annoyed.

"You *expecting* more?"

"I don't know what I'm expecting, but I hope it's not any more of these."

CHAPTER EIGHT

By three that afternoon, Hilary was knocking at the door of the Thackery home. Having chased down two false leads already, she was determined to seek out at least one legitimate contact before the day got away from her. Since Mathesson and Thackery had spent a recent evening together, Jim Thackery was a possible contact and perhaps even the carrier. She had to be sure. Maybe she might get lucky, and a lot of investigative work could be avoided.

Mrs. Thackery answered the door. She was a woman in her forties, slightly overweight with a robust complexion and wearing a two-piece suit. "Yes," was all that she said, but the single word actually said who are you, why are you here, I'm in a hurry.

Hilary explained who she was, and once she mentioned Gordon Mathesson's name she was invited in. As they walked back toward the kitchen, Mrs. Thackery apologized for the "messy house."

"Gordon didn't look so good when I saw him," the woman said. She offered Hilary a cup of coffee but she declined; the potential epidemic had already made her too tense.

"When did you see him?" Hilary asked, sitting down at the kitchen table and watching Mrs. Thackery pour herself some coffee.

"Oh . . . last week, I think. John, my husband, sees him all the time. They're old drinkin' and fishin' buddies. How serious is it? Harriet called and told me he was in the hospital. Poor man. She sounded frightened. Is there anything I can do?"

"I don't think there's much you can do at this point. He's in pretty serious condition and I think they're staying at her sister's home. I do need to talk to your husband, though."

"My husband? He just left town."

"They were together last night, weren't they?"

The woman nodded. "They took off for some secret drinking place. I never know where."

"Then there's a chance your husband might have picked up the same organism." Hilary saw that she had alarmed the woman and quickly added, "It's only a remote chance, but I should at least check him."

"I just saw him four hours ago. He looked healthy as could be."

"I'm sure he must be, but I still need to check him. You must have some way to reach him."

"He said he'd call tonight. He's on a buying trip for antiques. That's our business. He's somewhere in San Francisco, but right now he could be calling at any one of a dozen places. Once he starts wandering about, he loses track of time and gets lost for hours. How quickly do you need to see him? He's not going to come down with this immediately, is he? Not after looking so good this morning? I imagine I could get him on the phone tonight."

"Do you know which hotel he's staying at?"

"Always the Fairmont." Mrs. Thackery stood and

went to an address book next to the phone. "I'll call, but knowing him I'll bet he's out." She had to dial twice before reaching the hotel, and there was no answer in her husband's room. "He probably dropped his bags off and left right away. He gets excited," she explained, nervously fidgeting at the pages of the address book.

Hilary forced a smile. She had obviously frightened the woman. If John Thackery was infected, they'd have to hope that he either called home or sought out a physician. "I'd try not to worry," Hilary said, trying to reassure her. "I'm sure he's fine. This illness doesn't spread that easily."

"There is something you can do if I find him, isn't there? I'll try every antique shop I know of. I've gone on these trips with him before and there are certain ones that he likes to visit, where they know him. But there are others that he just walks in and doesn't say a word. If they don't know he's a buyer, sometimes he gets better deals."

Hilary continued to smile and her tone was sympathetic. "Do the best you can and call me as soon as you reach him." She handed Mrs. Thackery her business card.

As she started toward the front door, her pocket beeper buzzed. It was a message from the coroner's office, asking her to call.

Before returning to his project in the laboratory, Ogden decided to check on the two cases of meningitis in the CDU. Three people, one of whom was dead, in less than eight hours—it was highly unusual, and the least he should do was keep track of their progress. A peripheral involvement was all he could afford, however, and he assumed that the detour would only take a few minutes.

When he arrived on the third floor, Mr. Mathesson's condition was worse than the hospital notes reflected. He remained comatose with an extremely stiff neck, his fever curve had stayed above one hundred and four degrees and his blood pressure edged along the border of shock. These findings in themselves might not have alarmed Ogden—the disease was only a few hours old and the antibiotics hadn't had a chance to work—but when he pulled Mathesson's sheets back, he saw that both feet were a deep blue and ice cold. It looked as if he had clotted off the blood supply at midcalf, and Ogden immediately had Joanna Yates summoned.

The resident came in a hurry from the fourth floor, where she was helping to treat a three-day-old child with pneumonia. When she saw Mathesson's dying feet, she appeared just as surprised as Ogden and almost defensive. "They were cool, but not dead like that," she explained quickly. "I'm sure that I felt the pulses there. I thought it was because of the low blood pressure, but I didn't think this would happen."

"It shouldn't. He is getting penicillin, isn't he? Twenty million units a day?"

"I saw the nurse give the first dose myself. The orders have been written. Clotting can happen with meningococcus, can't it?"

"Sure, but not usually this bad, and certainly not after treatment has been initiated. I think you'd better repeat that spinal tap."

"We were going to do it at four—"

"Do it now. I think we'd better check those results before he loses any more of his body."

Yates called for a spinal tray and a nurse to assist her while Ogden went down the hall to check Marcey Mathesson. He felt himself getting angry with Yates, but he knew that she was competent and was doing her best. He was actually irritated with himself for not becoming involved earlier. This was a disaster.

He put on a fresh gown, mask and gloves, as he had before entering Gordon Mathesson's room, and found Marcey lying quietly in bed. He tried asking her a few simple questions about her age and school, but her an-

swers made no sense and she kept wanting to go back to
sleep. She was not the same person who had come into
the hospital a few hours before.

"I heard you were up here," Paige interrupted,
sticking his head inside the door and holding a surgical
mask over his nose and mouth. "Couldn't stay away,
huh?" He was joking, but Ogden's countenance
remained serious.

"Glad you came by," Ogden answered as he tried
without success to bend the girl's neck forward. "Was
she like this when you saw her?"

"No, Mike, not at all." Paige sounded surprised, and
concerned. "She looked pretty good, as a matter of
fact. We even debated on doing the spinal tap." He tied
his mask and reached for a gown and gloves to put on.

"Well, there's no question now," Ogden said as soon
as Paige was inside the room. Pulling her sheet back,
she saw that her chest and abdomen were covered with
the telltale lesions.

"Jesus, has she changed! None of those were there a
few hours ago, Mike. I looked and couldn't find a
one."

"Her father's worse than this. What is going on? Are
you sure you guys are even treating the right organism?"

"It couldn't be anything else . . . I'm sure of it."
Paige looked anything but sure. "The Gram stain was
classic. We even did a C.I.E. for the hell of it and it was
positive for meningococcus too—"

"Well, something's wrong. I told Yates to tap Mr.
Mathesson and I want her tapped also, right away."

"I agree," Paige answered, shaking his head in disbelief.

Both spinal taps only took a few minutes and when
they were done, all three—Ogden, Yates and Paige—
went downstairs to the bacteriology laboratory to
watch.

The fluid that was collected from both patients was yellow and cloudy, although Gordon Mathesson's specimen was considerably more turbid than his daughter's. Yates handed the tubes to the chief technician, who placed a small drop of Mr. Mathesson's fluid on a special slide that was crisscrossed with etched lines. After taking selected counts, he used a calculator to get the average number. Gordon Mathesson's was twelve thousand, more than double the number gotten on the first tap. When they checked Marcey's, hers was seven hundred, a tenfold increase.

"That's not possible," Yates said, and turned to Ogden. "Is it?"

"Not in my experience."

The technician proceeded to place a small aliquot of fluid in the chemical analyzer, and while the machine was clicking away he set up the Gram stain. After smearing a drop of fluid on several slides and drying them over a Bunsen burner, he stained them with four different chemicals. When he was done, Ogden was the first to view them. What he saw in the several microscopic fields were heavy concentrations of bacteria that were growing inside and outside of the white cells that were supposed to be fighting them. "I agree. It looks like meningococcus, but it's not acting like any I've seen before."

Paige looked next, then Yates.

"What about the cultures?" Ogden asked the technician.

"It's way too early to tell much, I'm sure."

"Let's take a look anyway. Now when will you be doing the fermentation studies?" Ogden asked, referring to the tests based on the meningococcal organism's ability to ferment dextrose and maltose, but not sucrose—another way to distinguish it from similar bacteria.

"Not until late tomorrow."

"What else could this be?" Paige asked. "I doubt it's a gonococcus."

"A mutant. Or a resistant strain," Ogden offered as an unwelcome alternative.

"A resistant meningococcus?" Paige said. "That's almost unheard of."

"I know, but so are two patients deteriorating despite the appropriate antibiotic. Either your penicillin's bad, which I doubt, or this bug's resistant."

"Or maybe the dose just isn't high enough . . ." Paige suggested lamely.

"I suppose, but until we know why, I think it would be wise to add on a second antibiotic like chloramphenicol, and increase your penicillin at the same time. Between the two guns, we ought to kill it." Ogden sounded confident as he left for his laboratory. He had no way of knowing that he was up against something he'd never seen or heard of before.

CHAPTER NINE

It was almost four-thirty when Hilary Walters pulled up in front of the apartment building where Tina Hudson had been found dead. After turning off the ignition, she paused for a minute to study the diagram that she'd drawn on a legal pad. The case was getting too complicated, too many names, too many possibilities, to keep straight without it.

Mrs. Trumbell
(drama teacher)

Mrs. Fitzhugh
(lady in wheelchair)   Mr. Thackery (neighbor) Wife

Szlenko   Gordon Mathesson   Marcey
(Russian courier)

Gerald Katzenbach   Van Horn   Lynda
(long-haired missionary)   (Customs inspector)   Jamey

? name
(Indonesian businessman)

Tina Hudson
(dead girl)

• • •

For the moment, Tina Hudson did not fit into the
scheme, unless, perhaps, she'd been a passenger on one
of the planes or a friend of the Mathesson family. So
far, all Hilary knew about her was what the coroner's
office had read off her driver's license: age, eye color,
address.

The building's exterior was deceptive. Outside it
seemed old, slightly unkempt with faded white paint
and cracks in the stucco walls, but inside it was obvious
that it belonged to an exclusive class. The entryway was
monitored by a television camera, and the furniture
visible beyond the glass door had an antique quality
with burgundy velvet upholstery and thick carpeting.

As Hilary entered, she stared up at the camera's dark
lens and wondered if someone might be watching her.
The idea of not knowing gave her an eerie feeling. She
looked for either mailboxes or a list of residents, but the
hallway walls were bare except for the camera and a
lone buzzer next to the door. She pushed it and stepped
forward, expecting to be let in. Above her head, the
camera followed, whirring as it moved and tilting down-
ward for a better view. She pretended to ignore it.

Over a minute elapsed as she waited with her hand
poised on the doorknob. The lobby beyond remained
dark and quiet. She knew someone was around, but
they weren't answering. Annoyed, she pressed the button down and kept it in.

"Okay, okay what do you want?" a woman's husky
voice exploded from a hidden speaker in the ceiling.

"I'm from the Health Department. I need to see Tina
Hudson's apartment," Hilary answered, directing her
response upward.

"What's the name again?"

"Tina Hudson."

"There's no one who lives here by that name."

Hilary pulled out her notes. The address was the
same. Either she had copied it incorrectly or the woman

was lying. "Did she ever live here?"

"No, no one by that name has ever lived here. Sorry." The woman's tone indicated she was finished speaking.

"The girl's dead," Hilary said quickly, and waited.

There was silence on the other end.

"I have some questions that I need answered."

"Are you with the police?" the voice asked.

"No, the Health Department." She took out her ID card and held it up to the camera.

After a moment, the door buzzed and it unlocked electrically. As Hilary entered, a heavyset, bleached-blonde woman came from a distant hallway to meet her. In her hand was a half-smoked cigarette.

"We can't take any chances around here." Her breath smelled of alcohol. "If you're a policewoman, you have to tell me, you know." The woman waited, then continued. "Now, what's this about Tina again. I just saw her a little while ago. Maybe an hour or so. Somebody beat her? Drugs? No, that wouldn't bring the Health Department out here, would it? Usually, you're interested in the clap. That's not it, is it?"

"No one beat her, and there weren't any drugs that I know of. Weren't you here when the fire department came?" She was surprised that the woman didn't know why she had come.

"Fire department? We haven't had a fire here. You sure you got the right girl, honey?"

"The paramedics didn't come here, break down the door and find Tina dead from gas?" Hilary asked. As she spoke, she spotted a man peering out through a partly opened door. He was wearing a brimmed red hat, and his close-set eyes regarded her suspiciously, almost maliciously.

"I think you've got the wrong place. No fire department's been here," the woman went on. "Not for no fire, anyway."

"But there is a Tina Hudson who lives here, right?"

"Maybe she comes to visit. Lots of people come and go around here. I dunno."

"This girl's five foot six and a hundred and twenty pounds, with brown hair and brown eyes."

"You got the wrong girl. Tina's got blonde hair and green eyes." The woman stopped short for a moment, realizing she had slipped, and then got angry. "Is this some kind of trick to get in here?" As quickly as she raised her voice, she lowered it again. Coming down the steps behind her was a seemingly well-to-do gentleman with a buxom brunette on his arm. They were both laughing, and when they reached the doorway the brunette kissed him on the cheek and waited as he walked to an emerald green Ferrari.

From the beginning, Hilary had suspected that this woman was a madam, but now she was certain. The brunette alone had prostitute written across her swaying chest. "Tina works here, doesn't she?" she asked once the coast was clear again.

"I don't have to answer any of your questions and I think it might be best if you left now," the woman replied. She started to open the lobby door, indicating that Hilary should leave.

"Look, I'm not with the police. I have no connection to them. A girl's dead and she had Tina's ID. I need to know who she is. This may not involve Tina at all."

"That's your problem, not mine." The woman opened the door as wide as it would go.

"When will Tina be here? I just need a few seconds," Hilary pleaded as she stepped into the outside hallway.

"I can't help you. Good-by." The door closed as the woman took a deep drag from her dwindling cigarette and turned away.

Before returning to his research laboratory, Ogden stopped by his office to call home. It was getting late, and with both the meningitis outbreak and the research project on his hands he doubted that he would leave for several hours.

Mrs. Anderson, his housekeeper, answered. The phone had rung several times and when she finally picked it up, she sounded as if she were in a hurry.

"What's wrong?" he immediately asked.

"Peter's been in another fight. He's got cuts and scratches from stem to stern. That boy of yours just can't stay out of trouble. You're going to have to talk to him."

"I will," Ogden promised, thinking to himself, *as soon as I have time*. "How bad off is he?" The boy was the smallest in his class but had the largest mouth, a combination that frequently got him into fights.

"I've seen worse. He's in the bathroom waiting for me to clean him up. No broken bones this time, but I'm not sure why."

Ogden laughed although he really didn't think it was funny. He'd spent hours trying to teach the boy how to get along with others—that is, when he had hours to spend, which was rare. He was fortunate to have found Mrs. Anderson. She'd raised four boys of her own, but he still missed putting in more time himself. Each year he had promised himself that he'd be around more often the next and yet, there was always more to do. He thought ruefully of Les Paige's repeated advice over the last year and of his own sharp replies. He knew this had to stop, but not yet. Not this week. "I'm afraid I'm going to have to work late again tonight," he said hesitantly.

"Again." She sounded like a disappointed wife. "Why don't you at least come home for dinner. A break would be good for you, I'm sure."

"Tell Peter I'll catch him in the morning and to stop fighting or he'll have me to deal with."

"I'll tell him that you love him instead," came the answer. She always knew what to say.

• • •

After leaving Tina Hudson's supposed apartment, Hilary went directly to the County Morgue to verify her information on the dead girl. Obviously someone or something was in error and this was too deadly a disease to be chasing down the wrong people.

When she arrived, the waiting area was crowded, and from the back of the room came the sound of a young woman's desolate sobs. The morgue was filled with untimely deaths and its waiting room filled with mourners. As a doctor, it was something Hilary was used to, something she had learned to block out of her mind a long time ago. She went directly to an opaque, sliding glass window and knocked until someone answered.

"I need to talk to someone about a girl's body that was brought in here earlier today. Someone gave my secretary her name and address from a driver's license, but it was wrong," she explained, showing her ID card to a bearded Hispanic in a short white coat.

"The name?" he asked, opening a thick log book on the desk top. The first sheet had fifteen names recorded since midnight. They were mostly car accidents, but three were homicides and one a drowning. "It's been a busy day," he explained. He grinned at her, recognizing that she was as inured to the morbid atmosphere as he was.

"Her name's Hudson."

The man ran his fingers down the page and stopped halfway. "Mary Hudson?"

"I was told Tina, but maybe that's it."

The attendant continued moving his fingers down through the other names, but when he came to the end, he said, "Mary's the only Hudson we got here, but maybe this is the case where we got the names wrong. It happened on the other shift." He pointed out that the previous clerk had tried to erase the ink and then written a different first name on top. "I think the paramedics took the wrong purse." The man leaned out of the window for a moment and then pointed to the crying girl in the waiting room. "That's her sister over there. Maybe she's Tina."

As Hilary approached, she saw that the girl looked like a fifteen-year-old with heavy makeup. She was wearing a tight, shiny silver dress that rested revealingly high on her thighs. Her hair was blonde, just as the driver's license had said, and lying next to her was a short fur coat and a beaded purse. There was no question in Hilary's mind that this girl worked the same apartment building that she'd just come from.

"Tina, I need to ask you a few questions about your sister," she said, sitting down next to the girl.

"You a cop?" the girl asked, looking up at her with red-rimmed but suddenly wary eyes.

"No, just the Health Department."

"That's good. I'm not in the mood for cops right now . . . what is this, anyway? My sister was healthy. I seen her last night and she looked good. She's never been sick."

"These things are unpredictable." Hilary tried to sound sympathetic.

"I don't understand it, not any of it. Jesus, I come home and some creeps have busted down my door, there's stuff all over the place and nobody tells me a thing. At first I thought it was the pigs who busted in, but they say she was sick. I can't believe that. If there's some kind of shit going on, I want to know."

"Nobody's trying to pull anything over on you," Hilary explained, trying to calm the girl. "She had meningitis. An infection around the brain that can kill someone in a matter of hours. The paramedics who broke in were only trying to save her."

"They didn't do a very good job, did they?" She started crying again.

"It was too late . . ."

"I just can't believe this. My sister was healthy. She was always the healthy one in the family. Me, I always

got the colds, once pneumonia even. But Mary, she
never got anything.''

"It looks like her luck didn't hold out. I need to know
where she got it.''

"Ya, I want to know that too,'' the girl answered,
blowing her nose in an already damp Kleenex.

"Were you roommates?''

"I was thinking about moving in with her. I sleep
there during the day anyway, and all my stuff's there.''

"Does she do the same kind of work that you do?''
Hilary asked, adding that she'd been to the other
building.

"No, not Mary.'' The girl laughed for an instant.
"She was trying to get me to leave. She didn't approve.
We never did do things the same way, but we always
stuck together. We're all the family we got. Our folks
died when we was younger. Daddy used to drink and
one night he set the house on fire with a cigarette. Mary
smelled the smoke and we got out in time. They didn't.''
The thoughts brought tears back to her eyes.

"I'm sorry . . .'' Beneath the profanity and tough exterior, she saw a lost person who needed to talk.

"It don't matter. That was a long time ago. Ain't
nothing you can do now. We moved in with an aunt.
She was awfully old, an old bitch about everything in
her house, but she didn't give a shit what we did on the
outside. It didn't matter with Mary anyway. She was
always reading the Bible or going to some church
meeting, but not me. That religious stuff wasn't for
me.''

"What kind of work did Mary do?'' She assumed
that the girl could talk for hours about her past, but
Hilary couldn't afford the time. There were contacts
who had to be reached.

"She was waitressing, but she got fired. The boss was
a dirty old man. Tried putting his hand up her dress
every time she bent over. Mary didn't go for that and he
canned her.''

"How long ago?"

"Two weeks."

"And what's she been doing since?"

"Collecting unemployment and going to church, I guess. I don't see her but for a few minutes some days."

"She have any boyfriends?"

"She don't date." The girl laughed. "Here I make my living . . . well, you know how, and she don't date. Strange, ain't it?"

"Anyone come by to visit her?"

"She had a friend come by yesterday. A man, but not a boyfriend, not a lover, you know . . . I heard them laughing when I came out for something to drink. I never seen him before."

"She didn't tell you his name?"

"No. I didn't ask either. Just some long-haired dude who probably goes to church with her."

Gerald Katzenbach, the long-haired missionery? Hilary wondered. After jotting down a few notes, she took out a throat swab to culture the girl's throat and explained that if the culture turned out positive she'd have to know the names of any men she'd been with.

"I can't tell you that! You crazy?"

"You have to understand how important this is—" Hilary broke off when she saw the man with the red brimmed hat from the apartment building approaching them.

"This lady botherin' you, babe?" he asked Tina, his gaze meeting Hilary's.

"No, she's just a doctor."

"What's she want then?"

"Nothing that concerns you. Just about my sister." The pimp didn't appear to believe her.

Bending down to speak directly into Hilary's face, he spoke very deliberately. "I seen you twice today, twice too much. You been around too long."

"I merely need to—"

"Listen lady, I don't give a damn what you merely

need to. Stay away. You're a doctor. You'd better worry about your own health.'' He took the girl by the arm and led her toward the door. She glanced back at Hilary, her expression frightened. Then she was gone.

CHAPTER TEN

Before leaving the Medical Center grounds, Hilary decided to make a few telephone calls and check on the two Mathesson cases. She still had four names on her list of suspects: the Russian courier, who seemed unlikely; the Oriental businessman, whose cough could have easily spread the germs but whose name and whereabouts were unknown; Mr. Thackery, who might be ill but was somewhere in San Francisco; and the missionary youth, who now became the object of her search. Although the evidence pointing toward Gerald Katzenbach was flimsy, it was thought-provoking nonetheless. If he were the carrier, he could have given it to Gordon Mathesson at Customs and later to Mary Hudson. It could be a perfect tie-in.

At first, she tried finding his name in one of L.A.'s five telephone books, but, not unexpectedly, he wasn't listed. There were a lot of Katzenbachs, but none of them reported having any relatives named Gerald. She turned next to religious organizations, and on her fourth call, to a Baptist group, she connected. According to the woman who answered, Gerald Katzenbach was due back any day, but no one there had heard from him recently and the only address they had on file was in Kenya. Hilary thanked her and left her name and phone number, insisting that they have him call her at the Health Department as soon as possible.

After checking with Mrs. Thackery, who had not been able to locate her husband, she decided to take a break for dinner at the hospital cafeteria. She needed a moment to collect her thoughts. Usually, she made a point of avoiding hospital food, but tonight it was too convenient and she knew that if she went home, she'd probably not want to leave. As she passed through the line, she picked up a chef's salad, a side dish of cottage cheese and a cup of black coffee, and found a quiet table to herself.

As she ate, she reviewed the flow sheet. She'd worked eight hours and hadn't progressed an inch. So far she had no idea where Mathesson had gotten the illness, whom he might have given it to—except, perhaps, his daughter—or how he had contracted it. A big goose egg, she thought. She liked clear-cut answers and this was all a blur. It was frustrating. The only hope now seemed to be the results of the throat cultures she would have in the morning.

By the time her mind returned to the food, her coffee was gone and she couldn't recall drinking it. As she went to the line to pour herself some more, Joanna Yates entered with her intern, Dr. James, trailing behind. "You heard about the Mathesson girl?" she called out.

"I got the message a couple of hours ago," Hilary answered.

"There's more to it than that, though." Yates spoke excitedly as she loaded her tray with something from every section. "The bug's resistant. At least that's what it looks like." After paying, she followed Hilary back to her table and James drifted off to join two other interns.

"To rifampin? I hope not, that's what I've been taking myself." Hilary had never heard of a resistant meningococcus.

"Well, so far just resistant to penicillin."

"Maybe, but I doubt it," Yates said, explaining how the cell counts in both spinal taps had increased and how both cases had worsened despite high doses of antibiotic. "We may even make the medical journals with this one."

"That's all we need—a penicillin-resistant bug."

"They're on chloramphenicol now. That ought to cover it." Yates dug into her food with vigor and then changed the subject. "Did you hear about our little rabies epidemic? I imagine it's already been on the news."

Hilary shook her head.

"NBC came down with camera and reporters. Some fifth grade class went out spelunking . . ." Yates stopped to laugh, enjoying her story before she even told it. ". . . and two boys caught a bat somehow and those little devils set it loose in the bus. Thirty-five screaming kids in a rickety school bus pulled in here with a half-crazed teacher and driver. It was really wild."

"All thirty-five were bitten?" Hilary asked in disbelief. If it were true, her stocks of vaccine might be too low.

"No," Yates reassured her, "only one, and that's not definite—it could have been a scratch from anything. The teacher thought everyone was bitten, though, and the news people were down here in a flash. For a while there, I thought we might make the national news. Now it'll be local. Not enough bites."

"Be thankful."

"I suppose," Yates answered, sounding disappointed. After a few more chews, she resumed another story, obviously eager to tell someone about the unusual cases she'd seen.

Hilary listened to the resident's accounts, interested in them but even more interested in Joanna Yates's enthusiasm over them. Yates was an able doctor, she guessed. She was also ambitious and young, which accounted for her enthusiasm for the clinical aspects of diseases, an enthusiasm that often swept aside consideration for the afflicted patients and that might be seen as insensitivity even among doctors. Hilary shared her fascination with offbeat or baffling cases. But enthusiasm, excitement? No, not anymore. She was only a few years older than Joanna Yates, but those few years of experience made a difference. And she had never been blindly ambitious, except maybe for a while, after she and David Kerr had split up. And now? She was startled when she suddenly realized that she had accomplished what she had set out to achieve, that she was happy with her new job. She had worked so hard to get to this point in her career that she hadn't recognized it when she'd reached it. . . .

Once the two had finished, Yates headed off to admitting while Hilary went upstairs to check on the Mathessons. She was hoping to see some improvement—that the chloramphenicol was working—but essentially their condition remained the same. It might be too early, she thought, rationalizing that at least they hadn't deteriorated.

As she reviewed the charts and spoke to the nurses, she was repeatedly struck by the odd fact that Ogden had not become involved. It ran counter to his reputation and certainly to his duty. She had met him only a few times, but he had struck her as being unusually conscientious about his service. She decided to seek him out in the research laboratory and found him leaning over a microscope.

"You know about the mini-epidemic, don't you?" she asked, more abruptly than she intended.

"Yes, of course," he answered, startled. Then he

smiled when he saw her face. "So they've got you involved already. I'm sure you'll have everything under control quickly."

"I hope. You heard about the resistance?" She continued in a serious vein despite the friendly reception.

"If it's really resistance. Sometimes meningococcus can be hard to treat."

"I don't understand why you're not involved, not worried like everyone else."

"I am, but we've had three cases of meningitis before at the same time. In fact, we had a dozen viral cases here last fall." Ogden walked across the room, picked up a test tube and came back. "Is there something else you think we should be doing?"

His question threw her. His involvement probably wouldn't change anything and she realized that her annoyance grew more out of her own fatigue than his attitude. "I'm sorry," she said after a moment's reflection. "I just think that this may be the tip of an iceberg and especially hazardous if the bug's resistant to penicillin."

"That would bother me too, but I bet we've seen all the cases there'll be. Besides, we've got other antibiotics, assuming it really is resistant."

"Maybe." Hilary sighed and then wandered over toward Clarence, who immediately woke and bared his teeth. His abdomen was covered with bandages and there was an intravenous line dripping into one leg. "What's he got?" she asked, keeping her distance. "He looks like a train hit him."

Ogden smiled. "He stood his girl friend up and that's what she did to him."

She couldn't help smiling. And even Ling, who was trying not to pay attention to them, started laughing.

"Your research?" she asked.

"Yes," Ogden responded and went on to explain the experiment's protocol.

"Well, at least now I see why you've been distracted," she said when he finished. She meant well, but Ogden became defensive.

"Hardly distracted. I'm here if anyone needs me: No one's been ignored. No one's suffered."

"Oh, I didn't mean distracted. It was a poor choice. Sorry. I'm sure your work here is more important than the hospital right now. At least until this thing gets worse."

"It won't."

"I hope you're right, but I'm not so sure," Hilary answered as she backed toward the door. She was afraid if she stayed they might get into an argument. His blue eyes looked tired, and he was probably just as edgy and fatigued as she was. "I'll keep you informed, Dr. Ogden," she said.

"Dr. Walters—"

She turned from the door and found Ogden smiling at her.

"Call me Mike. It's a new cure, used for treating resistant doctors and irritable researchers."

Hilary laughed. "I might just try it, at that." When she left the lab, she felt considerably less gloomy and turned her mind to the tasks ahead with fresh energy.

Once across the way, she telephoned the Russian consulate and left word for Szlenko to call her back. It was six o'clock and he had just left his office.

Barely an hour had elapsed after Hilary's departure when the telephone rang in Ogden's laboratory. On the other end was Dr. Yates.

"You're not going to believe this, but I think we've got ourselves another case." She sounded worried.

"Another meningitis?"

"Another *meningococcal* meningitis. This time it's one of our own staff. His wife just rushed him in here. He's the orderly who first saw Gordon Mathesson outside the main admitting room, before anyone knew the diagnosis.''

"That's impossible. No one catches this disease that easily. Did you call Dr. Paige?''

"He's on his way back from home, but he said you would want to know about this one also, since he's an employee of the hospital.''

"I do, thanks, but have Paige call me after he sees the man. I can't leave.'' Ogden hung up wondering if he should go and feeling bad that he wouldn't. He was in the middle of critical calculations. He didn't want to stop, but could hear Hilary's remark about "distraction'' going through his mind. He told himself that this was only one more case, that Paige could easily handle it and there really wasn't any need for two attending men. But it was hardly convincing. If he took a look, it would only take a few minutes. And since he was planning to work late anyway, he could afford the extra time. Besides, if he didn't go, he'd worry all night and the nagging guilt of years of compulsion was persuasive.

When he arrived, Yates had already suited up and was starting to numb Clagston's lower back for the spinal tap. The orderly was lying on his side, fully awake and complaining that the light overhead was making his headache worse. After going home from his shift that morning, he'd been asleep until mid-afternoon when his son returned from school. They were going to fly his new plane, but as Clagston had stood up from his bed, the room started spinning. A moment later, he became nauseated and had to lie back down. From that point on he was unable to raise his head off the pillow. Noises, lights and voices all bothered him and he had intermittent sieges of vomiting.

At first, Clagston thought it was the flu—he'd seen many similar cases in the emergency room this week—but his headache moved to the back of his neck and his fever climbed to one hundred and five degrees.

He tried taking aspirin, but the tablets wouldn't stay down. Despite his condition, however, he put off seeing a doctor until the vision in his left eye blurred and dozens of purplish spots cropped up on his chest. His wife called a friend to help carry him out to the car and over to County Hospital.

The spinal fluid that Yates extracted had a yellowish tinge. When the results returned from the laboratory, they had their third case of meningitis in their hospital, and the fourth for the day.

Patient: Clagston, Murray, age 31
PF Number: 246–27–891
Spinal Fluid Analysis
Drawn: 1905

	Result	Normal Value
Description	yellow, turbid	clear
Amount received	8.0 cc	variable
Cell count		
Total white count	2100	less than 10
Percent neutrophils	95%	0%
Percent mononuclears	5%	100%
Total red cells	2	0
Protein	98	15–45 mgm/100ml
Sugar	24	45–80 mg/100ml

Gram stain: many Gram negative diplococci, intracellular and extracellular consistent with the *Neisseria* species, probably meningococcus.

Meanwhile, Hilary had returned to the Mathesson house. Now, with Marcey being ill, she needed to know about the girl's contacts also. She had tried getting the information in the hospital, but the teenager was too confused to answer her questions.

Mrs. Mathesson opened the door and immediately became alarmed when she saw Hilary's face. "Something more has happened, hasn't it?" she asked.

"No, not any more than you already know. Can I

come in?'' The woman was so worried that she had remained frozen in the doorway.

"Of course, I'm a bit edgy, you know.'' She stepped aside and directed her toward the living room.

"I need to know about Marcey's contacts. She mentioned that she had a boyfriend. The name Joe came up, but I'm not sure. Is that the boy? Are there any others?''

"Joe Paulus is someone she's been hanging around. He lives about three blocks from here . . .''

Hilary wrote the name on her notepad.

". . . but she has dozens of girl friends who she sees every day at school. There's Rhonda Bailey, Carey Lenhardt . . . Judy Rotman . . . Karen McMillan.''

"Has she seen them in the past two days?'' Hilary asked as she copied the names. Now, not only did she have to deal with Mr. Mathesson's occupation and dozens of potential exposures, but Marcey's school as well. The disease could be traveling in any number of directions and the chore before her was getting more difficult rather than easier.

"Every day,'' came the answer she expected. "She sees them every day.''

Just then Hilary's beeper buzzed and she asked to use the phone. She assumed that it was the Russian consulate returning her call, but it was Mrs. Thackery instead.

The woman was frantic. "They just called me from San Francisco. My husband's been in a hospital all day.''

"Did they say what was wrong?'' Hilary asked, hoping that it might be a car accident or some food poisoning.

"The doctor said it was meningitis. He's in isolation.''

"What hospital is it?''

"Kaiser . . . I think he said Kaiser Permanente. I was so shook up, knowing how bad Gordon is, that I'm not sure. What should I do? I can pack a bag in five minutes. I can't leave him up there alone. Maybe I can catch a plane up tonight if it isn't too late. If not, maybe I can drive. We've driven there together before. Takes six hours—"

"Don't do anything yet. No need to panic." Hilary tried calming her, but noticed something peculiar out of the side of her eye. The Mathesson boy was passing through the room and she saw a purplish spot on his arm that resembled the purpuric spots of meningitis. "Let me call up there and see what's going on," she said, waving for the boy to stop. "I'll call you right back."

"How long? I'm too nervous just sitting here by the phone." She wouldn't let Hilary off.

"As soon as I can. Please, just stay in your house until I get back to you. I'm just across the street at the Mathessons' and I'll call you back as soon as I can."

After Hilary hung up, she asked the little boy to come closer to her. Hesitantly, he came forward. At first glance the spot looked like a bruise, but she found a second spot further up his arm and a third on his neck. As she lifted his T-shirt to look at his stomach, Harriet Mathesson came across the room to see also. Suddenly, both women became alarmed. Dotted across his abdomen, just like the others, were the meningococcal spots.

"He's got it too, hasn't he?" the woman asked, automatically putting her hand across his forehead and finding it warm. "I thought your medicine was supposed to protect us!"

"It is, but maybe he didn't get it soon enough." It was the truth, but it was the wrong thing to say. She wanted to console the child, who'd been frightened by their alarm, but she kept her distance because she was beginning to wonder whether she herself was really protected. "I think you'd better get him to the hospital immediately. I'll call ahead and tell them you're coming."

Before Mrs. Mathesson could get a coat on and find the car keys, Mrs. Thackery was ringing their doorbell. "Have you called San Francisco yet?" she asked as Hilary answered the door.

"I haven't had a chance, but I'm going to in just a minute," Hilary explained, wanting to solve one problem before tackling another.

"I've already packed a bag. I think I'd better get up there. I'll call back after I find him if you want," the woman anxiously said as she entered, unaware of the stress she was adding to an already tense situation.

"Please, Mrs. Thackery, just have a seat for a moment and I'll make the call."

As the neighbor grudgingly sat on the living room couch, Harriet Mathesson came hurrying past, pushing Jamey ahead of her and beckoning Lynda to hurry. "Did you hear Jim is in the hospital too?" Mrs. Thackery started to tell them, but the three scurried out to the car and in a few seconds were racing toward the hospital.

"I'm sure it's Kaiser, now that I think of it. Can you see if I can talk to Jim?" the neighbor asked, seeing Hilary heading toward the telephone.

"I'm calling the hospital here first," Hilary explained, annoyed at the woman's persistence.

The hospital operator paged Dr. Yates, and fifteen seconds later Hilary was explaining that the youngest Mathesson was en route.

"This is crazy. We may run out of beds if this keeps up," the resident responded, adding, "but we'll have the antibiotics drawn up by the time he gets here."

As Hilary hung up her beeper buzzed again. "Jesus, what's going on here?" she muttered, shutting the box off and quickly calling her answering service. She wasn't getting a chance to get organized. In the background, Mrs. Thackery was impatiently staring at her.

"Two calls, Dr. Walters," an unfamiliar woman's voice repeated. "The bacteriology laboratory at the County Medical Center says they have another meningitis case you should know about, and Mr. Korlov of the Russian consulate returned your call. He wouldn't give me a number to call back on and said for you to call his office in the morning. He sounded annoyed."

"But I need to speak to him tonight," Hilary said, as if the operator were responsible.

"I'm sorry, doctor, but that's all he said."

Disappointed, Hilary thanked her and hung up wondering who this newest case was. If her calculations were correct, there were now six cases altogether, including Jamey Mathesson and his father, but most worrisome was the fact that this epidemic, if it was to become one, had now extended to a second city. She could only hope that Mr. Thackery hadn't exposed anyone in San Francisco . . .

"Are you going to call now?" Mrs. Thackery asked. Hilary had momentarily forgotten that she was there.

"Oh, yes," she answered, and a few seconds later she was talking to an emergency room doctor at Kaiser Hospital.

"We admitted him about an hour ago," the physician explained, sounding hurried. "He came in with a stiff neck, fever and a headache. It looked like meningitis from the beginning, so we tapped him. Fortunately for him the count was low, barely two hundred cells, and of course they were polys. At least we caught him early."

"The Gram stain shows Gram negative diplococci, suggesting meningococcus?"

"Yes, how'd you know?"

She told him how many cases they had in Los Angeles already, how rapidly the organism appeared to be spreading and that there was the possibility of resistance. It was imperative that Kaiser reach all of

Thackery's contacts as quickly as possible.

"We don't have the facilities to do that, especially at night. His family's down there with you. Those are the people that really need to be treated, not any casual contacts that he might have had up here. He's only been in town a few hours."

"Under normal circumstances you'd be right, but this bug's more aggressive than usual," she said, trying to impress him with the seriousness of the problem.

"I wouldn't even know who to contact or how. My waiting room's overflowing with people who have to be seen, not potentials. We don't even know if it's the same organism that you have down there."

"I'm sure it is."

"We'll check the cultures. The results will be back by morning."

It looked as if he wasn't going to help. She asked him to hold a moment and dug through some papers in her purse. Buried in the pile was a list of all the important names in the state who were connected with the Health Department, and under San Francisco she found Dr. Thomas Judd's number. "Call Dr. Judd," she requested. "He's with the local office there. Tell him to call me back if he has any questions."

"I'll try to get him first thing in the morning when I get off duty."

"Never mind. I'll do it. We can't wait until morning. By then there might be a lot more people stricken."

When she reached Judd, he was dozing on a couch at home. Once he was fully awake he seemed to share her concern, but also felt that it could wait until morning. She persisted, however, until he told her he would do a preliminary check. As she hung up she knew she was right. Time *was* running out. Atlanta would have to know about the new cases and it was likely that she would need additional help shortly. . . .

In his San Francisco apartment, Dr. Thomas Judd turned over on his couch and went back to sleep.

CHAPTER ELEVEN

Twenty-five minutes after he left home, the Mathesson boy arrived at the admitting area. Joanna Yates had relayed Hilary's message to Les Paige and both physicians were waiting as Harriet Mathesson hurried in with the boy. She was out of breath as if she'd run the entire distance rather than pushed the speed limits.

Jamey was whisked away into isolation as his mother and Lynda were shown to the waiting room. A few minutes later a spinal tap was done and they were soon informed that his results were similar to the others—probable meningococcal meningitis.

Patient: Mathesson, Jamey, age 7
PF Number: 345–87–053
Spinal fluid analysis
Drawn: 2010

	Result	*Normal Value*
Description	clear	clear
Amount received	5.5 cc	variable
Cell count		
Total white count	46	less than 10

Percent neutrophils	98%	0%
Percent mononuclears	2%	100%
Total red cells	2	0
Protein	58	15–45 mgm/100ml
Sugar	42	45–80 mgm/100ml

Gram stain: rare Gram negative diplococci, intracellular and extracellular consistent with the *Neisseria* species, probable meningococcus

Les Paige couldn't believe what he was seeing as he peered over the technician's shoulder. It was an early case, evidenced by the low white count, mildly elevated protein and slightly depressed sugar, but it was definitely positive.

"Do you think we're going to need extra help tonight?" Yates asked.

"I don't know," Paige said after a moment's thought. "That's a question I'll probably have to put to Mike Ogden. The real question now is what to do with the two remaining Mathessons. I can't help but think that they'll be back with the same disease. It's just a matter of time. The boy was taking rifampin. Maybe he hadn't had enough yet, or maybe he already had the disease when we started him on it. But I'm not so sure it's working."

"They both look good. The girl's only got a cold and her mother thinks she's getting it also. We've checked them several times."

"Maybe you ought to take one more look while I go and talk to Mike. See if they'll stay here tonight for observation or at the Holiday Inn across the street. That way we can check them early in the morning again. And if there's trouble before then, they'll be nearby. Whatever we do, we should try to isolate them somewhat."

Yates set off for the waiting room and Paige headed toward Ogden's laboratory. He had barely stepped off the curb, however, when he spotted three nurses coming from the direction of the nurses' dormitory. They seemed to be struggling, and once they were clearly in view he realized that two girls were supporting a third in between them. He watched for a moment. The sick girl's neck was hung low and they had to stop twice while she retched. Drunk? No. The three nurses were dressed for work and they were definitely heading toward the Contagious Disease admitting area. When they reached the side door, Paige decided to go after them.

When he caught up to them in the admitting area, Joanna Yates was talking to the two nurses while their friend was moved into an isolation room. "What is it?" he asked her, keeping a few feet away.

"Mary said she had a headache that was much worse than any she'd had before," one of the nurses explained. "She took two pain pills with codeine and then got sick to her stomach. At first we thought it was the narcotic, but she kept throwing up. She said her neck was getting stiff too. That worried us. When I was a student nurse, I saw some cases of meningitis. Her temperature was one hundred and four and I thought we'd best get her here immediately. Maybe it's just a virus, but we didn't want to take any chances."

"It's good that you didn't," Paige commented. "What department does she work in?"

"The main emergency room. She works graveyard. We all do. We were going out to a movie before reporting in, but then this happened."

Clagston's name suddenly flashed through Paige's mind. "Did she take care of a meningitis case early this morning?"

Neither girl knew.

When Yates and Paige entered the isolation room, Nurse Mary Mitchell was lying on her back with one arm draped over her eyes. "They always get alarmed when I feel sick," she explained, sounding embarrassed about being there. "I'm sure it's—" she stopped in midsentence and asked for an emesis basin.

Both physicians stood by in their protective garments as the girl repeatedly retched, but everything that could be expelled had already come up.

"God, that hurts," she whispered hoarsely and lay back, holding her stomach.

Paige began his examination by bending her neck, but she grimaced in pain almost immediately.

"That hurts too, but it's not what you're thinking. It's not meningitis. I've seen spinal taps before and I definitely don't want one myself."

"I'm afraid we might not have a choice," Paige said, signaling for the nurse to undress the girl. "You know Murray Clagston?"

"Sure. He works the same shift. Why?"

"Did you take care of the same case of meningitis that he did?"

"What case was that?"

"The one that came in a recreational vehicle and transferred down here."

"For an instant maybe. We saw the patient out in the parking lot and moved him to CDU right away. You don't think I caught this from him, do you?"

"I don't know, but Clagston's been admitted with meningitis and he only beat you here by a few minutes." Once the girl's vital signs were checked and her temperature confirmed at one hundred and four degrees, Yates set her up for a spinal tap, remarking that she would soon be able to do these with her eyes closed. Fifteen minutes later, the results returned:

Name: Mary Mitchell, age 23
PF Number: 345–87–111
Spinal fluid analysis
Drawn: 2045

Description	*Result*	*Normal Value*
	slightly turbid	clear
Amount received	6.5 cc	variable

Cell count

Total white count	204	less than ten
Percent neutrophils	99%	0%
Percent mononuclears	1%	100%
Total red cells	7	0
Protein	63	15–46–mgm/ 101 ml
Sugar	36	45–80 mgm/100 ml

Gram stain: rare organism seen, but these appear to be a Gram negative diplococci consistent with the *Neisseria* species, probable meningococcus

It was the seventh case of the day.

It was after nine in the evening by the time Paige finally made it over to Ogden's laboratory. As he entered, he ran into Tom Ling, struggling with an ill-looking German shepherd who refused to be moved.

"We had a call from a vet in Santa Monica," Ogden's assistant explained. "At least this one doesn't bite."

As Ling forced the stubborn animal into his kennel, Paige proceeded toward the main lab and Ogden.

"Sorry to interrupt," he said, pulling up a stool next to Ogden's workbench. "But there's some new problems that have come up and I need to talk to you."

"Sure." Ogden sounded receptive as he marked his place in a lab book and set his pen aside. "You look worried."

"I am. These meningitis cases are getting out of hand. We just put two more patients in the house, a nurse who worked with Clagston in the Mathesson van and the Mathesson boy. Yates tells me that a neighbor of theirs is hospitalized in San Francisco also. I have this depressing feeling that things are about to get out of hand."

"You really think it's that bad? So far every case is a legitimate close contact."

"I wish I knew, but I don't. Even if you're right, just a few more admissions will put bed space here at a premium. We'll need additional nursing staff, which only you can order, and we may need additional residents on duty. Besides their usual admissions, Yates and James have been running nonstop since early this morning.''

"Then call the resident and intern on backup. They're supposed to be available at times like this. And call Mrs. Dawson, the nursing supervisor. She should get you the extra help. In fact, if there's really a problem, one of us will be hearing from her.''

"It's not quite that easy,'' Paige continued. "I really think all hell's going to break loose. We might as well start wearing gowns and gloves around the clock here. This bug seems to be resistant to penicillin, it might be resistant to rifampin, and it's spreading like a common cold.''

"That's pretty speculative. I'm sure the usual precautions are adequate.''

"I don't think so, not anymore.''

"There's never been a meningococcus that was multiple resistant.''

"There was never an atomic bomb before Hiroshima either. Things change.''

Ogden stopped short of arguing. He had seen cases pile up like this before, and one of his responsibilities was to keep the staff cool until the problem was over. It was obvious that Paige was distressed—possibly with good reason, but more likely just from a relative lack of experience. From Ogden's standpoint, everything still looked adequately under control. He decided to take him into his confidence a little. "Look, Les, to be honest, I can't drop everything right now. I need you to run things in the unit. We just got another dog in—this one's perfect for the experiment—and we'll be starting our tissue and blood analysis tonight. If it all looks as good as it seems, we'll be treating him tomorrow.''

"If we keep getting a meningitis case every hour, there won't be a need for a cure for cancer.''

"Oh, hell, that's not going to happen. You know that. They're all close contacts and easily explained.''

"What about that girl in the morgue?"

Ogden hesitated. It was a cogent question. "If there's a good connection, Walters will probably find it. Maybe the old man snuck off for a quickie behind his wife's back. Maybe she's one of those rare cases that crop up every year and there's no connection at all."

"I don't know."

"Look, I'll be here most of the night. If things get worse, call me, but if you can hold down the fort, I really need your help. In another week, I'll be out from under the pressure of the grant decision."

Paige agreed to try, but as he left the laboratory he was annoyed and found himself questioning Mike Ogden's professional opinion for the first time in their friendship.

Meanwhile, Gordon Mathesson's condition continued to deteriorate. At 8:00 P.M. his blood pressure barely measured 80 over 50, his pulse was extremely rapid and weak, his temperature hovered around one hundred and five degrees and his feet were purplish-blue. Worried that he was going into full-blown shock, Yates ordered a further increase in his intravenous fluids, but an hour later his pressure had fallen further to 70 over 30 and his kidneys had ceased putting out urine—the latter an indication that none of his vital organs were receiving enough blood. After conferring with Paige, she and James decided to put a catheter into the man's heart to properly assess blood flow and his need for fluids.

First she cranked the foot of the bed up so that Mathesson's head was the lowest part of his body and his neck veins bulged with blood. Then she took a large-bore needle and carefully inserted it into the jugular vein just above the collarbone on the right side. As she popped in, a gush of blood shot out the back end of the needle, which she quickly capped. She dilated the opening and inserted a long plastic tube with a tiny balloon on the end.

The balloon easily slipped through the hole, and once it was inside she inflated it so that the flow of blood would carry it back to the heart and through to the lungs. As she passed the tubing, she watched the overhead oscilloscope, whose pattern told her where the balloon was located. It took a few twists and manipulations, but eventually the balloon slipped through the right chamber and stopped in the vessels of the left lung. The readings clearly indicated that he'd had enough intravenous fluids. Any more, in fact, would be harmful. Instead, she'd have to use an infusion of dopamine—a medication that artificially elevates blood pressure.

The infusion was started at the lowest therapeutic doses and slowly increased until Mathesson's pressure readings returned to a level of 90 over 60, where she left him. It was too early to know if his kidneys would resume normal function, but his general color was improved and his feet seemed a little warmer. Through it all, Mathesson remained comatose, unresponsive to noise in the room or even needle pricks. As Yates stepped from his room, she doubted that he'd make it.

There was another admission downstairs and both Yates and Paige were summoned. Although this wasn't a case of meningitis, it was hardly a welcome relief. It was a nineteen-year-old laboratory technician with fulminant hepatitis. The girl was a trainee in the chemistry laboratory two months prior when she stuck herself with a needle that had been used to draw blood from a heroin addict. Knowing that addicts frequently carry the hepatitis virus, she was checked by a hospital staff physician, thought to be in good health, and was given a shot of gamma globulin to protect her. Two months later, however, she began developing joint pains and high fever. Four days later, her eyes suddenly turned yellow and she had trouble keeping food down. The same physician saw her again, diagnosed hepatitis, and told her to take a couple of weeks off to recuperate.

Normally, this disease is short-lived and easily tolerated, but hers wasn't. Two days after the office visit, she became confused and couldn't eat at all. Her entire body was jaundiced and her urine was as dark as tea. Liver tests indicated that she now had fulminant hepatitis, the worst of all possibilities, and the physician moved her to the Contagious Disease Unit.

When Yates and Paige examined her, she was extremely lethargic, barely able to open her eyes when they called her name and not fully aware of where she was. She'd lost fifteen pounds in less than a week and her liver had shrunk to half its normal size, essentially chewed up by the aggressive virus. To Paige, the outlook appeared hopeless, but he immediately called for a kidney specialist to put her on dialysis. By removing the destructive elements in her blood, there was a remote chance that they could buy some time, but the prospects looked poor. The only alternative he saw was a liver transplant, an experimental procedure not done at their hospital. And the only way they could transfer her to Colorado for the operation was if Ogden made the call. Paige was annoyed to find his hands tied, and by now he was tired and frustrated enough to wonder why the responsibility shouldn't be his rather than Ogden's. Mike Ogden had his research and all the glory that went with it—Paige stopped himself short with this thought. It was the end of a long day, he reminded himself, and at least he could go home to a wife and kids. Once things settled down here, anyway.

CHAPTER TWELVE

When Hilary returned to the hospital she found her hands full. Not only had the number of patients increased, but the list of contacts was now simply unmanageable. There was no question that she needed help, but before calling she wanted to be organized. After finding a desk, she tore out the old flow sheet and started another, this time using smaller print to accommodate the number of names.

Mrs. Thackery

Mrs. Trumbell

Mr. Thackery*   ?

Mrs. Fitzhugh

Wife

Szlenko	*Gordon	Marcey*	boyfriend (Paulus)
	Mathesson	Lynda	girlfriends

Gerald Katzenbach   Jamey*   School friends

Indonesian Businessman   Murray Clagston*   Wife
                                                      Son

                          Customs officials
                              Mary Mitchell*

                                                      Cunningham
                                                      Riley

Mary Hudson*———Tina Hudson

*Cases with meningitis

Among the more important people to contact was
Marcey's boyfriend, but even her girlfriends were
potential victims. The same was true for Jamey's school
friends. Both of the Clagstons had to be cultured and
treated, and if the boy was infected another school was
threatened. Then there was Mary Mitchell, who had
been inconveniently promiscuous today. Not only did
she have intercourse with Dr. Cunningham, but after
leaving the dorm she hurried across town and jumped
into bed with an advertising executive by the name of
Mark Riley. Both men were now in jeopardy, but since
Cunningham was on duty in the main building she
decided to see him first. Before leaving, however, she
called in a second investigator, Dr. Michael Meno, and
considered calling a third.

Dr. Cunningham was assigned to the sixth floor, a
medical service, and as Hilary exited from the elevator
she found the ward in a shambles. All of the rooms were
full and there were patients lying in beds up and down
the hallway. Medical personnel were racing about everywhere, seemingly disorganized. One intern was screaming on the phone that he had a heart patient who needed
a bed in the intensive care unit, while the nurse on the
other end of the line was apparently telling him that all
of their beds were taken. Another resident was yelling
from one of the rooms to his student and telling him to

get a surgeon down stat for a ruptured appendix. He was angry that the emergency room had sent an obvious surgical abdomen to a medical floor where nothing could be done.

Hilary approached the central desk and waited while the ward clerk was speaking to someone on the phone. The girl was laughing despite the havoc about her, and it was clearly a personal call. She saw Hilary standing in front of her, assumed that she was probably a patient's relative, and merely swung her chair around and lowered her voice.

A typical County employee, Hilary thought to herself. The hospital floors were full of personnel who didn't care about anything other than the time clock and their paychecks. The overwhelming number of patients bred the indifference and civil service protected it. After six months' probation as a new employee, no one could be fired.

"Excuse me!" she finally interrupted, thinking she might grab the phone away if she didn't respond.

The clerk spun around with a surly look and told her friend to hold on. "What is it?" she asked.

"I'd like to know where Dr. Cunningham is."

"He's tied up with a patient. Are you family? If so, you'll have to wait down the hall." The clerk pointed toward a distant couch and then resumed her conversation.

"No, I'm a doctor on staff here, and if you don't get off the damn phone and specifically tell me where he is I'll be sure that your name's turned in tomorrow morning!"

The clerk said a hurried good-by and set the receiver back in its cradle. Looking through the admission sheet, she saw that Cunningham's last patient was an old alcoholic. Hilary gave her a curt nod and went to the patient's room, where she found a tall, blondish intern standing over a quivering, obese, unshaven alcoholic who had just filled a metal basin with bloody vomitus.

"Get me that Litton tube stat!" the intern shouted over to the nurse.

Hilary introduced herself, but the intern was more concerned about the bleeding drunk than with her reason for being there. "This son of a bitch isn't going to stop!" Cunningham reached up and opened the IV line all the way so that the fluid in the bottle could rush in. "And get me two more units of blood. He's losing it faster than I can give it back." He said the last few words to Hilary and then returned his attention to the drunk. "I told you this would happen if you drank again. Don't you think we have better things to do than patch you up every other month?"

"Dr. Walters. Health Department. I'm here about Mary Mitchell," she inserted, not willing to wait any longer.

The intern suddenly stopped everything he was doing. "Don't tell me she's got gonorrhea! I should have known. It figures. There's always something to ruin a good thing."

Hilary smiled but before she could explain, the nurse returned with the units of blood that Cunningham had ordered and a long, red tube with a large yellow balloon on the end, the Litton tube.

"I don't know where he's bleeding, but it's a good guess that it's from varices. We proved that he had them on X-ray last admission," the intern said, referring to the bulging veins that alcoholics get in their esophagus once the liver scars down. "If you want to talk about Mary, you'll have to do it here. I've got to get the balloon down to put pressure on the spot so that I can get to the other eight patients I received tonight. This alky has put me hours behind. One of these days I'm going to just let him bleed to death. He's trying to do that anyway."

Hilary immediately glanced down at the old drunk, but his dirty face remained placid, pathetic, and oblivious to the intern's callous remark. Beside his scalp on the stained pillow were dozens of jumping lice.

"Mary's been admitted to the hospital," she went on as Cunningham took the balloon end of the tubing, lubricated the tip with an ointment and then forced it through the man's right nostril. "Now, swallow, dammit!" he shouted as he threaded the tubing down the back of the alky's throat and down toward his stomach. Halfway down, the gagging drunk reached up for the tubing, but Cunningham pushed his hands away.

"Aren't they wonderful," Cunningham remarked sarcastically. "Every goddamn time I'm on duty I get one of these cases." The intern picked up a large syringe and pumped air into an opening in his end of the tubing. After inserting 300 cc's, he tugged on the tubing to be sure it was secure, made it taut, put a wire mask over the drunk's face and then tied his end around one of the crossbars. "Let's hope it's in the right spot," he said, breathing a sigh of relief.

"About Mary," Hilary resumed. For the moment the case was under control and he was free to talk.

"You don't have to worry about me," he explained as he washed his hands in a closet-sized bathroom. "I always take an antibiotic after intercourse, especially if I don't know the girl well. You never know who's got what. And if she's that easy, she must be easy with others. A little tetracycline p.f., post . . . well, you know, wards off those worries."

"It's not gonorrhea."

"The same's true for syphilis."

"It's not syphilis either," Hilary answered as they walked out into the hallway. "She's got meningitis. Meningococcal meningitis."

"You're kidding!" The young physician was stunned.

"Did you have contact with anyone since her?"

"Sexual or otherwise?"

"Any type of intimate contact?"

Cunningham grinned. "Only what you see around

you. I didn't sleep with any of them, if that's what you want.''

"I should hope not.'' She smiled back, but looking around she estimated there might be fifty people he'd come in contact with, counting patients and personnel. They might have to be added to her list. But for now, she cultured his throat and started him on rifampin.

At 10:00 P.M. that evening, another ambulance arrived at the Contagious Disease Unit. The patient was a transfer from a Pasadena hospital and his history indicated that he was one of the paramedics called to Mary Hudson's apartment. Moments after he arrived, he began convulsing, biting his tongue and flailing his arms and legs about. He was covered with the typical meningococcal spots, and once he was subdued his temperature was measured at one hundred and six degrees.

At 11:14, Mrs. Clagston came racing back to the hospital with her son in her arms. Although Hilary's second investigator, Dr. Meno, had given them both the antibiotic, the boy had only received one dose and he arrived with a high fever and a headache. At first it looked as if his problem was merely an inner ear infection, but a prompt spinal tap proved that he too had meningitis.

At midnight, Dr. Paige was just settling down in one of the hospital's sleeping rooms when he received a call from the County Morgue. A team had just brought in a businessman who'd been found dead in his hotel room, covered with the purplish lesions. So far the only information they had on the man was that he'd arrived two days before and that he represented a copy machine business.

As Paige started across the parking lot toward the morgue, he detoured back to Ogden's laboratory first. Too much was happening, too fast. As he entered, Ling and Ogden had their backs to the door and didn't hear him open it. "Three more cases!" he announced, startling them both. "Two in the house and one about to go into the deep freeze. I knew it would only be a matter of time before this got out of hand."

"So is everything else around here tonight," Ogden answered, frustrated by several bothersome delays and a mound of paperwork accumulating on his desk. Every answer had created a dozen difficult questions. "You look like you could use a cup of coffee. I know I can." Ogden headed toward a small electric pot. "Les, it's only been three hours since we talked."

"Coffee's the one thing I don't need. We have two more cases in the house, and if this keeps up you may have to postpone your project. I'm sorry. I know what you asked me and I know how badly you need the time, but the logistics of caring for so many critically ill patients may soon be overwhelming. I doubt that our unit can handle much more." He sat down at Ogden's desk, arms folded, determined to stay put until he got through to his colleague.

"Everybody's taken care of so far, aren't they?" Ogden poured himself a half cup of coffee.

"So far, yes, but we're averaging a case an hour. By morning we may have ten more people."

Ogden leaned back against the countertop and for a moment appeared to be debating what to do.

"Mike, I'm going to need *your* help," Paige said after a few seconds.

"Okay, suppose I go over the cases and stay down here tonight. It's close to quitting time anyway." He paused to see if Ling objected, but the other scientist didn't say a word. "My experience is that an outbreak like this will die off as quickly as it started, but I'll see what I can do to help."

Paige seemed relieved. A few minutes after he left for the morgue, Ogden walked back to the hospital. He was annoyed both with what seemed like excessive alarm on his associate's part and the timing of the outbreak of the disease. A week earlier or two weeks hence, he'd be free

to hold Paige's hand on this, but not now, not when his
entire research project was on the line. Granted there
was a problem, but he felt certain that it would easily
pass and that it would be handled just as well without
his involvement.

Before sacking out on his office couch, however, he
reviewed the newest charts and examined the patients.
Everything seemed in order. All diagnoses were correct
and everyone was receiving the proper medications.
Nonetheless, a few things did bother him. He was struck
by the speed with which the disease struck; incubation
periods were supposed to be longer. And then there was
the business of possible resistance. This was particularly
worrisome, and if it turned out to be true he wouldn't
need Paige to tell him to forego his research.

At 1:45 he was starting to fall asleep when he was
startled by the phone. On the other end was a physician
from Orange County Hospital who was calling about
Joe Paulus, a youth who had been admitted to their
hospital with meningitis. His parents had informed him
that his girlfriend, Marcey Mathesson, had been admitted to L.A. County with the same diagnosis. Ogden
confirmed the story and advised the physician to cover
him with two antibiotics.

At 2:20, he was shocked back to reality again by the
main intercom. Waking the entire hospital, the voice
was paging him, Yates, James and Paige, all for an
emergency in the intensive care unit. Gordon Mathesson
had suddenly stopped breathing.

Joanna Yates was the first to arrive, but she was
closely followed by the others. As they all gowned outside the room, a nurse inside was frantically squeezing
an Ambu bag over Mathesson's face. The color of the
man's body was a deep blue.

"He just stopped breathing!" she quickly explained
as they entered. "I was changing his IV site when I
heard this funny gurgle. He hasn't been breathing well
for quite a while, but the respirations were adequate un-

til now. There was no indication he'd stop like this.''

Both Yates and Ogden pulled out their stethoscopes and listened to the man's chest. The air from the bag could be heard moving through his bronchioles, but just barely. It was obvious that he needed more.

"Get me an endotracheal tube!" Ogden ordered the nurse. Dr. James took her place at the end of the bed and rhythmically squeezed air into Mathesson's body. "And call respiratory therapy stat for a respirator!"

Ogden took a curved metal instrument, pried the man's mouth open and shoved a stiff rubbed tube through the opening to thread it down into his lungs. The passage went smoothly. The respirator, a three-foot-high box whose top was a collage of dials and warning lights, was turned on and began pumping one hundred percent oxygen into the failing body. Above, on the oscilloscope, Mathesson's heart rate slowed, and his color gradually changed from blue to ashen gray to pink.

He was breathing again, but only because of a machine.

CHAPTER THIRTEEN

A few seconds past six thirty, Ogden awoke in an uncomfortable position on his couch with an ache in his back from the soft cushions. He had only gotten three hours of sleep, five less than his usual and, he knew, an hour less than he needed to function reasonably. Years ago when he was an intern, four hours seemed to be the magic number. If he got less, even a few minutes under that four-hour mark, he found himself dragging by midday. Perhaps it was partly psychological, he thought, but with a mere three hours under his belt he knew that he'd have trouble later in the day.

He kept an extra set of clothes in his office closet, but had to shave and shower in surgery. "I'm too old for this crap," he muttered, eyeing the gray streaks in his hair as he moved the razor along his chin. The shower had made him appear well rested, but his mind was clouded and his muscles fatigued. He didn't like the feeling, especially with all the problems that he had, and he hoped he could take a break later for a nap.

Yates and her intern were already seated at the long conference table when he arrived in the cafeteria. They both had been working the entire night and they had dark circles around their eyes. In contrast, their replacement, Dr. Larry Frank, a tall, lean man with curly brown hair, looked particularly fresh and was eager to start. He'd heard about the epidemic and was eager to jump in and help.

The customary procedure each morning was for the admitting team from the previous twenty-four hours to describe their new admissions to the other interns and residents as well as to Dr. Ogden. There was a standard protocol. They'd begin with the patients' present complaints, go on to the relevant parts of their history, add in any abnormal physical findings and laboratory data, and then, in summary, offer their impressions and plan of therapy.

This morning every case except one—the technician with fulminant hepatitis—was meningitis.

As the other physicians listened to Yates's presentation, they could hardly believe what they were hearing. Not only were the number of cases extraordinary, but after Gordon Mathesson's respiratory arrest he had begun bleeding from his stomach, requiring three units of blood. And Murray Clagston had gone blind from the disease.

"How many more do you think there'll be?" Frank excitedly asked Ogden the moment Yates was done. Behind him, Paige was quietly sitting down with a cup of coffee in one hand and a danish in the other.

"I don't know, but—"

He was interrupted by Paige. "It might go as high as eight million. That's the population of this city, isn't it?"

Several residents laughed, thinking that he was joking, but stopped when they saw that Paige's expression remained serious.

"I'm sure it won't be eight dozen. Nothing like it," Ogden went on. "I suspect there'll be one or two more at the most. Three, if we're unlucky. These outbreaks never spread like you think they might. Last year we had a small epidemic of shigella dysentery at Pacific State Hospital. Thirty dehydrated, retarded kids with non-stop diarrhea. They took up the entire fourth floor and it required two teams of nurses just to stay ahead of the dirty diapers. Everyone thought it would spread to the other hundreds of kids in the institution, their attendants and everyone's relatives, but as usual it didn't.

"Then, two years ago, we had that diptheria outbreak. Fifteen people were hospitalized with necks so swollen they couldn't swallow or speak. The index case was a nine-year-old boy who died, but every one of the others walked out after a week or so. These small outbreaks always happen in big cities, probably because we all live so close together. But they're always short-lived."

"But what if this one isn't?" one of the residents asked.

"If it isn't, we'll have to earn our pay and deal with the problem," Ogden answered. "We'll just double up on the call schedule. Two interns and two residents on every night."

"Let's hope it doesn't," James remarked, rubbing at his eyes.

As the house staff left to do their morning scut work, Paige moved to a chair next to Ogden. "It's not going to stop, you know. You're just fooling yourself if you think otherwise."

"You're a pessimist. I think you've been reading too many science fiction magazines," Ogden teased him, but he was beginning to have some doubts.

"Or you're too much of an optimist. I've been watching this thing spread. The point is, Mike, whether we get ten more or a hundred, we're at the mercy of this thing. We haven't been able to cure a single one of the patients who have it. Our own staff are getting it. And we haven't even been able to *retard* the damn thing—with penicillin, with rifampin—"

"Les, it's only been twenty-four hours since this started."

Paige set down his coffee mug like a justice's gavel. "I rest my case," he said, and got up to go get some sleep.

After making the rounds on the meningitis cases, Ogden stopped by the bacteriology laboratory. It was on his way to his research laboratory, where he still hoped to spend most of his day. At the entrance, he ran into Dr. Walters coming from the opposite direction.

"Seven cases in the house here, two others elsewhere and two known dead." Her tone said I-told-you-so.

"You sound like you've been talking to Les Paige. The two of you are going to be pleasantly surprised. We're probably at the tail end of this outbreak."

"You really don't believe that, do you? I'd like to think you're right, but I can't agree," she said as the two entered the lab.

"Everybody wants this to be an epidemic. My interns and residents are excited, like little children going to Disneyland. My staff's expecting the roof to cave in and Paige is about to put on a sandwich board predicting the end of the world. I admit we have more cases than usual, but at this moment that's all it is."

"Maybe you're right, but I'll have to see a change to believe you. I've already added two more investigators and we've switched to using phones. There were too many contacts to visit each one personally. We may have to close down a few schools."

"Hilary, if you shut down a single school prematurely and unnecessarily, you'll scare every parent in the city. The news of a meningitis outbreak will travel a damn sight faster than any disease."

"And if I don't and you're wrong, you may have every parent and child in here as patients . . . or maybe in the morgue after it's too late."

"Wait—hold it." Ogden held his hands up. The discussion had quickly gotten heated. "I merely want you and everyone else around here to go easy until we're sure of what we have. No need to alarm everyone from Orange County to Oxnard if this ends just like every other meningitis epidemic before it."

Hilary felt like saying more, and in fact her face reddened with annoyance, but she stopped and took a deep breath instead. She respected his opinion, but she just couldn't agree and there was no purpose in arguing. Instead, they turned their attention to a lab tech who was examining the three Mathesson cultures. The agar plates from Gordon Mathesson and his daughter Marcey were covered with hundreds of pearly gray specks—colonies each representing millions of bacteria that resembled meningococcus—but Jamey's plate barely had a hint of any growth.

"His is too early to tell," the technician explained, pointing out that they'd set up Jamey's culture only twelve hours before.

"What about the fermentation studies?" Ogden asked, crossing the room to a workbench where several test tube racks were laid out. The tubes that contained a red material were the sugar lactose, while those that were yellow were glucose or maltose. This pattern of fermentation was proof positive that the meningococcus was the offending organism.

While Ogden studied the tubes, Hilary unloaded another incubator full of plates marked for the Health Department.

"The plates that show any growth at all look like the same organism," the technician remarked. "You don't need fermentation studies on all of them, do you?"

"All of them?" Hilary exclaimed. She had been hoping to find one positive among the lot and thereby pin down the carrier. Now she learned that two of the Customs officials, one of whom was Van Horn, were positives, as well as Mrs. Mathesson, Lynda Mathesson,

Mrs. Thackery and Tina Hudson. Since they were all contacts, it was possible, but the number still seemed incredible to her.

"I don't think you're going to have an easy time with this bug," the technician added as he directed them both to another countertop. "First of all, this son of a gun grows on everything. Meningococcus, at least the typical meningococcus we see around here, only grows on blood agar at ten percent carbon dioxide and high humidity. This character loves everything." The man pointed to several different colored petri dishes that were covered with the same pearly gray specks. "It also grows much more rapidly than any I've seen. Our counts show the colonies to be double and triple the usual concentration. The thing must be reproducing at record speed, and if that's not bad enough, it's also resistant to most of our antibiotics."

The technician handed Ogden his worksheet.

ANTIOBIOGRAM

Antibiotic	sensitive	inde-terminate	resistant
Penicillin			+
Ampicillin			+
Methicillin			+
Cephalothin		+	
Cephalexin		+	
Clindamycin			+
Minocycline			+
Cefamycin			+
Tetracycline			+
Erythromycin			+
Chloramphenicol		+	
Polymyxin		+	
Rifampin		+	
Gentamycin			+
Tobramycin			+
Carbenicillin			+
Ticarcillin			+

Amikacin	+	
Streptomycin		+
SXT		+

"That's impossible," he said after a moment of study. "You're saying that this organism isn't even *sensitive* to anything we have? The best you can find is an indeterminate rating, meaning that they might be sensitive?"

"No, meaning that they probably aren't, but we don't have enough data yet."

Ogden couldn't believe what he was looking at. It was the worst antibiotic profile he'd ever seen.

"They've all been double-checked," the technician went on to explain, groping for an answer. "But maybe it's too early. The culture's only twenty-four hours old and perhaps another day will show a reversal. And my tests don't cover the gamut of antibiotic doses. At higher serum levels in a human the bug might be sensitive."

"Possible, but not likely," Ogden remarked, intently studying the petri dishes where the antibiotics were tested. Within each circular container and lying on top of the agar film were twenty tiny paper discs. Each one had been soaked in a different antibiotic and had the drug's abbreviation printed on top—Pen for penicillin, Amp for ampicillin. Under usual conditions, a bacteria that was being studied would grow everywhere on the agar plate except near the antibiotic disc to which it was sensitive. Indeterminates would have scanty growth, resistant strains normal growth. On these particular cultures, however, the organisms covered the plate from one edge to the other and there was only a slight thinning near the indeterminate discs. A purist might have even called them resistant also—something Ogden was prone to believe.

"Now what?" Hilary asked curtly as she watched Ogden. He had suddenly become as alarmed as she had been. Alarmed and angry. Not only were these bizarre bacteria killing his patients, but they were also about to kill his cancer research.

"I assume that your contacts are already on rifampin?" he asked.

She nodded. "So am I, for that matter." She was thinking how she might have been more careful if she had known.

"I'm not sure it's going to do you or them any good, looking at this profile. There may not be *any* prophylactic drug. I hate to say it, but you're right about closing those schools. Just do me a favor. Try to keep this low-key. I'll let the Center for Disease Control know right away. Maybe we'll be able to tap their stock of vaccines."

As Ogden left the bacteriology lab, there was an urgency to his pace. Adrenalin had covered the fatigue of not sleeping. He had too much to do and his thoughts shot back and forth between the demands of his own research project and what he might have to do if the disease continued to spread. He still had hopes that it wouldn't, but they were only wishful thinking. He now suspected that they were in for some trouble.

CHAPTER FOURTEEN

The Contagious Disease Unit came alive as the intercom blared out "Code Blue, Third Floor. Code Blue, Third Floor." Everyone was supposed to respond. Code Blue meant cardiac arrest and every intern and resident in the building came running.

Ogden had just returned to the building and suited up when he heard the page and darted up the two flights of steps. When he arrived, a ward clerk standing in the hallway directed him toward Gordon Mathesson's room. Inside, Joanna Yates and two other residents with their gowns barely tied were beginning cardio-pulmonary resuscitation. His heart had stopped completely; the monitor above his head showed a flat line that was intermittently broken by the rhythmic chest compressions administered by Yates. "Get me adrenalin on an intracardiac needle!" she shouted, and a nurse handed her a syringe with a long needle.

It took a couple of seconds to localize the exact spot on the chest wall and then Yates stabbed the needle deep into the heart chamber and injected the medication. Everyone waited. The flat line changed to a very slow beat, barely one every five seconds, then increased to one every other second, and then ventricular fibrillation, a sawtooth pattern that was also life-threatening.

"Charge up the defibrillator!" Ogden ordered an aide as he grabbed the two paddles and laid them on Mathesson's chest. He asked everyone to stand back and then fired a two-hundred-watt shock that singed the man's skin and caused his body to convulse.

As Ogden removed the paddles, the original slow rhythm returned, sped up . . . and then converted to ventricular fibrillation again. He ordered the machine recharged and he shocked him again. This time the charge left deep red marks where the current had passed.

"Give him an amp of bicarb! No, give him two amps, and get some lidocaine started," Yates ordered a nurse who had just arrived. A second resident took Yates's place in case more chest compressions would be necessary.

For almost a minute, Mathesson's rhythm normalized on the scope and everyone began to relax. His blood pressure became measurable and his color started improving. During the injection of the second amp of bicarb, however, an occasional irregular beat appeared. It didn't seem threatening until the occurrences rapidly changed from once every twenty beats to every six and then every other.

"Get that lidocaine in him stat!" Ogden shouted to the nurse who was doing the injecting. "Forget the bicarb. Give the rest to him after the lidocaine."

The nurse quickly set the first syringe on the nightstand and injected the lidocaine directly into the intravenous tubing, but the irregularities continued and two minutes later converted to ventricular fibrillation a third time. They were forced to shock him again, and this time they injected procainamide, a medication similar to lidocaine. As Ogden stood at the bedside with the paddles still in hand, the new medication was tried and his rhythm stabilized. Every beat on the scope was similar to the one before it . . . every beat occurred at regular intervals . . . every beat carried blood to his ailing body. His blood pressure returned as before, and with it came some semblance of normal color. As they hooked him up to the respirator and large volumes of oxygen were pushed into his lungs, however, they could hear the grating sound of broken ribs rubbing together. The broken ribs were a painful but common post-resuscitation side effect and everyone knew that they would heal in time—if the patient survived.

As the additional personnel from other floors cleared the room and Mathesson's nurse was left to clear away the medication vials, dirty needles, used alcohol swabs, bloody sheets and reams of EKG paper, Ogden stepped to the patient's bedside to assess his condition. He had the feeling that they might be supporting a corpse. Indeed, all four extremities were flaccid, dropping like lead weights when he lifted them. There was no indication that he felt pain and both of his pupils were widely dilated and unresponsive to light.

"I'm sure he's dead," Ogden remarked to Yates and the nurse. He was referring to an invention of modern medicine—brain death, wherein the heart and lungs of a person can be maintained artificially, but the brain tissues themselves are beyond recovery. "We'll go ahead and get an EEG to prove it, but I'm sure he's dead."

Harriet Mathesson, unnoticed during the crisis, had walked onto the floor and gone to her husband's doorway to see what the commotion was all about. She knew it was a mistake to have come. The moment she peered inside, she couldn't leave. She saw everything that they had done and felt every blow to his chest as if it were her own. When she overheard Dr. Ogden say that he was dead, tears flooded her eyes and her legs started to give way. Hilary Walters was there to catch her.

"I knew it when I saw everyone running upstairs . . . I

knew it had to be him," she sobbed as Walters helped her back to the waiting room. Her daughter Lynda was standing at the entrance, and as the two embraced each other their grief-stricken cries echoed down the hallway.

As soon as Ogden left the bedside, he scrubbed and joined them, embarrassed that his frank diagnosis had been overheard.

"He was a good man . . . he didn't deserve this," Harriet Mathesson said through shuddering lips. She reached into her pocket for a tissue, and after wiping Lynda's eyes she wiped her own. "Is there any chance that you're wrong?" she asked Ogden. "Isn't there anything you can do?"

"We're doing everything we can. Everything that we know. Before we talk about disconnecting any of the life support, we'll check an EEG. Maybe there'll be some electrical activity, but I really doubt it. If he were to survive at this point, he'd be rather severely handicapped, I'm afraid. I doubt that he'd want that."

She agreed, and after taking a moment to gather her thoughts she asked about Marcey and Jamey. "This same thing isn't going to happen to them too, is it?"

"No, they're different, Mrs. Mathesson. Your husband's case was much further along. Neither of the kids is as bad. I'm sure we'll be able to help them," he answered, afraid that she was right.

The EEG machine was brought to Gordon Mathesson's bedside, but after the tiny electrodes were inserted into his scalp, the tracing was flat. Legally, the patient was dead, but Ogden ordered that the procedure be repeated in twelve hours. It was more wishful thinking than a realistic expectation, but there had been a few recent reports about tracings that had changed and he did not want to take any chances.

In addition to Gordon Mathesson's sudden deterioration, there were other problems brewing on the floor. Marcey was also slipping. The purple spots on her torso were coalescing into large blotches and her hands were turning blue from the wrists down. Murray Clagston was more confused, Mary Mitchell had had two convulsions within five minutes of each other and the paramedic was going into shock.

The change in the patients' clinical conditions worried Ogden, but he was even more concerned that the repeat spinal taps had also deteriorated. Marcey's white count in the fluid had gone from 72 cells to over 5,000, with a hundred percent increase in the protein content. Murray Clagston's cell count rose from 2,100 to 3,500 with a fifty percent increase in protein, and Mary Mitchell's count rose from 200 to 4,600 with a comparable increase in the chemistry value. These were all serious changes suggesting that the infection was not under control and that their lives would soon be in jeopardy if the process wasn't reversed.

The only patient among the lot who appeared to be holding his own was Jamey Mathesson, but everyone assumed that it was just a matter of time. When Ogden visited him, the boy acted more like a child with a cold—runny nose, cough, aches everywhere—but the high fever and meningococcal spots remained unchanged and the repeat spinal tap showed a slight increase in his white count. It wasn't nearly as high as the others, but it was still up.

After leaving Jamey's room, Ogden went directly to his office to call Dr. Bellows in Atlanta. He was beginning to think that he should have called sooner. Small epidemics from a variety of causes were common across the country, of course, and even minor changes in antibiotic resistance weren't surprising. This, however, was different somehow and he worried that his preoccupation with the research had temporarily blinded him. He could hear Paige's warning from the previous night. But strangely enough, it was the image of Hilary Walters, her dark eyes flashing with suppressed anger over his stubbornness, that was the strongest rebuke.

"Don't tell me you already have another breakthrough," Bellows joked as he answered. He was just on his way out for a business luncheon, he said.

"We've got a breakthrough all right, but not the kind I had been hoping to report." Ogden's tone was serious as he went on to explain the series of events since Gordon Mathesson's admission.

"To be honest, I've been expecting something like this," Bellows replied after a slight pause. "But I never thought the resistant organism would be meningococcus. It's always been sensitive to antibiotics, and it couldn't be a worse disease to happen with. Are you sure your antibiotic discs are properly saturated? Sometimes they change with age, you know. Last year we had a false alarm with a *Hemophilus* strain and it turned out to be technical only."

Ogden agreed that errors were always possible, but pointed out that most of the patients were also worse.

"I suppose that's really the proof of the pudding," Bellows said, breaking off for a moment to tell his secretary to cancel the luncheon. "Have you serotyped the organism yet?"

"We're still defrosting the antiserum. It'll be another hour or so before we can pin down the species. What's the status on vaccines if we need them?"

"The status isn't good, Mike, but it really depends on which species you come up with. We have a reasonable supply of vials for Type A and C, but vaccines for B are on the short side. There was a small outbreak of B at an Air Force base in Wiesbaden, Germany, last month and we shipped half of our stock overseas just to be safe. That was two hundred doses. It takes weeks to produce the antigen for the vaccine; nature won't go any faster. How many contacts do you think you'll have?"

Ogden stopped to figure. This was the first time he had given much thought to the actual numbers. "A couple of dozen at least. I'll have to check with Dr. Walters and my own staff. The problem isn't the number so much as the fact that this organism seems to spread a lot faster than you'd expect. We already have a few casual contacts with positive throat cultures. If we have to vaccinate more than just intimate contacts, the number might go into the hundreds."

"Hundreds?" Bellows repeated skeptically. "God, I hope not. If that's true we couldn't send you enough vaccines even if it were Type A."

"What if it's not any of the species that we know? It's not behaving like any that I've seen before. The lab data's different. The transmission pattern is bizarre. It might turn out to be a mutation or something that someone's concocted in an experimental laboratory."

"I doubt that," Bellows answered, but grew silent when Ogden mentioned that one of the contacts was a Russian courier. Hilary Walters had told him of the man's odd behavior at the airport and that she still hadn't been able to trace him.

"We gave up germ warfare, but we don't know if they did," Ogden concluded.

"It's still not possible," Bellows asserted. "I doubt that the Russians have the technology to develop an organism like this. I can tell you no one in the United States could do it. At least not yet."

"I guess it is pretty farfetched. We're all beginning to grope for answers at this point."

"Well, I'll have someone at the State Department look into it, just to be on the safe side. What about your patients? What are you doing for them?"

"We're using combinations of drugs and higher than usual dosages, but I'm not sure what to use. Any suggestions?"

Bellows was quiet for a moment before answering. "I'm not sure myself. Usually the antibiogram tells us."

"That won't help here."

"I know. I suppose the best thing to do is to use three or even four antibiotics on every patient. Vary the doses and split the patients into groups to see which combination works. In fact, I'd even give some of them direct injections into the spinal canal. Meanwhile, the most important aspect is analyzing this organism. Make sure we find out where it came from, how it picked up this multiple resistance pattern and what weaknesses, if any, you can detect. That's right up your alley, isn't it? That's what you were doing when you were here with us."

"Not quite the same—"

"Damn close, at least as close as anyone else in this country. Does your lab there have the equipment to follow through?"

The hospital's bacteriology laboratory didn't, but Ogden's own research facility did. "Yes, we can do it, but it'll mean stopping my cancer work," Ogden answered slowly. He had hoped that Tom Ling would carry on the experiment in his absence, but with the equipment shifted that would be impossible.

Bellows detected Ogden's concern. "I'll see what I can do when the grant committee meets, but for now I don't think you have any choice."

"No, I don't."

As Ogden was speaking to Bellows, Hilary Walters was talking on a different phone at the nurses' station. She had placed another call to the Russian consulate.

"I called you last night," she began, annoyed by Korlov's delay in taking her call. "I'm with the Health Department and we have a serious outbreak of meningitis in the city. The organism is resistant to most of our antibiotics and our index case is a Customs inspector who had contact with your courier two days ago. I'm worried that he might have contracted the disease or carried it in."

"Which man was that? We have several couriers coming and going." The consul spoke with a thick accent that was difficult to understand.

"Szlenko. Victor Szlenko."

"Mr. Szlenko has already returned to the Soviet Union and he looked quite well when I saw him. I'm sure there is no problem." His tone indicated that the conversation was now concluded.

"When was that?" she persisted.

"Ms. . . . ah, Dr. Walters, that is information that I don't need to share with you. Particularly over the telephone. Diplomatic courtesy, you understand. You can take my word that the man has returned home and is in excellent health."

"You can't be sure with this organism. Are you still in touch with him?"

"I would know if he were ill. If there is anything new, I'll be glad to pass it on through my secretary. Thank you for your interest." He started to hang up, but Walters held on to him.

"It's possible that he's only a carrier. He might have the bacteria in his throat or sinuses and not be ill at all, or he might have caught the disease here and become sick any moment. Someone should check him over and let me know right away."

"That might not be possible. I have been called back to Moscow on important business. We are leaving this afternoon."

"Then have someone in your office notify me—"

"The office will be closed while I am away."

"There must be some way. This is vital information. Perhaps you can notify the American Embassy in Moscow and have them forward the information."

"I shall look into it. Good day."

As the consul hung up, Hilary was puzzled by his reluctance to help, and especially by his pointed lack of concern. She had the feeling he was hiding something.

Her next call went to Dr. Raynor in Atlanta, who also seemed surprised that they were dealing with a resistant meningococcus. Her facts were too convincing to overlook, however, and when Hilary finished he offered to send two members from his staff out to help her. In addition, he suggested she keep all of the contacts on rifampin until there was a proven breakthrough, that she quarantine every contact possible, and lastly that she play this outbreak down if word got to the press. He was afraid that meningitis nowadays could prove as frightening as the plague was centuries ago.

As soon as she got off with Raynor, she began phoning every contact who had a positive throat culture. Her first call went to Mrs. Thackery, but no one answered. Next, she tried the two Customs officials and advised them to leave work immediately. On the third call, which was to Tina Hudson, she was interrupted by her beeper. A local general practitioner in Tarzana was trying to reach her. Gerald Katzenbach had come to him for an exam and mentioned that the Health Department was looking for him. The missionary was afraid that they knew he was being treated for tuberculosis and might send him back to Kenya, but as it turned out he was already on rifampin, Hilary's prophylactic drug. Since the practitioner said the boy looked well, she suggested that he merely culture his throat to be sure and send the specimen to her lab. There didn't seem to be any reason at the moment to see him personally—not if he'd been taking the medicine as prescribed, even though it was for a different disease. And if it were true that rifampin was ineffective, there was nothing she could do for him or for any of the other contacts.

CHAPTER FIFTEEN

Doctor Frank's admitting day began mildly despite Gordon Mathesson's cardiac arrest. He and his intern were able to make rounds with ease on their four cases in the hospital, and there was even some talk that the epidemic might have ended. No one was sure they believed it, but at least there were no new cases reported.

His first case on the floor was a sixteen-year-old girl who had been admitted with brucella, a disease that she caught by eating contaminated meat in Mexico. She'd been back in the States for several months, but had been running fevers off and on for weeks and suffering joint pain. Now that the diagnosis was made, however, and appropriate therapy initiated, she was expected to go home within a few days.

His second case was a three-year-old boy with Reye's syndrome, a severe neurological disease that appeared to be caused by the chicken pox virus. A few days before his admission, he broke out in the blisterlike sores that characterized chicken pox, but he also had a headache and had become increasingly confused. Now he was comatose. The pressure inside his head had grown to such intensity that a team of neurosurgeons had to remove a portion of his skull to drain some of the spinal fluid. At the moment, the outlook was grave and his parents had not left his bedside for hours.

The third case was that of a forty-five-year-old man with leukemia and pneumonia. He was being treated with six separate medications, three for each disease. So far, his body didn't have enough normal white cells to fight off the infection, and unless his bone marrow rallied he'd be overwhelmed with the bacteria very soon.

The fourth case was the most tragic. It was a four-day-old baby with herpes viremia. The child had been born at home to a counterculture couple who adamantly opposed an in-hospital delivery. Instead, they stayed at home and used a poorly trained midwife who never noticed that the mother's birth canal harbored the herpes venereal disease. Under proper conditions, the child would have been born through a caesarean section, but instead it had traveled through the infected cervix and contracted a disease that few infants survive. At the moment, all systems—heart, lungs, kidneys— were failing and the child was near death.

Despite the complexities of each case and the need to discuss them with family members, rounds only took Larry Frank an hour, and after discussing the day's scut work with his intern he left for the hospital library. He had always been lucky on admitting days, getting only a small number of admissions that were usually interesting cases, and he was beginning to feel confident that his luck would continue.

An hour and a half elapsed before he was called out, but the case was an easy one. Waiting in the admitting area was a nervous mother with her two-year-old boy who'd been having diarrhea for several days. The woman looked fatigued, probably from changing diapers all night, but the child was smiling and seemed well. After examining the child, Frank reassured the mother that he probably had a stomach virus; if she modified his diet, the runs would stop. She seemed satisfied and he hurried back to his books in the library.

At noon, just as he was starting to leave for lunch, he got his second call. This time it was a seven-year-old girl who was covered with a faint reddish rash that was typical for measles. The girl looked miserable, but there wasn't any treatment. He guaranteed the mother that she'd be well in three days and headed off for a leisurely lunch.

Halfway through a ham sandwich, however, Frank's name was paged stat. An ambulance was on its way in with a meningitis patient. The paramedics had reported over the radio that the man's blood pressure and pulse were unobtainable and that they were beginning cardiopulmonary resuscitation.

Frank immediately summoned his intern and the two physicians rushed to the admitting area, pulling on masks and gowns. They could hear the ambulance siren toning down and the sound of its engine as it backed up to the entrance. The rear doors flew open, and a moment later a stretcher was racing the man into one of the isolation rooms. One paramedic was pounding on his chest while the other struggled to steer the cart.

"No blood pressure and no palpable pulse!" one of the paramedics reported. "We couldn't get an IV started on him. All of his veins are collapsed." Their patient was an Oriental man with purplish spots across his face and thick pus exuding from beneath his eyeballs.

Once the man was shifted onto a bed, Frank grabbed a long intravenous needle and stuck it in just below the man's collarbone, hoping to hit one of the major veins and thereby give them a quick portal for medications. His stab missed, however, and caused a portion of the man's right lung to collapse. He quickly shifted to the other side of the bed and inserted a new needle, paying more attention to the landmarks this time and finding the subclavian vein. In the interim, the oscilloscope showed an extremely rapid pulse interspersed with frequent abnormal beats.

"Give him a push of lidocaine and two amps of bicarb," the resident called to a nurse, who quickly removed the medications from an emergency cart.

"Where'd you find him? What's his name?" Frank asked the nearest paramedic as he injected the drugs. But before he got an answer he turned back to the nurse. "Get me five million units . . . no, make it ten million units of penicillin, a gram of chloramphenicol and fifty milligrams of gentamycin." These were antibiotics that Ogden had advised him to use.

"His wife said that she found him like this and she tried doing CPR on her own. She really didn't know how. He was home ill and she had just come back from the store. His name is Leon Yong."

"Do you know anything else about his health?" Frank asked as he tossed the used syringes aside and watched Yong's feeble heart rhythm on the oscilloscope. For the moment, it appeared stable.

"She said something about a heart condition, maybe a heart attack a few years ago, but he's been in good health ever since."

Just as the nurse was about to take his blood pressure, however, the patient's rhythm went into ventricular fibrillation.

"Get me the defibrillator!" Frank shouted.

As the nurse charged up the machine, he laid the paddles on Yong's chest. When she signalled, he fired. The shock made the oscilloscope pattern bounce for a second, but when it returned Yong's rhythm was normal.

Meanwhile, the admitting clerk had received another emergency radio call, and she came to the doorway of Yong's isolation room. "We've got another ambulance coming," she called out. "Their estimated time of arrival is three minutes. It's another case of meningitis and they're doing CPR."

"There's no way I can handle two of these at the same time," Frank exclaimed. "Get someone else down here!"

"Who?" the clerk asked, but Frank's attention was diverted by Yong's rhythm, which had changed back into ventricular fibrillation. He called for the paddles again.

"Who should I call?" the clerk repeated, her voice rising in exasperation.

"Call anyone . . . call the resident who's on call tomorrow . . . he's supposed to be on backup . . . I don't know," Frank said, his attention on attending the dying man. As he fired the shock, the jolt jarred the intravenous line loose and the fluids began to run off into the sheets. . . .

The hospital intercom boomed out with an emergency page. "Dr. Yarrow . . . *Dr. Yarrow* . . ." The ponytailed resident was eating his lunch and dropped his fork noisily onto his tray. "I'm not *on* today!" he muttered as he went to a wall phone. "Someone's got the damn admitting schedule all screwed up again."

A minute later, however, Yarrow was on the run toward admitting. Once the clerk explained that Dr. Frank was tied up with a cardiac arrest and another meningococcal CPR patient was on the way, he understood. He was unable to find his intern, and he was alone when he arrived at admitting, where the second ambulance was unloading a case similar to the previous admission. The man was close to forty years old and he too had purple spots across his face and pus oozing from his eyeballs. He had been found in an alleyway.

Working in separate isolation rooms, the two residents battled changing heart rhythms and varying blood pressures. Both patients were comatose and neither seemed to be responding to their intensive efforts.

Mike Ogden, working downstairs in the bacteriology laboratory, had heard the page for Frank, but ignored it until he heard the emergency page for Yarrow as well.

Alarmed, he ran up the stairway and was astounded by what he saw. Cardiac arrests were rare occurrences in the unit, thank God, but at the moment there were two. Both had meningitis and both appeared to be nearly terminal.

Seeing that Yarrow was shorthanded, Ogden gowned and entered his room. The man upon whom he was working was barely breathing, and as Ogden approached the heart beat slowed to zero—a flat line on the scope. They injected adrenalin through his chest wall into the heart, then calcium, then adrenalin again, but none of the stimulants worked. Less than ten minutes after the patient arrived, he was pronounced dead.

The two physicians tossed their contaminated gowns into a hamper, scrubbed and regowned, although the pile of fresh gowns was getting low. They entered Frank's room, where the pattern continued to be the same. Yong's breathing had ceased, and a minute later so did his heartbeat. Adrenalin and calcium failed to revive him.

The second day's onslaught had begun. Before the nurses could clean up the rooms and move the two bodies to the morgue, two more cases came in. The first was Dr. Howard Cunningham, who walked over to the unit on his own power. He had been working all night on the admitting service, and during the morning he began feeling some muscle aches. At first he attributed them to fatigue—he had been awake for thirty straight hours—but they steadily worsened. And when he checked his temperature, the thermometer read one hundred and three. He didn't have the typical headache or any noticeable spots, but he remembered Mary Mitchell's diagnosis and wanted to be checked.

Both Larry Frank and Mike Ogden examined him, and when neither physician could explain his elevated temperature they proceeded with the spinal tap. The results were not surprising. He too had meningitis.

The second case was a six-year-old boy who turned out to be a schoolmate of the Clagston boy. He had been playing on the swings at school that morning when he started vomiting and couldn't stop. The school nurse noted a fever and a stiff neck, called the parents and immediately sent him off to the unit.

By the time the child arrived, his retching had become so severe that he tore his esophagus at the junction of the stomach. Now he was throwing up solid blood, and he had to be raced off to surgery with transfusions pouring in through two intravenous sites and the triple antibiotics through a third . . .

Before the child was taken off to surgery, Mike Ogden had looked down at his agonized face and had been caught off guard with the sudden memory of Karen's painful death. He was startled, for he had long since learned to guard himself from this kind of association. But then the boy was only a year or so younger than Peter . . .

He went to the nearest phone on the corridor to call Mrs. Anderson and tell her to keep Peter home from school, but the busy lights for every one of the five available lines was lit up. He stood for a moment, looking at the chaos gathering around him, and then raced off to place the call from his office.

Work on the meningococcus began immediately in Ogden's research laboratory. While Tom Ling hurriedly cleared the workbenches and set up new equipment, Ogden recruited two additional technicians from the hospital's main lab. Both were highly experienced in bacteriology and were willing to put in the number of hours necessary. At the moment, it looked as if they'd be working around the clock until they got an answer.

Their first step was to further characterize the offending organism. Seemingly, the bacteria met all of the standard criteria used to identify the meningococcus— Gram stains, colony appearance, chemistries, fermentation studies and culture requirements—but because of its peculiar behavior and aggressive nature Ogden wanted to be sure before proceeding. After selecting a typical colony from Gordon Mathesson's culture plate, they subjected the tiny speck to the scrutiny of a scanning electron microscope.

Photographs of the organisms magnified them to 200,000 times their actual size—to grapefruit size—and just as one would expect with meningococcus, the organisms turned out to be bean-shaped and grouped in pairs. They were prokaryotic, meaning that they lacked most of the characteristics of higher class cells, having no nucleus and showing only a strand of DNA. Their outside cell wall was typical for all members of *Neisseria*, the genus to which meningococcus belongs.

In Ogden's mind, the organism had to be meningococcus—the evidence was too conclusive—and much to his dismay its species was soon shown to be Type B, the only group for which Bellows had told him there was a shortage of vaccine. It now was imperative that he find a weakness.

CHAPTER SIXTEEN

Hilary Walters had been trying to reach the Hudson girl by phone. At first there was no answer, and then she got a continuous busy signal as if the phone might be off the hook. After several attempts, she decided to drive to the girl's apartment instead. Now that Tina Hudson had a known positive throat culture, it was critical that Hilary get the names of her clientele. If she were to judge by Tina's youth and beauty, the number might be considerable.

When she arrived outside the apartment door, she could hear the TV playing and it took Tina several minutes to answer the bell. When she opened the door, she looked ill.

"Bad night?" Hilary asked, entering without being asked.

"Something like that," Tina answered, closing the door and slowly walking toward the couch. She was slightly hunched over and each step seemed to be an effort.

"Are you sick?"

"No, just a stomachache. I've got to get some sleep.

Why'd you come? I thought we were finished."

"Your throat culture was positive. You're carrying the same bacteria in your throat that killed your sister. You are taking the medicine I gave you, aren't you?"

"No, not yet, but I plan to," the girl replied wearily as she rolled to her side and crossed her arms over her stomach.

"Why not?" Hilary angrily replied. "You saw how serious this disease can be, how deadly. You saw what it did to your sister."

"I know, I know, but I haven't been able to keep anything down. I tried. Honestly, I did. I've been throwing up all morning."

"Maybe I should take you over to the hospital and have someone check you over," Hilary said, concerned now that it might be more serious than Tina was letting on.

"No, I'll be all right," she insisted. "It's just a cramp. I've had it before. It'll go away."

Hilary asked if she had any other symptoms, but the girl steadfastly maintained that her illness was minor. At last Hilary gave up, pausing for a second before she said, "I'm sure you don't feel like talking about it, but I need to know the names of everyone you slept with in the last three days."

Tina started to laugh, but stopped short as if in pain. After a moment, she spoke, "You're kidding. You think I keep records or something? I don't know half those dudes and I certainly couldn't tell you the names of the ones I do. Not regulars."

"You have to!" Hilary insisted. "Some of their lives might be in danger. Some of their families. This thing spreads very easily."

"If I tell you then my life's in danger too. That's just not done in my business."

"It's all in confidence." Hilary's voice was low, urgent, as she went on. "I won't tell anyone where I got the names. I'll make up stories if I have to."

"If someone finds out, my ass will be in a sling."

"I guarantee no one will find out."

"I don't trust your guarantees."

"I can't believe you can *be* like this. This disease might spread across the city if you don't help me. You really want someone else's death on your conscience?"

"I don't want *my* death on my conscience, and that's what it'll be. You have to watch out for number one. You saw my pimp, in the red hat?"

Hilary nodded.

"That son of a bitch gets crazy if he even *suspects* someone of selling out on him. And I do mean crazy. He even carries a knife in his boot and I know people that he's cut on before—girls who were so scarred that they had trouble working again. He wouldn't think too highly of me if I was to tell you any names. Or you either, for that matter."

"I'm not afraid, and you shouldn't be either. He'll never know."

"He'll know. Tony can smell it in the air." The girl struggled to her feet, grimacing as she rose, and walked across the room to the dining room table, where she opened a pill vial and popped one of the tablets into her mouth. "See, I've started your medicine. Now I've got to get to bed." She turned abruptly to walk toward the door, but stumbled and fell back against one of the chairs.

Hilary quickly jumped up to steady her. "You need medical attention. Let me take you to the hospital."

Tina started to resist, but the pain had temporarily paralyzed her. After taking a deep breath, she said, "Only if it don't mean I have to help you."

It wasn't a compromise that Hilary welcomed, but she agreed. After helping Tina put on a bathrobe, they started down the stairwell arm in arm. Halfway down, they heard footsteps approaching. A second later, they saw the brim of a red hat and Hilary felt Tina stiffen against her.

"Well, what have we here? The Bobbsey twins?" the pimp said with a wide grin. "Aren't you two buddy-buddy?"

"Tony, she's just trying to help me. I'm sick."

"Sick in what way, baby? Maybe, I can help you . . . like I always do." His tone was solicitous but there was a glint of something else in his eyes as he turned his gaze to Hilary.

"This girl needs to get to a hospital," Hilary explained. She tried to usher the girl past him, but their way was blocked.

"Well, why don't you run along and I'll see to it. I always take care of my people, Miss Lady Doctor."

"Tony, I know your doctors. I'm going with her," Tina insisted, but she broke off on the last word and sagged against the wall as her cramps started in again.

Both Hilary and Tony reacted instantly, but Hilary was nearest the girl and got to her first. She put her arm around Tina to help her stand, then froze when she saw Tina look past her and gasp. As Hilary turned to face the pimp again, she saw that he had not moved to help the girl at all. He had bent down to pull the knife from his boot and now held the shiny blade in front of him.

"You ain't goin' nowhere with her," he said.

"You've got to let us pass," Hilary pleaded, staring at the knife. "She's too sick."

"I really don't think so." The pimp started toward them, forcing them back upstairs and waving the blade inches from Hilary's breasts.

"Tony, this is crazy!" the girl screamed out. "She's just trying to help me."

"Sure, baby. So am I." He slowly backed them up the stairs toward Tina's apartment.

Hilary had dropped her right arm from Tina, letting her walk on her own just ahead. As they backed up the stairs, Hilary was turned slightly so that her right side and her shoulder bag were away from the pimp. Moving carefully, scarcely daring to breathe, she inched her hand upward, keeping her shoulder hunched down so that Tony would not perceive the movement, until she could put her hand into her bag. Fumbling through its contents, her eyes still on the pimp, she almost breathed a sigh of relief when her hand at last closed around a small cylinder.

They were at the door to Tina's apartment now, and Hilary's fingers had removed the cap on the cylinder. Suddenly she spun to face the man, drawing the cylinder out of her bag to fire the spray directly into his face. He screamed, clutching his hands to his eyes as the chemical mace took effect, and in that instant Hilary grabbed Tina's hand to pull her past the man and race back for the stairs. He took a wild swipe at them with the knife, but he was blinded and in pain. They skirted the blade easily and ran down the stairs for the car.

Tina was slumped into the seat beside Hilary as they sped toward the hospital, the girl's eyes closed and her attention focused inward on her pain. Hilary was still panicked, her heart pounding, and she kept thinking she saw a car following them in the rearview mirror. But as her fear gradually subsided she thought back to the day she had told her father about her new job and he had insisted that she carry some kind of protection when she was out in the field on her cases.

She had been on the job exactly one week when a gift-wrapped package containing the cartridge gun had arrived, along with a well-meaning but overly cautionary note from her father. At the time she had thought it silly to believe that she would really be able to whip the gun out and use it in an emergency. Now she was glad for the sentiment that had made her carry it with her in spite of her feeling that it was impractical. . . .

Dr. Frank was in the admitting area, and he examined Tina once she had changed into a hospital gown. The area that she was complaining of was the right lower quadrant of her abdomen. It was exquisitely tender when he palpated it and the muscles above were rigid. Had she not had an appendectomy scar, he would have presumed that it was appendicitis. Now he was left with the female organs as the cause, and he called for a nurse to assist him with a pelvic.

Tina lay back with her heels in the stirrups and her knees far apart as Frank slowly slid a metal speculum between her labia and into the vaginal vault. Twice, she screamed out in pain, but he continued on. Once the speculum was opened, he saw yellow pus exuding from her cervix. After taking a small amount of the discharge for culture and smear, he removed the speculum and inserted two fingers to feel her tubes and ovaries. Her right side was definitely inflamed and he could barely touch her there without causing her to practically jump off the table.

Once he was done, Frank took one of the slides to a small lab near admitting, did a Gram stain and, after the slide was dry, viewed it under the microscope. Hilary stood by, and after a moment he announced, "What else would you expect a prostitute to have? It's gonorrhea."

"Gonococcus at one end and carrying meningococcus at the other—even if she hasn't come down with it. She's a walking petri dish, isn't she?" Hilary remarked. She returned to Tina's room and found her sitting on the edge of her bed and looking worried. "You've got P.I.D.—pelvic inflammatory disease," Hilary announced, but Tina didn't understand. "Gonorrhea— you know, the clap."

"Still?"

"What do you mean, still?"

"I just got shots for it last week, but then it was just a discharge. It never hurt like this."

"Maybe you've got one of the resistant strains. We'll have to give you a different antibiotic. Now, can you tell me those names?"

"I'd like to, but I can't. You saw that knife. I should

never have come with you. He's got an awful temper.''
As she spoke, she went to the window and peered
through the blinds. Parked a half block away was a
silver Cadillac. "He's out there," she said, pointing.

Now Hilary understood the real reason the girl had
looked so worried when she came into the room. "I'm
going to call the police," she said, exasperated and a little frightened herself.

"That won't do no good. There's others jus' like him.
If I don't get out of here, he'll kill us both for sure."

"Just stay here. I'll get rid of him."

Hilary quickly went to a phone in the hallway, but as
she was dialing the girl hurried out of the isolation room
and slipped out the nearest exit. When Hilary returned
to the room and found her gone, she immediately
chased after her. She got out to the street just in time to
see the Cadillac screeching around a corner, with Tina
inside.

When Hilary finally returned to the third floor, she
was angry and frustrated. She could no longer rely on
Tina for information and now her mind was going
through several scenarios on how the disease might have
spread. Assuming that Mathesson was the first
case—and there was some real doubt about that
now—he could have given it to Van Horn and the other
inspector, to his daughter and son, to Mr. Thackery and
to Tina Hudson on his secret night out. An alternate
theory, however, was that Mary Hudson was actually
the first case and that she gave it to her sister, who was
only a carrier and had ultimately spread it to Mr.
Mathesson, Mr. Thackery and possibly the dead
businessman from St. Louis. And yet, if Mr. Mathesson
or Mary were the first cases, where did they contract it?
For the moment, she didn't know. And with the enormous work load ahead, she wondered if she ever would.

Her thoughts were interrupted by her beeper, and
when she called in to her secretary she was told that she
had a message to call the Russian consul. Surprised, she

took down the number and dialed immediately.

The call was answered by a man who explained in an unaccented voice that he was Korlov's assistant and had been asked to relay a message to her. "Mr. Korlov wishes me to make up for his . . . abrupt manner when he spoke to you last. He was preoccupied, you understand, with preparations for his trip, but he wants you to know that he has seen Victor Szlenko in Russia and that he was in perfect health. He wants to assure you that he appreciated your concern and your diligence in carrying out your job."

Hilary thanked him, gratified by the call but in a hurry to get on with her investigation now that she knew the call brought her no closer to a solution. But the man was not to be cut short.

"Were there many others you had to contact?" he asked, his voice all polite concern.

"Yes, but it doesn't pose any serious threat. In any event, we have one of the top medical researchers working on it," she said, torn between the need to reassure the man and downplay the epidemic and her impatience to end the conversation. "Dr. Ogden has it well under control."

"Dr. Ogden . . . ?"

"Yes, Dr. Michael Ogden, at County Hospital." At last she was able to get the man off the phone, and after thank-yous on both sides she hung up and got back to work.

CHAPTER SEVENTEEN

The admitting area remained busy all day. As soon as one emergency arrived, received a spinal tap and was begun on antibiotics, another followed. Dr. Cunningham was barely in his bed upstairs when Mark Riley, Mary Mitchell's second lover, was transferred from another hospital with identical symptoms. On Riley's heels came the second paramedic from Mary Hudson's apartment, and forty-five minutes later one of Marcey's girl friends was admitted. It looked as if there was going to be a steady flow, and an order came down from Paige for all personnel to wear gowns, gloves and masks at all times.

Most of the afflicted patients already upstairs were also worsening. None of the antibiotics selected appeared to be working, not even used in combination or in varied routes of administration. Mathesson's blood pressure had sunk to shock levels and her kidneys were threatening to shut down. The first paramedic was now struggling to breathe and suddenly started vomiting clots of blood. Mary Mitchell's pulse had become dangerously irregular and Murray Clagston had slipped into a deep coma.

Down the hall, the waiting room kept filling with anxious friends and relatives, including Harriet and Lynda Mathesson, whose colds made them look even more weary and frightened. Everyone had his throat cultured and then was sent home on rifampin to be quarantined. Although there was some doubt that the antibiotic could actually prevent the disease, it was still being prescribed in hope that it might at least slow it down.

The number of admissions and the work involved in coping with the severity of the symptoms were taxing the CDU's staff and resources, and Ogden decided to take a closer look at the unit's situation. Every bed in the unit would soon be filled if they continued to receive patients at this rate, but that was only one part of it. Everything involved in patient care would be affected. They might need more nursing personnel, aides and lab technicians, and he also had to consider the supplies of antibiotics, intravenous fluids, respirators, heart monitors, oxygen tanks and tubing, urinary catheters and even food, although few of the meningitis cases were able to eat. . . .

He left Ling in charge of the lab and went to the wards first. Between the third and fourth floors there were only five open beds left. There was a chance that two patients might be discharged by evening, but even seven beds were inadequate. The only alternatives available appeared to be either refusing new cases once the unit was full or moving the less ill patients to wards in the main hospital. The latter choice was risky because the nursing personnel in the main hospital was inexperienced with this type of infection. Still, he doubted that the unit could refuse sick people. . . .

After checking each chart, he proceeded to the Department of Respiratory Therapy, where he spoke to the chief therapist. At present all four respirators were in use, but the one belonging to Gordon Mathesson was expected to be freed up soon. There were four backup units stored in the basement and Ogden suggested that the therapist have them serviced and ready to go. They weren't the newest machines, having been around since the polio epidemic in the fifties, but they were considered reliable. Of greater concern was the fact that the department did not have enough therapists to man eight respirators.

In contrast, the CDU's pharmacy appeared to be well stocked. As long as the ordering physicians stuck to the more common antibiotics like penicillin or chloramphenicol, their supply seemed endless. But now methicillin and gentamycin were being used, and these antibiotics were never kept in large volumes. Even the main hospital had only a short supply, and Ogden suggested that the pharmacy contact the respective drug companies and order additional stocks immediately.

Ogden's last stop was the office of Mrs. Duncan, the nursing supervisor. She had been on the phone all day trying to get extra help, but the hospital—in fact the entire county system—had been shorthanded for months and the best that she could procure was one additional nurse per shift. They both knew that was not enough. Some of the sicker patients were requiring a single nurse to themselves. The prospects looked grim, but she promised to bring in aides to do nursing work if necessary. Under the present circumstances, it was better than having no nurse at all.

His final consideration was how to plan physician coverage. He had already mentioned the possibility of doubling up, but only in jest. Now it appeared to be a necessity. He went to his office and drew up a new schedule wherein two teams, each consisting of a resident and intern, would be on duty at the same time, one team handling the admissions downstairs and the other the patients upstairs. In addition, he and Les Paige would alternate nights at the hospital. If further manpower was needed, he'd call in some of the attending men, the physicians in private practice who taught part time.

Hilary Walters was downtown at the school board. She wanted three schools closed—Marcey's, Jamey's and the Clagston boy's—and the superintendent readily agreed. "No need to take any chances," he kept repeating, even though there was no evidence that the disease was spreading there.

Afterward she returned to the unit, where she learned about the first definite rifampin failure. The patient was Inspector Van Horn. He had taken the antibiotic exactly as directed, and yet, despite the presumed protection, he began developing a headache and a fever. He immediately drove himself to the hospital and a subsequent spinal tap confirmed the diagnosis.

"What am I supposed to give these people if rifampin doesn't work?" she asked Ogden after tracking him down in his laboratory. Old Mr. O'Malley was just leaving, looking disappointed after being told that the experiment on his dog couldn't proceed for a few days.

"You might as well as give them aspirin or codeine for their headaches as far as I know."

"A lot that'll do. You're supposed to be the expert."

Ogden laughed sardonically. "Expert at real things, real diseases, not something like this. Have you tried minocycline? That's the other antibiotic we sometimes use for prophylaxis."

She reminded him that the drug was also in the resistant column.

"Then you'll have to wait for the vaccines with the rest of us or hope that we can find some quick miracle in the lab."

"How many doses did Bellows have?"

"Two hundred," he replied in a disillusioned tone. "And there's no guarantee that the shot will work. It should, the serotype's the same, but who knows with this damn thing."

"Well, whoever we give it to had better keep it a secret," Hilary suggested. "If word gets around that there's a cure and the supply is limited, you're liable to have a riot here. Nobody's going to want their family to go without."

"God, I never thought of that," Ogden mumbled, realizing that he was in a similar predicament with his son, but he also knew that he couldn't make an exception for Peter. "We can't immunize everyone who needs it or wants it, and my staff has to be first. I suppose if we do it quickly, in one big swoop, and use up the doses before anyone realizes it, there won't be any arguments."

"Your staff? Hospital employees are already protected by their masks and gloves. Clagston and Mitchell were flukes. I need every milliliter of those vaccines for contacts."

"We don't know that everyone's protected here. You can have what's left over, but we can't afford to lose vital staff to this disease. You can even skip yours if you want, but I wouldn't recommend it, Hilary. I'm not. Someone's got to be around to bury the dead when this ends."

Realizing that he was right, Hilary gave in and reviewed her findings with him—rather, her lack of findings. Ogden listened sympathetically, beginning to see what she was up against. The only light note of the conversation was when she told him of her escape from Tina Hudson's pimp, and they both laughed as she imitated Tony's shifty looks and menacing tone. But underneath the humorous vein she struck, Ogden sensed the fear she had felt.

As she was leaving, he walked her to the door of the lab and touched his hand to her back. "Do me a favor,

Hilary. Make sure you get a dose of minocycline when it comes in.''

She looked at him in surprise, then smiled. "You too, Mike."

At three o'clock, Les Paige was working in his office when an emergency call came in from a Pasadena doctor by the name of Thomas Larkin.

"We think we have a case of meningococcal meningitis here and I'd like to transfer her directly to your unit.'' The physician spoke quickly and sounded anxious.

"How sure are you of the diagnosis?''

"The Gram stain's textbook perfect, but I don't know much about the woman. She just dropped in with a headache. Said that she was exposed to some gas. Apparently a neighbor in another apartment tried to kill herself. A friend, I think. She's pretty upset. If she didn't have a fever, I wouldn't have tapped her, but the results are pretty conclusive. Can you take the case? We really don't have the facilities here to care for this.''

"Sure. Give her five million units of penicillin IV and a gram of chloramphenicol, take precautions and ship her stat.''

"*Both* antibiotics?''

"Absolutely. We've been seeing some tough cases. And don't waste any time.''

Suddenly it struck Paige that other hospitals in the city might be seeing additional cases and that each might be thinking that theirs was an isolated instance. If so, the numbers had to be determined and everyone should know about the severity of the problem. He called Michael Meno, Hilary's second investigator, to pass on the information he had and tell him how they were now treating the disease. Meno had already begun to call other hospitals in the area, at Hilary's suggestion. Armed with his new information from Paige, he called U.C.L.A. first and learned that a geology student had just been admitted in critical condition. After advising them to use a minimum of two antibiotics and preferably four, he called Cedars-Sinai. There an attendant from the coroner's office was under observation for possible meningitis. His spinal tap results were equivocal but suggestive, and they were planning to repeat the procedure in four hours. Meno warned them of the organism's virulence and continued his calls.

At St. John's Hospital, Marcy Mathesson's English teacher had been admitted with an overwhelming headache. At first it was presumed to be a migraine, but the associated fever led to a spinal tap and the results were positive. Another M.D. had admitted a sailor who was home on leave. His connection was clearly traced back to Tina Hudson.

Other hospitals involved thus far included Daniel Freeman, St. Joseph's, White Memorial, Hollywood-Presbyterian, Good Samaritan and the Kaiser Permanente on Sunset Boulevard.

The most worrisome cases came to Kaiser—two toddlers from a day care center run by Mrs. Van Horn—and suddenly there was a major concern for the health of the twenty other children. Of all institutions, day care centers were the most vulnerable when a disease of this type cropped up. Meningitis had been known to devastate nursery schools.

Meno continued his calls, but he had no way of knowing that in the metropolitan area itself there were more than a dozen additional cases that had not been diagnosed yet. These were people who felt ill, but either weren't sick enough yet to call their physicians, or had been diagnosed over the phone for the wrong disease. A few had rashes, all had fevers and headaches, and it was only a matter of hours before they and many of their family members would be hospitalized.

Now that the organism had been shown to be an unusual type of meningococcus, Tom Ling and Mike

Ogden decided to see if there were any characteristics shared by the victims. As it turned out, little could be learned. Their ages varied from three years old to over sixty, women seemed to be affected as frequently as men, they came from different socioeconomic levels, ate different foods, had different hobbies and none had had so much as a cold for months. In addition, the exposure to the disease, the length of incubation time, some of the symptoms and even the outcomes varied. Gordon Mathesson would have lost his feet had he survived, Marcey's hands were in similar jeopardy and Murray Clagston might have become permanently blind.

After these tabulations, they culled all of the admitting data, now searching for a chemical clue, but here too they could find no answer. Everyone's white count was elevated, which was to be expected, all of the urinalyses were typical for meningococcal disease and the chemistry profiles—salts, proteins, liver function, kidney function—were normal in the beginning. The only thing to be learned was that a lot of normal people had come down with a disastrous disease—which was exactly what they knew before looking.

CHAPTER EIGHTEEN

At four o'clock that afternoon, a reporter named Terry Roberts from KNBC dropped in on the Contagious Disease Unit. Having heard about the school closures, she had already been to the school board, where the superintendent had told her about the meningitis epidemic. He referred her on to County Hospital for details. It was the word *epidemic* that excited her—it could mean a national story, and she also appeared to be first.

After Roberts and her cameraman parked their van in the ambulance zone, they barged into the admitting area as if they were on some life-saving mission. When they reached the main receiving desk, she asked to speak to "the doctor who's treating all these cases of meningitis."

Mike Ogden was paged.

"You'll have to clear any stories through our public relations office," Ogden said when he arrived, pointing toward the main unit of the hospital. "Reporters aren't allowed in here otherwise."

"We've already cleared it," Roberts answered with a

saccharine smile. "They told us to come straight here. Now, what's this about an epidemic? How many people are affected?" As she spoke she pulled a small pad of paper from her purse and the cameraman started setting up his lighting.

"There's no epidemic," Ogden quickly replied. He felt like refusing the interview, but someone had to play the disease down.

"That's not what we've heard. You're—?"

"Dr. Michael Ogden. I'm the head of the department here."

Roberts jotted a few notes and the camera started.

"Dr. Ogden, despite reports of a serious epidemic from the school board and other medical authorities, I understand that you disagree."

"Turn that thing off." Ogden angrily raised his hands to cover the lens. "Miss Roberts, this is dangerous and inflammatory. There's no epidemic. But if you even mention the word, some people will inevitably panic."

"There is an epidemic though, isn't there?"

"We have more than the usual number of cases admitted, but that's all it amounts to. We're making every effort to be sure it doesn't spread. That's all."

"Yet you've closed three schools and told families to keep their children at home?"

"The Health Department did that, not me. That's their domain and they're just being careful. They're only precautions."

"Rather extensive precautions, don't you think?"

"We're dealing with a serious illness. It demands extensive precautions."

"Dr. Ogden, I don't think you're leveling with me," she said, pensively rolling a pencil along her lower lip. "How many cases do you actually have here?"

"Seven or eight. If you broadcast that there's an epidemic, people will think that there are hundreds here."

She thought for a moment. "All right, suppose we delete the word epidemic and just stick to the facts."

Since she seemed to have changed her mind, Ogden invited the two of them back to his office for a more leisurely interview. He thought that he had convinced her to play the story his way, but she had other plans.

At five o'clock, the team of investigators from Atlanta arrived. Hilary and her staff joined them and began setting up a command post in the basement. They had brought several cartons of clerical materials and the two hundred doses of vaccine, all carefully packaged in double cartons, refrigerated by dry ice and protected by Styrofoam.

When Ogden came down to greet them, Hilary pulled him aside. "This is it, Mike," she said, handing him a list of names. "There's a hundred and thirty-six people, counting all three shifts, admitting, X-ray, both laboratories and even the kitchen and maintenance. That leaves me with less than seventy immunizations for friends and families of patients. It's not going to do much."

"I'm not sure giving it is going to do much either. It takes a minimum of four days to be fully protected once the immunization has been given. With this disease, you could contract it, be hospitalized, die and be buried before the four days are up. Despite the shots, strict isolation will have to remain."

As the investigators set up an assembly line for vaccination, the hospital operator began paging personnel from the two floors. One by one, everyone who was working that day was immunized. Afterwards, people from other shifts were called from home, and within two hours everyone except Joanna Yates had received the shot. She had been paged repeatedly, but had never answered.

Worried that something was wrong, Ogden immediately went to the third and fourth floors to find her. He was hoping that she was merely tied up with a case, but no one there had seen her in quite a while. He tried calling her home, but her roommate said that she hadn't seen her since yesterday. He rechecked the cafeteria and, lastly, the library. When he was a resident he had often napped among the bookshelves, and he was relieved when he finally spotted her in a chair behind a stack of reference books, her tall form slumped over as she snored away in the dark corner.

The woman physician woke with a start as Ogden shook her shoulder, but as she tried to focus on him, he could tell that she didn't feel well. It was something more than fatigue, and when he felt her forehead he found it warm.

"Just tired," she explained. "Thirty-six hours without sleep tends to creep up on you." She unraveled herself from the chair and stretched. As she stood and the lights hit her face, Ogden could see that she was covered with the purpuric spots.

Dr. Joanna Yates was the twelfth admission to the unit and the thirty-second known case of meningococcal meningitis in the city. She knew that once the disease became manifest, the giving of a vaccine was worthless, and she had a vivid image of the fate that awaited her. Ogden promised to do everything he could, but they both knew that everything was already being done for the others and that so far most of them were terminal.

Once the resident was bedded down and her antibiotics started, Ogden spent time in her room trying to figure out how she might have gotten the disease. Transmission of any illness to hospital personnel was a rarity, especially if they followed standard precautions. She claimed that she had, that she had scrubbed her hands thoroughly after dealing with each of the patients. The only logical explanation left appeared to be that the organism was transmitted in the same way as the common cold, spread by tiny airborne droplets that everyone sprays when they talk. If this was true, it meant that nothing short of quarantining the entire city would halt the epidemic.

In the interim, bed space in the unit was getting tighter. Joanna's admission had taken the last single-bed room and very few of the double rooms were open. Ogden immediately got on the phone and after several calls to different administrators was able to shift patients in the main unit and procure fourteen additional beds on the urology ward. It was far from ideal, but it gave him more time.

Afterward, he returned to his laboratory. The pressures of the day and lack of sleep were getting to him. He felt torn between priorities and irritable. Every second of his time was accounted for, and he barely managed enough time to call home and check on Peter. There were dozens of phone calls and a myriad of problems. When he wasn't in admitting or on the floor, he was hassling some logistic problem. Staff and relatives alike were all complaining. No one was satisfied with his answers, and he couldn't blame them. He was a researcher, not Moses. The nursing staff was already hopelessly overloaded and no end was in sight; the respiratory therapists were running from patient to patient, barely able to keep their equipment clean and functioning; and the pharmacists were working nonstop to keep up with constantly changing intravenous orders. Everyone turned to him for answers he did not have.

Hilary's command post in the basement had become unbearably hectic. Six more telephones had been installed and close contacts were being urged to come in for their vaccinations. A fourth public school and two more day care centers had been closed, and there were plans to quarantine all of the Customs officials at L.A. International Airport and replace them with fresh inspectors from Hollywood and Burbank.

At 5:00 P.M. Hilary was paged to come to the front lobby. Waiting for her were two CIA agents who quietly showed their identification cards and then asked to be shown to a private room where they could talk. "We're here at the request of the State Department" was the only explanation offered by the man who identified himself as Taylor. She thought the other was Lindberg.

As the two men followed her, they studied every individual they passed, every piece of equipment, every open room.

"This is the best I can come up with," she explained as she directed them into a small room where hospital linens were stored. "Every available room is being used for patients."

"It'll do," Taylor curtly replied, closing the door behind them and glancing at the half-empty shelves for a moment.

"What's all the mystery? Am I under arrest or something?" She forced a smile, but neither man's expression changed.

"Are you aware that you're being watched? You and everyone else here?" Taylor said, sitting on the edge of a cabinet as Lindberg stationed himself at the door.

"Watched by who?" she said, almost laughing at the absurdity of it.

"The Russians. We've already spotted their people coming and going a couple of times."

"What on earth for?"

"We have some ideas, but we're not entirely sure. Dr. Bellows notified the State Department about the Russian courier on your list of contacts. We weren't too concerned, but we had to make a routine check anyway. What we found was that both Szlenko and the Russian consul, Korlov, had suddenly gone back to Mother Russia—too big a coincidence to be ignored, under the circumstances. Then we discovered that you're being followed—maybe only because your questions about Szlenko made them nervous. But we also have to consider that they know something about the epidemic, that they might even be responsible."

"That's crazy," Hilary said, shaking her head in disbelief. "I can't buy it."

"Maybe. But unlike us, they haven't given up bacteriological warfare, and we have reason to believe that they started the cholera epidemic in the Mideast in '74 and the adenovirus epidemic in England in '78. Both epidemics began at seaports—just like the airport here, with lots of contacts and no way to trace the source. We need to know about your conversation with the Russian consul."

"There's not that much to say. He said the courier was back in Russia, that he was in good health. He even had his assistant call me again later to say that he'd seen Szlenko in Russia. He was very polite, actually, and concerned about the epidemic."

Taylor started at this information, then said, "Did he want to know anything? Did you give him any information whatsoever?"

"No, of course not. And I think this whole thing is just a coincidence anyway. No one could have created this monstrosity. It's not humanly possible."

"Perhaps. We're not scientists, but we're certain they'd do it if they could."

"But what about the courier? Rather dumb to be spotted if he really was planting an epidemic, don't you think?"

"Our information indicates that was a mistake. Someone got the wrong luggage. We're checking now, but we doubt that his name was Szlenko. The courier we know by that name fits a different description."

"I just can't buy it," Hilary repeated.

"We're not selling. Just being careful—and you should be, too. We wanted you to know you're being watched, and we want to be told about anything suspicious. Whatever their motives are at this point, it's clear that they're extremely interested."

After the agents left, Hilary pondered their disclosure for several minutes, still discounting the possibility that the Russians were involved in the epidemic but unsettled by the news that she was being followed. The hospital was full of strangers, but she had naturally assumed they were all relatives or friends of the patients. The problem was that everyone was wearing masks and gowns and it was impossible to know who belonged and who didn't. It was only now that she remembered having given Ogden's name to the consul's assistant, and while she doubted that the Russians were responsible for originating the epidemic she was nonetheless startled by the degree of concern she felt for Ogden. She drew out the card Taylor had given her and called to leave this information for him and then went off to find Ogden and fill him in on the CIA's theory.

An hour later, she was no longer sure that the agents' suspicions were so farfetched. Michael Meno had learned that Leon Yong, the man who died within minutes of his arrival, had been visited by a famous biological chemist from Taiwan. The scientist had been working on recombinant DNA in bacteria in order to make marketable hormones, such as insulin, growth hormone and ACTH, on a mass scale. In the U.S., research on genetically altered organisms was strictly controlled because of the potential for creating a dangerous organism, but the restrictions were less stringent abroad. If this visitor was also the "Indonesian businessman" at the airport, he might have carried the meningococcal organism here. She immediately asked Dr. Meno to drop what he was doing and track the researcher down. It was now imperative that she learn if the disease had come from the Russians or the Orient or was merely a fluke of nature.

CHAPTER NINETEEN

As the second evening came, problems intensified in the Contagious Disease Unit. Every bed was occupied and new arrivals were piling up on the admitting floor faster than they could be transported off to the converted urology ward. While they waited, they were bedded down in the hallway, separated from each other by movable screens, and all staff throughout the CDU continued their strict isolation measures. At this point, no one knew if the vaccines would actually work and no one was taking any chances.

Two teams of residents and interns were racing about with occasional assistance from Dr. Paige and Dr. Ogden. Histories were brief—essentially limited to: "How long have you been ill? Where do you hurt? Are you allergic to any antibiotics?"—and physicals were equally cursory, confined to major body systems. What was most important was the spinal tap and the rapid institution of intravenous antibiotics. Doctors' voices echoed each other down the hall with the same questions and the same orders.

By eight that evening, all three members of the Van

Horn family, the second Customs official with the positive throat culture, both nurses who had helped carry Mary Mitchell to the unit and Mrs. Clagston were hospitalized. All but Mrs. Clagston were critically ill.

At nine, Tina Hudson arrived by ambulance. She appeared moribund, suffering from severe abdominal pains, a stiff neck, an overwhelming headache and huge bruises, some of which came from a beating and some from the meningococcus. The beating was from a pipe. Once her chart was made up, the admitting diagnoses read: "1.) Gonorrhea—resistant strain; 2.) Meningococcal meningitis—resistant strain; 3.) Blunt trauma to head and abdomen with probable concussion; 4.) Fractures to both wrists." Before she was transferred to the main unit, Hilary Walters tried to reinterview her in her hallway bed.

"Tina, can you hear me?" she said loudly through her mask, looking down at a girl she barely recognized—eyes swollen shut, lips battered and her nose slightly deviated to one side. "I've *got* to know the names of your contacts."

The response was a moan.

"Do you know who I am?" she asked, leaning forward.

The girl whispered a "yes" through a mouth that didn't seem to move.

"Then tell me the names."

This time there was no response.

"Then tell me this much. Do you know a Jim Thackery or a Gordon Mathesson?"

"No—" Tina started to raise one hand to feel her face, but whimpered when she moved the broken wrist.

"I know you know them. Just confirm it for me. No one will ever hurt you again," Hilary pleaded.

"I can't," came a muted answer. Tears oozed through the bloodied eyelids and trickled down her distorted face.

The transport team arrived and Tina was moved onto

a stretcher and transferred to the main unit. Hilary couldn't help thinking that the girl was a major key to the epidemic, but without her cooperation it was impossible to prove. Hilary shuddered at the thought of what the girl had been through at the hands of her pimp, but an even greater source of fear was what lay ahead for the city if the epidemic went unchecked.

Meanwhile, upstairs a second EEG was run on Gordon Mathesson. Again the tracing was flat. Without commenting to the nurse in the room, Dr. Frank disconnected the respirator and looked up at the monitor above his head. Mathesson's heart rate quickened to two hundred beats a minute, where it stayed for a few seconds, became erratic with bizarre beats and then stopped. It was all over in less than a minute and a half. Frank and the nurse simply went on to the next patient, not a word spoken or a look exchanged between them.

Down the hall, Marcey Mathesson's breathing had become so labored that she was connected to a respirator, and in the room across the way the Clagston boy suddenly died. The nurse caring for him said that the youth had appeared stable a few minutes before she took her break, but when she returned, his heart had stopped. She had sounded the alarm, but resuscitation measures were too late. His pupils were fully dilated and he was beyond recovery.

As one person died in the unit, another was admitted to his bed the minute the room was clean. The usual twenty-hour "airing out" procedure was foregone. There was too little time; every bed was needed. Some drugs were in critically short supply, and as the crowding mounted, nursing personnel were being asked to work double shifts.

The Contagious Disease Unit was not the only hospital feeling the pressure at this point. The number of admissions to U.C.L.A. Hospital had risen to nine, and Cedars-Sinai had another seven. Every hospital in the city had at least one case; most had several. And now cases were cropping up in other California cities.

Bakersfield was the first to report in, with a ten-year-old Los Angeles girl who had been visiting friends in Tarzana. Another case report came from San Diego on an elderly woman who had just been taken off a Greyhound bus. In Fresno, it was a student from Cal-Poly; in Modesto, a farmer who had just sold his vegetables in Los Angeles; in Sacramento, a state legislator who had flown home; and in Riverside, a gas station attendant who was dating a girl in Burbank. In San Francisco, the total number of cases had risen to twelve, including Jim Thackery's wife, who had frantically driven up to be near him—and now lay in a bed across the hall.

There was no doubt in the minds of public health officials that the disease would continue spreading both east and north. Air travel being as efficient as it was, any number of people had probably contracted the disease in Los Angeles and could be halfway across the country a few hours later before any symptoms became manifest.

It was 10:00 P.M. when Les Paige walked over to the research laboratory and found Ogden staring out a window at the darkness.

"Think you might find the answer out there?" Paige said, past caring whether he hurt Ogden's feelings or not. The number of admissions had increased so quickly that he was worried that the urology ward would be overflowing by morning.

"You never know. We can't seem to find an answer in this place either." Ogden slowly turned to face him. He looked tired. "Not a damn thing we've tried so far has worked. Or if it killed the bacteria, it would also kill the patient . . . I don't know. It's heat sensitive, but to take advantage of that we'd have to raise everyone's body temperature to lethal levels—if that was even possible. The same's true for cold. We've shown that extremely high doses of certain antibiotics, especially combinations of cephalosporins and aminoglycosides, might work, but they'd turn the recipient's bloodstream into a channel of chalk. Carbon tetrachloride works like a charm, but with its toxicity we might as well give everyone a capsule of cyanide. This is a tough son of a bitch, the toughest I've ever seen, and right now I'm not sure we can beat it."

"Why don't you take a break? Give your mind a rest. Sometimes answers come a lot easier when you've had a chance to rest."

"Break? Now how much time would you say I should take? If I take four hours, maybe only ten people will die. Or maybe I can afford eight hours in trade for twenty-five lives? How many people are expendable for a few hours' sleep?"

"If you don't take a break and get away from it all, you might not be able to help anybody. Then hundreds will die."

"Either way . . ." he trailed off.

Paige had never seen Ogden so near defeat. "There must be something you're overlooking. Every microorganism has a weak point. If it's a living organism, it can't be invincible."

"That's what I keep telling myself. For the moment, we're working on plasmid analysis to see where the damn thing *came* from. Maybe that information will give us a clue. If it doesn't, at least the history books will be able to record where this bastard began. That is, if anyone's still around to write history books."

"Mike, you need a break. Go home. By now CDC in Atlanta is working on the problem too, and they've got ten times the manpower and equipment you have here."

"Except we have a day's head start and all of the cases. Twenty-four hours may be critical."

"Not if you're working in anger."

"I'm not angry!" Ogden retorted and then realized

his tone. "I'm just perplexed by it all, and worried."

"When's the last time you saw your boy?"

"Give me a break. I've been on the phone to him, and anyway I want him to stay put in the house until this is over. When's the last time you saw your family?"

"About the same as you, I suppose."

"So we're in the same boat. I appreciate your concern, and if things were different I'd take your advice." Ogden broke off, embarrassed now as he took in Paige's appearance. His normally immaculate suit was rumpled, his hair tousled and his face was strained. "What brings you here anyway? Certainly not to tell me to take a break."

"Urology only has five beds left."

Ogden had expected the crowding to intensify, but not this rapidly. "I guess that's the reason I can't stop." He picked up the phone and called the head administrator at home to ask for some more beds.

"We're already at capacity and my phone's been ringing off the hook all night," came an exasperated response. "Every department is having some problem. In fact, practically every hospital in the city has called, asking me for advice or equipment or both. And when it's not someone medical, it's a goddamn reporter. The whole country's just dying to hear." He gave a bitter laugh.

"That doesn't change the situation here. I've got to have more beds," Ogden insisted.

"Can you make do until morning? Maybe we can make some shifts then."

"I don't know if I can make it another two hours. If we don't get more room soon, you may find some of the meningitis cases in the lobby."

There was a sigh and a moment of silence. "All right. I'll get dressed and come back down. I can't promise anything. Everything's tight already. At least it'll be more peaceful down there away from this phone."

Ogden hung up. "I doubt he'll find it peaceful," he said, and walked with Dr. Paige back toward the noisy ward.

In Atlanta, Dr. Sidney Bellows called an emergency meeting of the epidemic committee of the National Center for Disease Control. This was a select group of seven scientists and physicians who met weekly to discuss real and potential health problems across the country. Generally, the meetings were routine, dealing with small outbreaks of hepatitis or influenza, but on two occasions in the past year, the group had been suddenly convened. The first time was for an encephalitis epidemic that had spread northward from the Yucatan and was threatening to pass over the Texas border, and they met again because of a typhoid outbreak that had begun in Mexico City during the spring holidays when thousands of Americans were vacationing there. In both instances, contingency plans had been developed to cope with the diseases if they spread into the United States, but because of rapid action in quarantining and treating the victims the contingency plans had never had to be activated.

The problem confronting them this evening was real. Although it was after midnight, the members gathered in a conference room had arrived within a half hour of being called. In addition to Dr. Bellows, who was the chairman, the group consisted of Dr. Charles Finnegan, the chief of Public Health Investigation; Dr. M. J. Frisbee, director of Microbial Research at the Center; Dr. Frank Walker, Public Health liaison and H.E.W. representative; Dr. Ellen Leech, director of the Infectious Disease Laboratory; Dr. William Ellmore, a Public Health Department pharmacist; and Dr. Christopher Edwards, an epidemiologist with a Ph.D. in microbiology.

Most of them had already heard about the meningococcus outbreak, and now Dr. Bellows proceeded to brief them on the true extent of the epidemic. "It looks like we might have found our super germ," he concluded grimly. "Mike Ogden reports that the cultures taken from his patients are resistant to every antibiotic we have and to every combination they've tried."

"Do you trust his results?" Dr. Frisbee asked. She was new to the CDC and had never met Ogden.

"Implicitly. He was here with us before you came. I know his work and I'm sure his lab is as good as ours."

"I still find his data hard to believe," she insisted. "Resistances to antibiotics are acquired one at a time. It seems unlikely that a single organism would assume the worst characteristics of a dozen different organisms *at the same time.*"

"That's true," Dr. Finnegan put in, "but we're now getting similar culture reports from other hospitals also. The meningococcus at U.C.L.A. is multiply resistant, and so is the one they've grown at San Francisco General."

"How bad is it?" Dr. Walker asked. He was expected to report to the secretary of Health and Welfare first thing in the morning. "Or maybe I should ask how bad is it going to be?"

"It's hard to say," Bellows answered. "But there's no question that it's extremely serious and getting worse. We expect two hundred cases along the western seaboard by tomorrow morning, and at least double that by nightfall. We might even have as many as a thousand cases. Its spread is exponential, and it moves from person to person easily. As I see it, we have two major problems at hand. The first is where it came from, although I doubt that matters anymore and—"

"It *does* matter," Finnegan interrupted, going on to review the information Hilary Walters had passed on to him after her talk with the CIA and with Meno. "If this is a Russian plant, our government's going to want to know. Or if it's a botched recombinant DNA experiment in Taiwan, they'll need to know that also."

"I doubt that the Russians or anyone else could do this. It's not technically feasible." Bellows put in. "How would the user nation protect its own population and keep the whole thing secret? They would not only have to synthesize this organism but an equally potent vaccine. I just don't see how."

"You doubt, but you don't know for sure," Finnegan replied. "They've done similar things before. It's a perfect way to destroy a country without firing a shot."

"Perfect, perhaps, but impracticable. I just don't see how."

"We have very little information about how advanced they are in biological warfare, except that they haven't given it up," Walker inserted. "After what we've seen here, anything's possible in my book. And if they are responsible, we need to retaliate and demand the antidote."

"Retaliate with what? Nuclear war?" Bellows said. "That's all we need, a nuclear holocaust and this organism around to pick off the survivors. This damn thing has to be a spontaneous mutation, a quirk of nature, and it could have been predicted. If it's any consolation though, I've already notified the State Department to look into it. My feeling is that the Russans are worried that it's going to spread to *their* country if we can't stop it here. We need to deal with my second point on how to contain it. Right now it's jumping from city to city at will."

"We could ban all travel—air, rail, truck, car, whatever," Dr. Leech suggested.

"Do you think you could have the secretary recommend that to the President?" Bellows asked Walker.

"I'll ask."

"Travel's only one approach," Edwards spoke up. "I think we need to do a lot more than just that. To be certain we control the spread, every school should be closed, whether the city is affected yet or not . . . every person reachable by radio or television should be urged to stay home . . . every case and every contact should be isolated. We need to do this for the entire country and we should start immediately."

"An approach like that would bring the country to a halt," Walker argued. "At the moment we're only dealing with cases along the Pacific. For Washington to follow our advice, we need to come up with something that's less disastrous than the disease. I agree with closing most schools, but only in affected states, and quarantining cases, of course. That makes sense."

"I'm afraid that I agree with Dr. Edwards," Bellows resumed. "This epidemic is on the verge of affecting the entire country. I recommend that Washington close down everything, including their own doors, before it's too late."

Everyone else agreed, and while Walker jotted down some notes they went on to discuss how they were going to research the organism in their lab.

Meanwhile, the late news in Los Angeles and San Francisco was full of stories about the "epidemic." Mike Ogden's interview, in which he had played down the problem, barely occupied a ten-second portion of one film strip while other more vocal physicians were interviewed in depth. One speculated that this might become a pandemic—an epidemic that could disable an entire country.

In Los Angeles, Mike Ogden, Ling and their staff worked through the night, taking short breaks for sleep and sustaining themselves on coffee and donuts. A total of three hundred and twenty cultures were set up, incorporating every combination of antibiotics and every other drug known to have the slightest antibacterial effect.

In addition, they began their study of plasmids, tiny strands of the chromosome material that normally carry information from one bacterium to another. In this situation, they were looking for the messenger molecule that was responsible for resistance—the production of specific enzymes by a bacteria to protect itself from threatening chemicals in its environment.

Plasmids had been only recently discovered, and under electron microscopy they looked like circular strands attached to the larger DNA molecule. In Johannesburg, where many organisms had become insensitive to tetracycline, plasmids had been found to carry the key to resistance. In Japan it was penicillin; in Mexico, chloramphenicol. No one knew how or why these message units came about, but like all organisms in nature which need defense mechanisms, bacteria relied on a form of organic communication.

The group of researchers collected bacterial colonies from the throat cultures of all the contacts and of anyone else initially considered a potential source of the epidemic. They placed them in separate test tubes and then, using a series of enzymes and a microbiological detergent, broke down the cell walls. Once this was accomplished, the DNA (the cell's genetic material) leaked out, along with the plasmids. Afterwards, these two components were separated by high-power centrifugation.

The procedure was long and tedious, but almost as simple as following a cookbook recipe if one understood the steps involved. Once the centrifugation was complete, they added a dye that fluoresced under ultraviolet light. In each test tube, two major areas were then able to be visualized—the top layer being the organism's normal DNA or chromosomes, and the layer halfway down being the plasmids

In the test tube, all plasmids looked alike, but once they were placed on a tiny agar strip and subjected to a small amount of electricity, they began to migrate to spots along the strip that were identifiable: penicillin-resistant plasmids, chloramphenicol-resistant plasmids, tetracycline-resistant plasmids, and so on.

Just as police work would compare fingerprints until they found a match, these plasmid patterns were compared with Gordon Mathesson's strip, one by one. After several hours, it became apparent that his multiresistant organism had been exposed to several other types of bacteria and had incorporated their separate patterns of resistance, none of which would be worrisome if taken alone but which had combined to create a devastating disease. As a Customs official who was exposed to ill people on a daily basis, he had been in an extremely vulnerable position for something like this to happen.

Matheson proved to be the first case, just as they had initially thought, but Ogden theorized that his meningococcus might have remained sensitive to penicillin if he had not come in contact with Tina Hudson—whose gonorrhea organism was resistant to penicillin and sulfa and readily passed on that resistance to other organisms. Resistance to tetracycline and four other antibiotics came from Mrs. Fitzhugh, who had been treated with several antibiotics in Greece and therefore brought back a highly resistant pneumococcus. Miss Trumbell, the teacher, had a small boil on her nose that harbored a methicillin-resistant staphylococcus, and she had fiddled with the sore, getting the bacteria on her hands and passing it on. The rifampin resistance came from Gerald Katzenbach, the African missionary, who had been treated for tuberculosis, and the remaining plasmids were found in Mr. Yong's culture. It was presumed that he was probably carrying a multi-resistant streptococcus.

The evidence was immediately shared with Dr. Bellows and Hilary Walters. It put the detective work to rest, but it didn't help find a cure.

CHAPTER TWENTY

By the morning of the third day, every radio and television station in Los Angeles and San Francisco was broadcasting news of the epidemic. It sounded as if war had been declared. A three-inch-high headline in the L.A. *Times* read: "MENINGITIS EPIDEMIC HITS CITY: SCORES DYING" and their entire front page was dedicated to news about the disease. People were being warned to stay at home, to keep their children indoors, to stay away from anyone who seemed the slightest bit ill no matter how minor they thought the problem was. All sources gave out a list of signs and symptoms to watch for, and most included directions on how to get help if it became necessary. Most of the information was accurate, but in the frenzy of getting the story out, considerable misinformation was also mixed in. The rash was described as reddish by some, hivelike by others. The headache described more often resembled a tension headache than it did the characteristics of one from meningitis.

The count on cases was difficult, not only because it was constantly changing but also because some hospitals were not calling the NCDC. Nonetheless, at 8:00 A.M. the reported cases numbered over one thousand, with half of them in Los Angeles and the others scattered up to the Canadian border and across to the Mississippi River. San Diego had eighty-five cases with thirteen deaths; San Francisco had one hundred and seventy with nineteen deaths; Sacramento, fifty-two with eleven deaths; Portland, forty-six with seven deaths; Seattle, thirty-nine with eight deaths; Spokane, twenty cases and five deaths; Salt Lake City, fifteen cases and one death; Albuquerque, ten cases and no deaths; Las Vegas, nineteen cases and one death; Reno, eight cases and no deaths; Denver, five cases and no deaths; and lastly, St. Louis reported their first case at 7:30 A.M. The rapidity of the spread had far exceeded Dr. Bellows's expectations.

In Los Angeles, most of the city's activities had come to an abrupt halt. People had panicked overnight. All public schools were closed and teachers at private schools were sending their pupils home the moment they arrived. The doors to City Hall and other government buildings were locked, and the rush hour traffic that had come into the downtown area was hurriedly heading back out as commuters heard the reports on their car radios. Shopping areas such as Westwood and Rodeo Drive were as deserted as on an early Sunday morning, with shops closing as quickly as they opened and very few people on the sidewalks.

By nine, L.A. International Airport had cancelled all incoming and outgoing flights. Planes already en route were refueled—their cabins kept pressurized and their passengers held on board—and then ordered back to their city of origin. By ten, the highway patrol had barricaded all major highways. Blockaded freeway entrances were flooded with anxious tourists wanting to get back home, but no one was allowed to leave the metropolitan area.

Against the otherwise desolate background of sparse

traffic and distant ambulance sirens, a few places were busy. In the few grocery stores still open, housewives flocked in and grabbed practically everything in sight. Bread and milk were the highest priority items, but all types of canned and bottled goods were quick to follow. When shelves were empty, fights began to break out.

In the poorer neighborhoods, gangs were beginning to roam—oblivious to the biological hazard—and looters were taking advantage of the unguarded and empty stores. Dozens of people would suddenly descend on a shop, break in the windows and clean out the stock long before police, who were already stretched thin, could arrive. There was little they could do but race from emergency to emergency.

In middle-class neighborhoods, the few people out walking were wearing masks or scarves over their mouths and noses, keeping several feet apart when they passed each other or stopped to talk. No one shook hands or touched one another. Some pedestrians, unsure how the disease spread and not taking any chances, were even wearing gloves. Few people understood what they were avoiding, but everyone knew that it was deadly. . . .

In Washington, meanwhile, Dr. Walker's late-night-call to the secretary of H.E.W. had led to an early morning meeting with the President. When they had set up the meeting, the number of cases was only two hundred, but now that it was a thousand, the President was worried about the health of the entire country. He immediately issued directives to close federal buildings west of the Mississippi, to shut down *all* schools across the country and to confine stateside military personnel to their bases. He sensed that more was needed, but deferred making any further decisions until he could meet with his cabinet and with Dr. Bellows, who was immediately summoned.

•   •   •

L.A. County Hospital was bulging at its seams. Every available bed was being utilized. Meningitis cases had taken over three different wards, and the uninfected patients who had been moved were occupying hallways on other noninfectious floors. Personnel was stretched thin, dwindling medications of all kinds were being dispensed sparingly, and meals came hours late, if at all. All elective surgery was cancelled, and every patient who could conceivably be sent home was discharged.

The Contagious Disease Unit looked like—was—a disaster area. The floors were wall-to-wall with patients, many screaming or crying out, others delirious and babbling. The conference rooms and auditorium housed patients. Pain medications were extremely low and all antibiotics—for what they were worth—were down to emergency reserves. Every respirator available was now in use, and one patient had died because of the shortage. Every heart monitor was hooked up; even equipment to do spinal taps was critically low.

Morale of the house staff was poor. Everyone was exhausted, and no end was in sight. All six residents and interns were on duty now, except Yates, and all were extremely busy. Tempers were short and it seemed to Paige that there was always an argument going on in the corridors. He did everything he could to keep everyone calm and organized, but he too felt the strain.

In a crowded corner room of the CDU, however, there was one unexpected occurrence. The Mathesson boy started improving. At first, his clinical change was overlooked—it was a relief to have someone not needing immediate attention—but the improvement was so striking that Paige summoned Ogden to the room. The boy's fever was gone and along with it, the spots, the stiff neck and the headache. In their place was a wide-eyed youth with sniffles who wanted to go home.

Ogden was not sure what he was seeing. He immediately proceeded with a spinal tap and personally carried the tubes down to the laboratory. It looked like the boy was out of immediate danger, and the results confirmed this and more.

Patient: Mathesson, Jamey, age 7
PF Number: 345-87-053
Spinal Fluid Analysis
Drawn: 1450

	Result	*Normal Value*
Description	clear	clear
Amount received	6.0cc	variable
Cell count		
Total white count	0	less than ten
Percent neutrophils	0%	0%
Percent mononuclears	0%	100% (if any cells present)
Total red cells	0	0
Protein	40	15–45 mgm/100ml
Sugar	60	45-80 mgm/100ml

Gram stain: No bacteria seen

Ogden was encouraged and puzzled at the same time. He checked on the boy's previous cultures and confirmed that they had indeed initially grown out meningococcus. He definitely had had the same disease and yet, somehow, he had had a spontaneous cure. He had received the same antibiotics as many others who were not cured, and all of his other admitting laboratory data was unremarkable.

Ogden checked and rechecked the boy's chart, reviewing the fever graphs, nurse's notes, medications, what he had eaten . . . everything he could think of. There had to be a clue in there, but he couldn't find it. He then re-examined the child's body from one end to the other, keeping Paige beside him in case he missed something. When he was done, all he could say was that it looked like Jamey had a simple cold, and under normal circumstances he would be sent home. Not this day, however. Not until more was learned. Suddenly James Mathesson had become a V.I.P.

Their next step was to repeat all of his blood tests. His liver tests were unremarkable, his kidney function was normal, there were no signs of diabetes, no derangement of his proteins, no abnormalities in his salts or gases, no abnormalities in his red or white blood cells. On paper, he seemed perfectly normal . . .

"The answer's in that kid's body somewhere!" Ogden told Ling as he paced his laboratory floor. "And we can't quit until we find it."

Ling agreed, but for the moment he was at a loss to suggest how they should begin.

Two hours after Walker's meeting with the President, Dr. Bellows was seated at a conference table in the White House with the chief executive and his cabinet. He'd been whisked away from his office by a military sedan, placed in the rear seat of an Air Force jet, flown to Washington and raced to the White House in a special limousine. During the rush he barely had time to collect his thoughts, but he knew what he wanted to recommend.

"Nothing short of a nationwide quarantine will stop this," he said, addressing the group. President Lansfield, a man with curly gray hair and bifocals, was seated directly across from him. "We've never seen anything like this before. We can't control it and none of our drugs are working. At the moment it appears to be one hundred percent lethal and it's spreading at an incredible rate."

Everyone was silent for a moment and then the president asked, "How long do you think it'll take to find a cure?"

"I wouldn't count on us finding one, sir. All of the manpower at the CDC and N.I.H. are working on it, as well as a dozen medical schools—and of course U.S.C., where it was first picked up. The only thing we have is a vaccine which probably will protect against it, but supplies are extremely short and even mass production couldn't get it out for weeks. By then half of the country could succumb.''

''You don't really think this epidemic could kill a hundred million people, do you?'' the secretary of defense asked, turning the pages of Bellows's situation report. It was stamped TOP SECRET.

''I think it could kill everyone who comes in contact with it—and without a strictly enforced quarantine, a hundred million lives might be a low estimate.''

''Surely modern medicine can do better than just tell people to hide in their homes,'' the secretary said. ''This sounds like something out of the fourteenth century.''

''I'm afraid that's all we can do. We need time. We've never seen anything like it. Even in the fourteenth century. I've been expecting a multiply resistant strain, but I never thought it would be this bad or this soon. If it goes unchecked, this epidemic might just become the dawn of a biological ice age.''

The group was obviously stunned. Turning to the secretary of the interior, President Lansfield asked, ''Can we manage a quarantine?''

''It doesn't sound like we have a choice. The economic consequences could be disastrous. I'm sure that industry could handle a day or two, maybe even a week of a special holiday, but not a month or more. The stock market would crash in about twenty minutes. Food would rot in the fields, people in the cities would starve and everyone would go broke from the lack of income. Maybe we should've had a contingency plan for something like this, but it's never come up. I don't think we can do it. There's got to be another answer.''

''I assure you there isn't any,'' Bellows inserted, but was stopped short by the secretary of state.

''I can't go for a quarantine either. If our economy

collapses, so does our military. You can't confine
soldiers to their barracks for a month, and without food
or supplies the situation becomes ludicrous. I think
you'd have anarchy everywhere. People won't put up
with a prolonged quarantine and I'm sure a few of our
enemies might be interested in capitalizing on our crippled state. A few weeks down the road would be a perfect time to attack. We have to come up with something
less damaging to the country."

"You can't afford not to," Bellows argued. "If you
don't quarantine the country, a military attack wouldn't
be necessary—and I doubt these real or imagined
enemies will escape the epidemic. It doesn't respect
ideologies any more than human lives. As cruel as it
may sound, we have to let the afflicted die off, isolate
everyone else, and put everything we can into producing
the vaccine."

"Putting every penny into getting the vaccine goes
without question," the president responded. "But shutting down the country seems too risky. I'll have to give
it some thought." He thanked Bellows for coming,
promised to get back to him, and added that he'd
probably go on the air to tell the nation about the
problem once he had a definite plan.

At noon, Mike Ogden was walking back into the
hospital for lunch. His gait was slow, having slept only
five hours in two days, and he was worried that he could
not keep up the pace. All three hundred and twenty
culture tests had failed to point to a cure, and he was
still pondering Jamey Mathesson's recovery. As he entered the building, he ran into Hilary Walters, who had
been helping out on the floors between her investigative
work. Like the rest of them, she had long since ceased to
pay heed to her appearance. Her chestnut hair was in
disarray and her dark eyes looked tired. As she walked
toward him, he saw that her usually purposeful manner
was gone.

"I hope you don't feel as bad as you look," he said, taking her hand. "You look terribly depressed."

"Marcey Mathesson just died." Tears filled her eyes. "It all seems so hopeless . . ."

"I know how you feel. It's everywhere, but we do have one chance if I can just figure it out. My mind isn't as clear as it might be. You know that the boy recovered?"

Hilary nodded and wiped her eyes with a tissue.

"That little s.o.b. has just got a cold."

Hilary shook her head, giving Ogden a sad smile. "I'm sure that it's good news to his family. They were hit pretty hard. At least his mother and Lynda haven't come down with it. Not yet, anyway. The worst they've had to contend with so far is a heavy cold. But the way things are going, it seems like only a matter of time before we have everyone in Los Angeles in here."

Ogden had seemingly tuned out, giving in to his fatigue, but he suddenly interrupted her, his expression intent. "Not both of them?"

"Not both what?" Hilary asked, startled.

"Jamey's mother and sister—they both have colds?"

"Why, yes—"

Ogden grasped her arm and hurried her down the corridor, ignoring her questions as he concentrated on some inner puzzle. His gait slowed only when their path was obstructed by two orderlies who were shifting the hospital beds in the corridor—one of the beds occupied by a still, white-sheeted form and the others by patients in the early but most painful stages of the disease. The sight of these patients seemed to jar Ogden back to his surroundings—although neither he nor Hilary noticed that a heavyset man in a brown suit had come to a halt just behind them and then nervously moved back a few steps, pointedly looking away from them.

As Ogden resumed his half-sprint down the hall, with Hilary in tow, he squeezed her hand and said, "I may be crazy, Hilary, but if I'm not you may just have given me the key. I've seen this with staphylococci . . . their natural enemy is a particular virus. Every time you put the two of them together, the bacteria's cell wall is punched full of holes and the damn things dies. That might be what's happening here . . . meningococcus being knocked off by that respiratory virus. I'll bet on it!''

As soon as they reached the laboratory, Ogden telephoned over for a nurse to collect a specimen of saliva from Jamey Mathesson's mouth and run it over to them. At the same time, he had Hilary call the two other Mathessons at home and ask them to come by the lab to drop off comparable specimens.

Cultures with the meningococcus and the cold virus were immediately set up and monitored hourly, but it would be a minimum of twelve hours—and probably as many deaths—before Ogden knew whether there was any basis to hope he had something new.

CHAPTER TWENTY-ONE

At 3:00 P.M. President Lansfield went on the air. After explaining what the epidemic was, he urged people to remain calm and tried to play down its severity. In an effort to contain the spread, he ordered all federal, state and local government buildings locked, all schools closed, all major highways barricaded except for delivery of food and necessities, and all airports shut down, and he recommended that all businesses take a prolonged holiday. People living in the country were urged to stay out of the cities and anyone living in the cities was asked to stay indoors. He suggested that anyone who must speak to strangers keep at least two feet away and to wear protective scarves when outdoors. For the moment, he said, most of his suggestions were voluntary, but if the disease continued to spread, he'd resort to twenty-four-hour curfews that would be enforced by National Guard units.

Over the next several hours, the disease continued its rampage, however. Cases were cropping up along the eastern seaboard as far north as Maine and down to the Florida Keys. Two separate SAC bases had stricken personnel, as did four Army training bases. For them the quarantine was too late. At 6:00 P.M., the U.S. senator from Arizona came down with the disease. He was in the Senate chambers when he became ill.

In the interim, foreign countries began taking note of the crisis. Most embassies were told to close their doors and both Canada and Mexico closed their borders, but it was too late for several countries. A G.I. returning from Seattle to Berlin had stopped off to visit several German friends before reporting to his base. After spending the night with fifty other recruits in his barracks, he came down with meningitis. In France, there was a similar occurrence with a college student returning to the Sorbonne. Not only had she exposed dozens of foreign travelers on her PanAm flight, but she had been out partying the night before she got sick. In Rio de Janeiro, an American pilot had carried the disease from Los Angeles. And in Capetown, an American tourist had brought it from San Francisco. Authorities in each of these countries were desperately trying to isolate all contacts, but the task before them seemed impossible.

By 9:00 P.M. that evening, Dr. Bellows had a new list of cases and he was on the phone urging the president to take more drastic measures.

	No. of New Cases	Deaths
Albany	12	2
Albuquerque	36	10
Atlanta	19	5
Baltimore	25	7
Boston	14	2
Chicago	48	12
Cleveland	9	1
Dallas	32	8
Detroit	41	13
Houston	22	7
Indianapolis	11	1

Jacksonville	5	0
Las Vegas	64	17
Lexington	12	2
Little Rock	14	3
Los Angeles	882	98
Miami, Fla.	9	1
New Orleans	17	4
Philadelphia	22	3
Phoenix	40	9
Pittsburgh	10	1
Portland, Me.	4	0
Portland, Ore.	79	19
Providence, R.I.	3	1
Reno	30	10
Sacramento	45	11
Salt Lake City	48	17
San Diego	46	16
San Francisco	307	56
Savannah	6	1
Seattle	86	21
Spokane	39	7
St. Louis	29	8
Tallahassee	6	1
Washington, D.C.	3	0
Other cities	198	31

Both Ogden and Ling kept a close watch on the new cultures. Every hour, colony counts were made and samples from each plate were scanned by the electronic microscope. Nothing was overlooked or considered inconsequential, and any hint of change was checked and rechecked.

Dr. Bellows was kept apprised by phone and teletype of their progress, but although he was aware of the staphylococcal-virus interaction he doubted that it would work with meningococcus. "Even if you're right," he told Ogden, "it may take weeks to prove it. You need controls, Mike. We don't know what culture medium would be proper to test it on, or what nutrients to add—and then, if it works in the lab, there's no guarantee it'll work on people."

Ogden disagreed. Bacterial resistance had been his area of expertise before switching to cancer research and he'd been living with and watching this particular organism for two solid days. "If it works in my lab, it'll work on people. I know what this thing likes and dislikes and it really doesn't make a damn bit of difference what you grow it on. Anything short of poison, it'll live, but to simulate a human body we're using human blood in the media. That boy's recovery wasn't a fluke. The only explanation has to be that virus. Everything else has been checked."

"Everything we know how to check, you mean." Bellows corrected.

"Everything we *need* to check. Just clear the red tape away, please, so that we can more quickly once the proof is there."

"There are a dozen agencies to go through—"

"We only need to clear the FDA. The rest can be bypassed. Come on, there won't be enough time to do repeated studies. If we're forced to meet their criteria, it'll take months and the country may be half dead by then."

"But you haven't *got* a cure yet, only a good guess. If you prove it, I'll personally cut that red tape, but for the moment I can't go off half-cocked because someone— even you, Mike—thinks that he's hit on a miracle cure. Get me some hard data, something solid and easily reproduced, and then we'll talk. Good night."

Ogden resented Bellows's attitude but at the same time understood it. By now, dozens of labs across the country and many reputable scientists were working overtime to find a cure and speed up production of the vaccine. The best that Bellows could be expected to do was to keep in touch with each of them and be ready to move if anyone actually succeeded. Until then, his main plan was apparently to persuade the president to order a strict national quarantine.

Just like the fourteenth century, Ogden thought as he
hung up. Head for the hills. . . .

During the first few hours of Ogden's experiment, the
bacteria flourished much as they had on previous days
when challenged. The areas where the cold virus particles had been added were overrun with rapidly
reproducing meningococci, acting as if the virus were
not even present.

"It's too early to jump to any conclusions either
way," Ling said tentatively as he filed the third set of
electron microscope photographs away.

"It's always too early or too late . . . the eternal excuse for failure," Ogden responded, disappointed and
worried. "Sorry, I hope you're right." He tossed his lab
coat across a chair and trudged out to check the
hospital. He did not want to believe that his theory was
wrong, but the evidence was mounting against him.

During the night a combined investigative team from
the L.A. Health Department and the U.S. Department
of Health had expanded their numbers and moved into
the auditorium. The patients housed there were shifted
to the conference room while fifteen telephones were installed and investigators continued tracking down contacts. The large room was thick with smoke as an increasing list of friends and relatives were urged to seek
medical attention or isolate themselves.

Hearing the clamor, Ogden stopped momentarily and
glanced inside. Hilary was seated near the entrance and
talking on a phone, but she smiled his way and waved
for him to wait. She watched him as she finished her
phone conversation, taking in the dark, gray-streaked
hair, the intent blue eyes and the quiet air about him.
She was genuinely pleased to see him, she realized. Once
she hung up, she quickly came to the door.

"Sold any coupons yet?" he said as he stepped back
into the hallway with her. "That's how I used to make a

few bucks when I was in high school."

"Right now, I wish that was why we were calling. People either don't believe us or they're panicked. Half of them don't even know a doctor's name to call in an emergency. I've been giving out a list, but I'm not sure why. No one can do anything for them. Not yet anyway." Her hand gently slipped into his and found it receptive. "Any luck on your end? That virus theory pan out?"

"As Tom Ling just told me, it's too early," he answered, looking at her. He was fatigued and lonely, he thought, but she really did look pretty and for an instant he let himself forget that she was another doctor. He felt as though he could confide in her as a woman and a friend, in spite of how little he really knew about her. He wanted to touch her face and caress her cheek with his hand, to say that things would somehow be all right, but the jangle of telephones in the auditorium behind her brought him harshly back to reality. "Tom's still at it in the lab, so it's about time that I check on how we're doing at this end."

"You don't really want to, Mike. Stick to the lab. It's not a pleasant sight. Find the cure first, then come back."

"On a white horse?" Ogden looked away. "There are only so many test tubes a man can look at in two days."

"What happens if you don't find a cure? What if that virus isn't the reason Jamey survived?" It was the question that had been haunting him since he had spoken to Bellows.

Ogden squeezed her hand affectionately, and sighed as he let go. "We can hope that someone else finds the cure. Otherwise, the only thing to be optimistic about is that the vaccinations of the unit's personnel will leave us the only survivors in the city . . . maybe the country."

"Sounds awful . . ."

"It is," Ogden answered as he started up the stairs.

"Catch you for coffee on my next break?"

Hilary smiled. "I'll look forward to it." They both knew there would be no more breaks.

She stood and watched him disappear up the stairs, but they both started and turned when they heard a scuffle behind them in the corridor. The two CIA men, Taylor and Lindberg, were struggling with a heavyset man in a brown suit who had been standing outside the auditorium and listening to Hilary's conversation with Ogden. Ogden came back down the stairs, drawing her away from the fight and standing protectively by her side as they watched Taylor and Lindberg subdue the man.

"I have diplomatic immunity," the man protested, trying to pull free. "My card's in my wallet. A Russian embassy card." Hilary recognized the voice; it was Korlov's so-called assistant, the man who had called with Korlov's apology.

"A little far from home, aren't you?" Taylor asked.

"I don't have to account for my actions," he said.

"And we don't have to look into your wallet either. Why don't we go downtown and talk about it?"

As Lindberg led the man away, Taylor approached Hilary and Ogden to explain. "He's the one we identified earlier, the one who was following you. There's probably others—or there will be soon."

"You know that we've proven where the epidemic came from? Not Russia," Hilary said, referring to Ogden's work and perplexed as to the Russian's motive in following her.

"Yes, that information reached us. But it appears the courier took back more than papers, and we think they've got an epidemic of their own and no way to combat it. That's why the Russians called you again, seemingly so concerned about your epidemic. And we later discovered that that little tidbit you dropped about Ogden started them tailing him too. Or him especially.

The Russians are going to be extremely interested in what you come up with here," he said, turning to Ogden. "In fact, we have information that they've got agents at several labs across the country, probably trying to get a line on the cure."

CHAPTER TWENTY-TWO

When Ogden arrived on the third floor and got into his protective garments, he couldn't believe how much worse things had gotten. The hallway resembled pictures he'd once seen of refugee camps. The entire length of the corridor was lined with beds and even the waiting room had two beds crammed inside. Every inch had been utilized. As he made his way toward the nursing station, he studied each patient. It was all the same, each critically ill, each confused and covered with the purple spots. Hilary's remark about it not being a pleasant sight was an understatement. To him, it was disaster.

The countertop at the station was cluttered with intravenous bottles and medication vials, and sitting amidst them Paige was working on a stack of charts. He looked up. "Welcome to the newest addition to the County Morgue." His eyes were reddened from lack of sleep. "We just ran out of penicillin and chloramphenicol. We'll be out of the remaining antibiotics by morning. It probably doesn't matter, though. We've also run out of intravenous tubing to administer it."

Ogden did not answer right away. He looked back up the corridor and then down toward the opposite end. Shaking his head in disbelief, he asked, "What are you doing about new cases?"

"When the beds are full, sending them home to die." Paige closed the chart and stood. Under normal circumstances a comment such as that would have stunned Ogden, but this day, it didn't. "There's nothing we can do even if we have room. One body goes out in a bag, and another comes in on a stretcher. In fact, I think we're keeping out people with other illnesses that we should be doing something about and throwing medications away on patients we can't help. Personally, I think we should clear out the place, send everyone home and just get some sleep. No one here can keep up this pace, especially if it's hopeless."

"We can't give up, you know that," Ogden chided. To his right side, he spotted a wide-brimmed, red hat. "Yours?" he asked.

"Hardly." Paige half smiled. "It belonged to our last admission. He died by the time he got up here. No next of kin."

Ogden couldn't help wondering if the hat had belonged to the pimp Hilary had described to him, or repressing the thought that, if so, the man had died as he'd deserved to. But there were also the victims like Gordon and Marcey Mathesson, Mary Mitchell, Murray Clagston and his son, and the boy who had reminded him of Peter . . . After staring at the hat for a moment, Ogden asked, "How many have died?"

"Honestly, I've lost count. Maybe twenty here, maybe more. Half were children. You can count the bags from the morgue. They sent us fifty and the pile's half down."

"I guess the exact numbers don't matter right now, but try to keep records as best you can." Ogden started to leave, but was stopped by the head nurse.

She was crying and tearfully reported that Joanna Yates had just died.

The epidemic continued spreading. By evening every city in the country had at least one case, and most of the larger cities had hundreds of victims. Analysis of the data indicated that the average length of survival was ten hours if untreated and only twenty-four if antibiotics were administered. Although a few cases managed to survive a full forty-eight hours, these patients were maintained on respirators and considered mental vegetables.

Overseas, the problem was also increasing. Germany now had twenty-two confirmed cases and France had diagnosed seventeen. In Madrid, an American tourist succumbed, but before the disease was recognized she had exposed dozens of people in her hotel and at the hospital. In addition, London had five cases, Rome three, Vienna four, Tel Aviv two and Cairo two. Governments from each of these countries were calling American officials for advice, but the only recommendation forthcoming was to quarantine everyone suspected.

In Washington, D.C., every embassy locked its doors and within hours virtually all international airports around the globe were shut down. Most of the Western countries closed their borders, and a few such as Greece and Portugal considered arming their border guards. All foreign travelers were avoided, but none so assiduously as Americans. Until proven otherwise, they were considered to be carrying the disease.

Ogden returned to the laboratory after picking up a cold roast beef sandwich and forcing himself to eat. An hour had passed since he had left and it was time to recheck the cultures.

When he arrived, Tom Ling had all of the plates out

and had lined them up along the bench top. "You know, it may be my imagination, but I think there's something going on." He tried to contain his excitement as Ogden glanced over his shoulder. "I'm not sure yet, but there's a hint of some slowed growth in some of these plates . . . the areas over the viral particles are thinner. They're still multiplying like crazy, but not nearly as fast as usual. Take a look."

Superficially, it looked as if Ling was correct, but Ogden took a few plates to a different microscope and began making his own counts. What was only suggestive to the naked eye, however, was definite close up. The number of bacteria in each of the treated colonies was lower than in the controls, and after making a few calculations he determined that the doubling time had been prolonged from twenty to thirty minutes. Something was affecting their growth and the virus had to be the reason. Ogden glanced at Ling, smiling as he saw his own hope mirrored in the man's face, and then turned his attention back to the plates.

"I think you're right," Ogden announced, clapping his hand on Ling's back after rechecking his figures. He wasted no time in putting through a call to Bellows, who was just leaving for another meeting with the full cabinet.

The moment that Bellows answered, Ogden said, "It looks like the virus might be doing it," and then quickly went on to describe their findings.

"It's not enough. Promising, I grant, but not enough. And suppose your theory's right—what am I supposed to do with it?"

"Spray the whole damn country with the virus. There must be millions of cultures stockpiled across the country. Every pharmaceutical house and university is working on a cure for the common cold."

"Spray the whole country?" Bellows said incredulously. "That's impossible. The area to be covered is just too large, and you'll lose a lot of the virus to winds.

And considering the large numbers of particles needed to infect one person . . . it would take tons of viral particles. Literally tons."

"Then distribute it through the mail or on some food staple like milk or bread. Have people congregate in movie theaters or churches or auditoriums and put it into the air conditioning systems. It's *got* to be possible somehow."

"I don't know." Bellows hesitated. "This would be an enormous undertaking no matter how we attacked it, and I'm afraid your evidence is just too flimsy. Has the virus actually killed the meningococcal organisms or just slowed them down?"

"Just slowed them down. But it's early yet." Ogden felt certain the full proof would soon follow. "What if we just spray Los Angeles? Make this city into a giant test tube of sorts? It's where most of our cases are."

"Still very difficult and there's no precedent for this kind of procedure. I'm sure there's enough viral stocks for a limited area and if it works we can distribute the rest through grocery stores or theaters or whatever. But I think the president's receptive to a nationwide quarantine and that's the only thing scientific evidence has shown would work."

"We can't afford to wait. You'll never have a perfect quarantine and God knows what the attempt will do to the country."

"Look, I'm as desperate as you are, but we can't afford to make a mistake either. What you're proposing could be dangerous. The very young and the very old could be killed by the cold virus."

Bellows was referring to the risk of viral pneumonia to those whose immune systems were not yet well developed or were aged, Ogden knew, but there was far more than that risk at stake now. "And everyone else may be killed if we don't," he argued.

Bellows was silent. He wanted to be careful. After a

prolonged pause, he asked, "How many cultures show this slowing?"

"Every one that we've checked and the controls are growing as usual." Ogden could feel that the scientist was shifting to his opinion.

"It's not a cure yet, you know." Bellows said tentatively.

"Not yet, but it could be. And even if all it does is slow down the disease it'll buy us some critical time. It might just give us that interval we need until the vaccines are ready."

Ogden's arguments were difficult to refute. An experiment in one city seemed reasonable, especially if President Lansfield also enforced the quarantine. Before hanging up, Bellows promised to look into means of carrying out the spraying and added, "We'll proceed only if that virus continues to inhibit the meningococcus. I want to know every change."

Time passed very slowly as Ogden and Ling monitored the changes in their cultures. Hilary Walters was used as an independent observer, checking the cultures without knowing which had been treated and which had not.

At 7:00 P.M., the bacterial doubling time in three of the treated plates had shortened to twenty-five minutes and Ogden became worried again. It meant that the meningococci might be adjusting to the virus's presence, just as they had appropriated the resistances of the bacteria with which they had combined. If it was true he knew that he should notify Bellows, but he put off calling. The trend was not definite and he "had to be sure." He found himself playing Bellows's wait-and-see game . . . At 8:00 P.M., the earlier change was indeed shown to be transient. On this check, there was a definite change toward longer reproduction times, and most of the treated cultures were ranging between thirty and thirty-five minutes. Under the microscope, the internal architecture of many of the bacteria was distorted. Although neither scientist could explain what they were viewing, both were in full agreement that the pattern was abnormal.

At 9:00 P.M., some of the bacteria in the virus plates were dying. *Dying*—it was a beautiful sight to Ogden, who had seen so much other death these past ninety-six hours. The colonies located nearest the virus populations had clear spots, and using photographs from the electron microscope Ogden proved that the viral particles were actually penetrating the bacterial cell walls. The meningococci were definitely under attack and seemingly helpless. Doubling times in other areas were approaching an hour and some colonies were now at a standstill. This was the proof that he had been waiting for—that Bellows had been waiting for. He ran to the phone on the wall of his laboratory.

"Dr. Bellows, the damn things are dying, dying like flies," Ogden excitedly reported after spending a frustrating half hour trying to locate the professor. "It's working. I knew that it would. You've got your cure. Now, someone merely needs to deliver it."

"How sure are you?" Bellows asked. Under normal circumstances, he would want to see the results himself. Obviously, that was impossible and his decision now boiled down to whether he trusted Ogden's work or not. "And suppose you're correct. We've still got to quarantine the whole country."

"I don't care if you tie everyone to their bedposts. We've got to spray Los Angeles. The data here is clear. Every culture with viruses added is dying, every one without is growing unchanged—"

"No exceptions?"

"Not yet."

"I wonder if we should try it out on a patient or two first?" Bellows asked, recalling the tragedy of the swine flu vaccine. "We can't afford to make a mistake—"

"We're not wrong and we haven't got time to experiment anymore. Your quarantine won't stop it. With cities as crowded as they are the meningococcus will keep going. You've *got* to spray," Ogden insisted. "I thought you said you would get the wheels rolling the last time we talked."

Bellows's end of the line was quiet for a moment and then, sounding as if he were late and in a hurry, he said, "Yes, Mike, I did. I put it in motion yesterday. I'm sorry I didn't tell you, but . . . well, I had a feeling that if I rode you hard enough for unequivocal results, you'd come through with something we could go with. I knew that there wouldn't be time for me to cross-check, for me to be on the scene, to be convinced myself. Hell, you know me. . . . But I know you, Mike, and it's good enough for me that *you* are convinced."

"Thanks." Ogden was moved, but now that his plan was about to be set in motion he was also a little afraid.

It was after 1:00 A.M. and raining in Washington when Bellows got back to the White House and was shown to a small study. A few minutes later, President Lansfield joined him, obviously just called from his bed and wearing a bathrobe over blue pants and a T-shirt. By the time he had turned on another lamp he was fully awake and eager to hear what Bellows had to say.

"Your message said that you might have a cure?" the president asked as he seated himself on a hard wooden chair across from Bellows. "It seems awfully quick, considering how pessimistic you were earlier."

"Earlier, there were reasons to be pessimistic, but there's been a breakthrough. If this is our cure, its discovery is almost as serendipitous as Fleming's moldy orange—the right occurrence and the right observer." Bellows's tone reflected pride as he went on. "We had a boy survive the meningitis in Los Angeles and Dr. Ogden, an old student of mine, was able to find the reason why. A virus, in fact, a common cold virus. Most organisms on earth have at least one natural enemy, and this appears to be the one that's lethal to the source of our epidemic.''

The president appeared both intrigued and relieved as Bellows continued his explanation. When the scientist was through, Lansfield leaned back and dug into the pocket of his robe for a pipe. "So what do we do?"

"I suggest that you attack the epidemic in two ways. Proceed with the quarantine, and enforce it. We can't afford to make any mistakes. Too many people will die and very quickly if you don't, and this way it'll buy us some time to spray Los Angeles."

"Like DDT?" The idea of spraying had taken Lansfield by surprise.

"Just like mosquito control in the Everglades. That's the only way we can distribute the virus quickly. It won't work for the entire country—it's too large—but the L.A. basin is surrounded by a very convenient ring of mountains that will keep everything within the area. I've already called the Department of Agriculture. We can have a dozen crop dusters in two hours if we need them and I've checked with several pharmaceutical houses. Viral stocks are adequate, but they won't give them up without some compensation. I need your help to push this through, and I need it tonight."

"How much money are we talking about?"

"Eighty million dollars minimum for the cold viruses, and whatever else it takes to refit the planes and get them into the air."

The president lit his pipe and began pacing the floor. "How certain are you that this will work?"

"I'm not sure at all. It's never been done before. We used to joke about treating epidemics with antibiotics from the air, but nobody ever thought that it might have to be done. There's no research protocol to draw on. The closest thing we've studied is biological warfare, and that's never been given a full-scale test either."

"Eighty million dollars . . . or maybe double that, on

an untried experiment? That'll be an expensive mistake. Politically, I mean.''

"It'll be a lot more costly if it could have worked and wasn't tried.''

Lansfield walked to the window and studied the raindrops sliding down the pane. "What about the rest of the country? How do you plan to treat other cities?''

"Differently. In the laboratory we give volunteers colds by using a nasal spray or putting them in an enclosed room for fifteen seconds with a nebulizer. Every town has a movie theater. That would be a way to treat if it works.''

"Why not do that in L.A.? It would be a lot cheaper.''

"Cheaper, maybe, but not if it fails. We still need to try to quarantine everyone we can. Convening people for inoculation might be the quickest way to spread the disease if the incubation period of the meningitis outstrips that of the cold virus. People have to stay put until we know the results.''

Lansfield was silent for a moment as he stared at Bellows and seemed to weigh the man and his words. "All right, we'll do it. I hope to God you're right.''

The logistics of implementing Bellows's proposal were considerably more difficult than the scientist expected, but within an hour a makeshift task force of cabinet members and their staffs, all called from their beds, was hastily assembled at the White House. The president's instructions were simple: "Get Los Angeles sprayed by morning no matter what it takes.'' Although several members doubted that they could act that quickly, everyone was willing to try.

They set up a communications center and Bellows began recontacting the pharmaceutical houses, but none of the companies were willing to accept his word that the federal government would reimburse all losses. Each call was followed by one from the secretary of H.E.W., and then by Lansfield, who finally convinced them.

"You may not have a damn company to run if this epidemic isn't stopped!" the president was overheard saying to one resistant executive, who replied that he was merely making sure.

Next came procurement. Here, estimates of the amount needed were literally guesswork. No one knew how many viral particles were necessary to infect a city the size of Los Angeles, but using data from animal studies on inoculum size in the laboratory and classified information on the defoliants used in Vietnam, Bellows made a rough calculation, added ten percent, and then ascertained that they would only need materials from two companies to start with. Once the numbers were turned over to the group, the secretary of defense arranged for military teams to pick up the special incubators from the two companies and transport them to Long Beach Naval Station, which was to become their staging area.

The third step was delivery and the only feasible vehicles were crop dusters. After obtaining a list of potential pilots from the files at the FAA, twelve men from the San Joaquin and Imperial Valleys were awakened and asked to fly their planes to Long Beach as well. Although they were all told that their planes were being used to fight the epidemic, specifics were withheld until they arrived.

In the interim, emergency crews at the Naval air station hastily began cleaning and sterilizing special stainless steel, pressurized tanks and attaching new sterile spray heads. When the viral cultures arrived, however, the containing media appeared too viscous to disperse adequately from the spray nozzles, and despite the addition of sterile saline, several engineers complained that takeoffs might be dangerous. Their concerns were promptly relayed to Washington, but the response was to go ahead. According to the secretary of defense, proper baffling could avert the danger.

The moment the crop dusters began arriving, they

were quickly equipped with the steel tanks and given a flight plan. Each pilot was told to fly at rooftop level and all were given self-contained breathing apparatus with special masks to prevent inhalation of an over-whelming viral inoculum.

By 5:00 A.M., the first flight was in the air and the remaining eleven followed within two hours, each pilot following a path that crisscrossed the city and extended from Long Beach to Valencia.

CHAPTER TWENTY-THREE

Hilary was sound asleep on Mike Ogden's office couch and Ogden was slumped down in a nearby lounge when a Yeoman Cropmaster flew over the rooftop of the Contagious Disease Unit, where the windows had intentionally been left open. The crop duster's single prop sputtered noisily above in the darkness, but neither person stirred. There was no smell to the barely perceptible mist that slowly descended on the hospital and spread to the surrounding neighborhood. Unknowingly, healthy and ill people alike began inhaling millions of viral particles.

Several hours earlier, Bellows had telephoned Ogden to tell him that their proposal had been accepted, but a tincture of obsessiveness had kept Hilary and him working an additional three hours—"just to be completely sure." Their concerns, however, were unnecessary. Every culture medium treated with the common cold virus had died. Afterward, the two had returned to Ogden's office for that coffee date once planned, but they had fallen asleep with their cups still two-thirds full—and with thoughts of getting to know each other better once the crisis had passed.

Just before seven, Ogden began to awake. Blurry-eyed and unaware that day had come, he resumed a conversation that had died in midsentence four hours before. At the time, he had been bragging about his son, how Peter had learned to read by five, play the piano by six and how much he had missed him the last several days.

"I imagine he'll be playing concerts by ten," Ogden muttered hoarsely. The sound of his voice jarred him fully awake, and he chuckled as he noted the hour and that Hilary's eyes were tightly closed. She was curled up at the far end of the couch, with both hands clasped together for a pillow.

For several minutes, he just stared. There was something about the quietness of a woman's sleep, the innocence of it, that suddenly intrigued him. He studied each curl of her chestnut hair and how it framed the soft features of her face, the movements of her breasts, rhythmically rising and falling with her slow breathing, and the shapely lines of her legs that tapered from the seductive fullness concealed by her skirt to slim, delicate ankles. As he watched, he suddenly felt an affinity and attraction that he had felt for no one since his wife's death. He realized that he had buried himself in his work, a laboratory for a coffin, and vowed never to let it happen again. Hilary Walters was not only attractive, but she was someone with whom he felt a closeness that he did not want to lose.

After standing, he quietly walked to her side and kissed her forehead. As he drew away, her eyes slowly opened and a smile crossed her face.

"That's a nice way to wake up," she said, stretching and pushing her hair back. "I must have dozed off. Have we cured the city yet?"

"I hope so, but it's early. Surgery has showers and clean clothes upstairs. Why don't I buy you a fresh cup of coffee and some breakfast, in say . . ." He glanced at his watch. "Fifteen minutes. Then we'll reassess the damages and prepare everyone for the onslaught of respiratory infections."

"Sounds good, Mike," she answered. She brushed her fingertips across his cheek, smiled and left.

Meanwhile, the president had gone on the air to announce the quarantine. In contrast to earlier statements, however, these were orders, not recommendations. Every school and business had to take a two-day holiday and every highway was closed until they could fully assess the virus's effect on Los Angeles. The only exceptions were medical and emergency vehicles. Although he never specifically said it, he implied that he might use the military to enforce martial law. The speech was repeated every fifteen minutes on all of the national networks.

By noon that day, every city street across the country was deserted. In New York, Fifth Avenue looked like a metropolitan ghost town. A few businessmen who had gotten the message late were hurriedly leaving their offices and all shops were closed. Chicago's Michigan Avenue was equally empty, with lone patrol cars checking storefronts and looking for possible looters. The only sound along Wilshire Boulevard in Los Angeles was the sound of an ambulance's siren swiftly moving eastward and then shooting north on Fairfax, and only on Sunset Boulevard did two all-night massage parlors have to be forcibly evacuated.

Along both coasts, all seaports were closed. Incoming ships were forced to stay at sea and those that were already docked had to pull in their gangplanks. Airplanes en route to the U.S. were diverted to airports outside the country, outgoing flights were cancelled, and those within the continental airspace returned to their points of origin. Trains and buses between cities were stopped at the nearest stations and all passengers were told to check into local hotels. Cars along major arteries were likewise stopped by police barricades and told either to return home or stay put.

At the same time, the military was put on a precautionary alert. Submarines in the Pacific and Indian Oceans poised their missiles toward vital Russian targets. Additional SAC flights were put into the air, U.S. troops at key NATO, Mideast and Far East bases were assembled near transport planes and all leaves were cancelled.

It was doubtful, of course, that the Russians would indeed take advantage of the U.S. paralysis, but the president wasn't taking any chances and he quickly let that fact be known through diplomatic channels. Not unexpectedly, the Communist bloc promptly put their forces on alert as well, and threatened to retaliate for any aggressive acts.

Both countries knew by now, however, that the Russians had a definite epidemic of their own in Moscow and Leningrad and were much more interested in how the U.S. curtailed its spread than in the military threat. Assurances had been given on both sides that they would cooperate in any breakthrough on a cure.

After breakfast, Mike Ogden and Hilary Walters began making rounds in the hospital. One of their first stops was in Mary Mitchell's room. The nurse was deeply comatose, her skin had a bluish tinge, punctuated by the huge purplish spots, and her right hand was cold. Any worsening of her condition would require a respirator—that is, if one was available—and unless the virus worked quickly in her case, she could easily die.

A few doors away, Murray Clagston was still on a respirator and requiring one hundred percent oxygen to aerate his failing lungs. His fever had remained at the top of the temperature graph and his vital signs were constantly changing. Intermittently, there'd be a minute or two when he was conscious, but even then he was confused and combative, and those episodes were occurring at wider intervals. Like Mary's, his skin was grossly discolored and all four of his extremities were threatening autoamputation.

In contrast, Tina Hudson seemed to have regained some strength, but Ogden thought that was due to the blood transfusions and not to a turnaround in the course of the disease. Her somnolent state was broken only by outcries from pain. Her complicated problems required a lot more nursing than was available and there were long periods when she went unobserved.

Dr. Cunningham was one of the few patients who were still fully conscious, although he was suffering from an overwhelming headache and repeated retching that resisted the usual antiemetics. When he was told about the spraying his response was: "I'd take five colds, maybe ten with pneumonia, over this damn thing."

The Van Horn family was housed together in a room on the next floor and each of them was suffering from headache and vomiting, but the purplish lesions were not apparent yet and they were able to retain some food.

The hospital corridors remained a shambles. No one had time to clean up. Dirty linens and used IV bottles were pushed into corners once waste containers overflowed. None of the beds were made and pickups of food trays were hours behind. Many of the nurses who were working were left over from the previous shift and few had gotten more than a couple hours of sleep. Although the police department had made a concerted effort to call in replacements from their homes, the influx was slow and the hospital work force continued racing from emergency to emergency rather than dealing with typical day-to-day problems. Even medications were stretched thin and many of the shelves in the pharmacy were empty.

"This must be what the end of the world looks like," Hilary said to Ogden when they disrobed from their hospital gowns and went downstairs.

"No, just a medical hell," he said tonelessly.

When they got to Ogden's office, he called home to check on Peter and to apologize for missing another evening.

"Don't you budge out of that house until I tell you to leave," he warned the youth, who acted more like it was a punishment than for his own good. "I'll be home tonight even if the police have to bring me." He affected an optimistic tone, but he was worried that it might be the last time that he'd see his son if the cold virus didn't work. A massive vaccination program was weeks away and he doubted that the quarantine would hold up. Within days the streets would be loaded with panicked people looking for food and spreading the disease with them.

"How sick are they, daddy?" the seven-year-old asked. "Why are all those people sick?"

"Baby, it's too hard to explain, but you remember how the chicken pox went through your school? How all of your friends got it and then you did? It's something like that, but much more serious. Now, you be good and listen to Mrs. Anderson. I'll be home somehow to see you." He emphasized the word "somehow" and forced a saddened smile, as if the boy could see him.

The phone rang as soon as he hung up and it was Bellows on the other end. "Well, you're on your way," the older scientist began. "The city's been saturated."

"Everything go smoothly?" Ogden asked.

"Considering the task before us, yes, but we lost two pilots. There were three crashes altogether, but one of the men walked away from his plane. The other two weren't as fortunate."

"Let's hope it wasn't in vain . . . How do you plan to monitor the effect?"

"You're the key. We have direct links to all of the hospitals in L.A., but you've got the most cases and the earliest ones. We'll need periodic updating. We've

already started working on plans to hit the rest of the
country if this thing works. Otherwise . . . well, I guess I
don't need to tell you.''

''No, that you don't. We've gotten baseline blood
counts and spinal taps on certain patients to follow for
change, but our staff's too short to be running extra
tests on everyone. We're even using lab techs to care for
patients now. I guess the easiest way to tell is if things
start leveling off. The Mathesson kid plateaued early
and then quickly improved. If any of these cases merely
stop worsening, that should be reasonable evidence. I
suppose we can look at the number of admissions too.
It's easily documented in the logbook.''

''Sounds good. Keep us abreast. We want to know
every change, good or bad,'' Bellows curtly responded
and started to hang up.

''What if they don't go well?'' Ogden quickly asked
but waited a moment for the answer.

''I guess you should just go home and stay put like
everyone else. I really don't know at this moment.''

Drs. Ling, Paige, Walters and Ogden spent the rest of
the day on the wards, helping with patient care, filling in
where staff was short, doing everything from injecting
what few medications remained and managing respirators to emptying bedpans and moving equipment. Every
time a patient seemed to be improving, they were disappointed to find that the change was always transitory.
Every time a patient worsened, they rationalized it away
as being too early for the cold virus to have worked or as
being due to a side effect from the medications or the
fact that the patient was beyond help. Complicated
graphs for charting blood pressures, heart rates,
temperatures, urinary outputs, white counts and
changes in mental states were set up, all looking for a
hint of improvement, but the curves tended to worsen
regardless of which parameter they studied and the information was reluctantly passed on to Washington.

By noon, Ogden's worries had intensified. Perhaps his proposal was in error and something else in the culture, such as a by-product of viral replication, had killed the meningococcus. Or maybe Bellows's calculation for the inoculum was too weak, or the winds had carried off the viral particles and now all was lost. His gut feeling was that he had been right—his medical accumen asserted it—but he was searching for proof, and all about him patients continued their unrelenting course to their graves.

At lunch, the only person who remained the least optimistic was Hilary Walters. "Even penicillin doesn't work that quickly on the most sensitive of bacteria."

"Unfortunately, penicillin doesn't work here at all," Ogden responded, stirring a bowl of tomato soup that he had little desire to eat.

"We checked and double-checked all of the data," she continued, trying to reinfuse some enthusiasm. "You want a miracle cure that also works in a miraculous time. I doubt you can have both."

"I'll take the former. I guess I'm just beat from all this. I feel like a man falling off a cliff and hoping that someone's put up a net in time to catch him." He knew she was right. Five or six hours was hardly enough time for the virus to even penetrate a person's mucous membranes and start reproducing, but he needed quick answers. The country needed quick answers.

At 1:00 P.M., they lost their first patient since the cold virus had been sprayed, and other evidence suggested that the trend was going to continue. But a half hour later, there was a clue that the virus might be working. Ambulances had been arriving every fifteen minutes and now, all of a sudden, the rate had slowed to every half hour. Ogden quickly got on the phone and called every hospital in the vicinity to see if they were witnessing the same slowdown or were merely getting County Hospital's overflow. None, however, had received any additional cases and they too noted longer intervals between admissions. Before notifying Washington, he called the ambulance company to make sure that they weren't merely short of help, but they confirmed that their calls had lessened.

"Either they're dying at home or something's working out here," Ogden reported to Bellows, but both men knew that it wasn't enough to go on.

At 5:00 P.M., a second break came and this time it was considerably more tangible. Mary Mitchell's blood count, which had been running in the high 30,000s, dropped precipitously to 21,000. A few minutes later, nursing reported that Murray Clagston's oxygen needs had lessened by twenty percent.

"It's still not enough," Ogden remarked to Paige, who had brought him the new information.

"Mike, what else could it be?" the other physician argued. "None of these cases have spontaneously remitted."

"True, but it's still not enough. No enough to start a national program, anyway. White counts can bounce around. So can oxygen needs. We still have to sit tight."

At six, just when Ogden was about to call for a police car to drive him home for a short visit, their third clue came from Dr. Cunningham's spinal tap—and this time the evidence was solid. The results from Cunningham's tap had changed just as bizarrely as the Mathesson boy's had. Whereas every previous spinal tap had had bacteria present, each with a worsening white count, now the number of white cells in the spinal fluid had dramatically plummeted and none of the meningococcal organisms could be seen. To be sure, a spinal tap was then quickly done on Mary Mitchell and the results on her fluid had changed in exactly the same way. Ogden immediately got on the phone to Washington and, barely able to contain his excitement, passed the good news on. They were right. The bacteria had a natural enemy. Although physically exhausted, Ogden was exhilarated and immediately went up and down the halls spreading the good news, including a stop in Dr. Cunningham's room to tell him about the cold he was about to get.

Over the next several hours, patients throughout the hospital began improving. The changes were slow but definite. Vital signs stabilized, heart rhythms normalized and fevers defervesced.

Outside the hospital, the ambulance dock was quiet. Quieter than it had been in days. . . .

EPILOGUE

During the following day, while most of L.A.'s population was hacking and blowing their noses, viral stocks began being distributed across the country and people were instructed to congregate at movie theaters designated by their local officials. Inoculums were put in the air conditioning units and people remained there for fifteen minutes at a time. Within four days, ninety-eight percent of the country had been protected. And although it wasn't a guarantee that the disease wouldn't return, it gave officials time to produce enough vaccine.

The total loss of lives was finally placed at twelve thousand, with another eighteen thousand disabled in some way. Mary Mitchell survived, but lost the use of her right hand. Murray Clagston remained blind. Tina Hudson became a paraplegic and a ward of the state. Mr. Van Horn was left with a twitching in one arm, but the rest of his family walked out in perfect health. And Dr. Cunningham returned to his ward duties the next day without any obvious aftereffects.

The total cost to the country's economy in lost production and manpower and in military and medical expenditures was not easily calculated, but experts finally put it at a quarter of a billion dollars. Had government agencies been prepared for such an epidemic, Bellows said at a news conference, the cost might have been one tenth that, but he knew that it was speculation only.

Hilary Walters, Les Paige, Tom Ling and Mike Ogden were among the few beneficiaries of the epidemic. All four were honored at the National Academy of Sciences and later at the White House.

Not unexpectedly, Ogden was eventually granted the funds for his cancer research. The latter would have to wait, however. He had other promises to keep. To Peter, to Hilary, and most of all, to himself.

Turn the page for a thrilling preview of

SEVEN MINUTES PAST MIDNIGHT

**the spellbinding new novel
by Walter Winward,
bestselling author of
HAMMERSTRIKE.**

"But for our premature surrender [in World War I], Germany would have gained an honorable peace and there would have been no postwar chaos. This time we must not give up five minutes before midnight."

Adolf Hitler to his generals, January 1945

PROLOGUE

November 1944

The Special Operations officer, whose real name was Greenleigh but who for the purposes of this trip was traveling under false identity and nationality documents, watched the plain-clothes German courier cross safely back into his homeland. Then the Englishman turned away. For better or worse, the operation was off and running.

There was not too much two-way traffic between Germany and Switzerland at that point in the war, and what there was was watched carefully by troops of the *Sicherheitsdienst*, or SD, the SS Security Police, on the German side. Most Germans who passed through the frontier post had legitimate business in the neutral country—at least, business that had been franked as official by a high authority, although it was common knowledge that the majority of it involved the transfer of currency to numbered accounts. In the depraved world of National Socialism, this was not regarded as unusual. If the war went badly, funds would be required to carry on the struggle at some future time; they would also be needed to provide members of the SS with living expenses elsewhere. And there was no doubt that Sturmbannfuehrer Klaus Bauer was an officer of that elite organization, even though one set of papers pronounced him to be a Swedish citizen. That too was legitimate, simply to avoid awkward questions on the Swiss side of the border. His real papers were franked by SS-General Kaltenbrunner's department, the RSHA, or Reich Main Security Office.

Nevertheless, the SD Untersturmfuehrer who readmitted Bauer to the Reich took his time, scrutinizing each page of the entry document carefully before finally allowing the Sturmbannfuehrer to pass through. Time of entry was noted as 12:22 P.M.

Being so close to the Swiss frontier, this part of Germany had been left severely alone by Allied bombers, and Bauer found it hard to believe that less than a hundred miles away some of the fiercest fighting of the war was taking place.

Halfway down the hill, making for the public telephone booth at the foot, he glanced over his shoulder. The SD Untersturmfuehrer was about forty or fifty meters behind, accompanied by a senior NCO. Both men were carrying MP 40 submachine guns.

Bauer forced himself to relax. It was coincidence, that was all. His papers were quite in order. If the Untersturmfuehrer had suspected that anything was amiss, he would have held him at the border post. They were going for lunch or a beer; it was that time of day. Still, it was better to be safe than sorry.

He stopped, making it obvious that he would wait for them to catch up. But the Untersturmfuehrer waved his hand negatively. Nothing sinister in that either. They simply had private matters to discuss, and he was far senior to either of them in rank. His presence would make them feel uncomfortable.

At the foot of the hill he entered the telephone booth.

Later it would be established that he spent six minutes on the phone, talking in an agitated fashion to the person at the other end. And so engrossed did he become in the conversation that he did not notice the Untersturmfuehrer and the NCO waiting for him until he hung up and stepped outside.

"You want something of me?" he demanded.

The younger officer seemed almost embarrassed.

"I'm sorry, Herr Sturmbannfuehrer, but I must ask you to accompany me to SD Headquarters. I have reason to believe that you are engaged in treasonable activities."

Bauer tried to bluff it out. "You will just about live to regret this impertinence. I am on important business for the Reich."

"Nevertheless, I must ask you to come with me."

Bauer nodded slowly, as though accepting the situation. He saw the other two visibly relax, and at that moment took to his heels.

Unfortunately, there was nowhere to run to, no side streets to disappear down, and the SD NCO had already been given his instructions coming down the hill. He fired a short burst from the MP 40 and at that range could hardly miss. When they reached Bauer he was quite dead.

A truck was called for and Bauer's corpse taken to SD Headquarters, where it was stripped and searched. His clothing contained nothing except his Swedish papers and his SS pass, which was strange in itself. No money, no photographs or letters, no cigarettes or matches. It took a sharp-eyed doctor to spot the ink marks on the inside of his left wrist and a magnifying glass to decipher the symbols. They simply said, LONDON—and gave some figures that were obviously a radio frequency.

In due course the papers pertaining to the case found their way to Berlin and into the In tray of Hauptsturmfuehrer Sepp Langendorf. Although an officer in the SD, Langendorf had desk space in the Prinz Albrechtstrasse HQ of the Gestapo, with which organization the SD was closely linked.

The report from the frontier guard stated that initial inquiries had revealed no trace of a permit being issued by the RSHA for Sturmbannfuehrer Bauer to visit Switzerland. Furthermore, there was no record that Sturmbannfuehrer Bauer actually existed. The name and papers were obviously fakes, but the dead man's true identity had not been established.

Hauptsturmfuehrer Langendorf resolved not to refer the case to a higher authority. He had a radio frequency and access to a listening post. All he had to do was wait.

By keeping the matter to himself he was breaking all the rules. Had he acted otherwise, the course of the war, and certainly the peace, would have altered dramatically.

ONE

Not entirely because of the freezing temperature and the bitter wind blowing the length of Wilhelmstrasse, most Berliners chose to walk with their heads down these days. It was better not to look, for the city was in ruins, a tribute to the accuracy of the terror bombers. Moldering walls with gaping windows reared up like tombstones amid acres of debris for as far as the eye could see. It seemed that the Reich Chancellery, stretching the whole length of Voss-strasse, from Wilhelmplatz to Hermann Goeringstrasse, was the only building left intact. Not many saw this as a miracle.

Those scheduled to attend the afternoon conference were already entering the Chancellery, the military through one door, Party members through another.

Once inside the high entrance hall they were faced with a bleak prospect, one made even drearier by the miserable illumination shed by the few remaining lights. The carpets, paintings and tapestries that had once graced the hallway had long since been removed for protection from Allied air raids. Most of the windows were covered with cardboard.

At the head of the corridor leading to the anteroom in the conference area, SS troopers of the *Fuehrerbegleitkommando*, Hitler's hand-picked personal guard, armed with machine pistols, demanded that all visitors, regardless of rank, hand over their side arms and open their briefcases. It was now January 27, 1945, but Count Klaus von Stauffenberg's attempt to assassinate Hitler six months earlier was still fresh in the minds of many. The extreme security measures applied to everyone. Even the last to arrive, Generaloberst Heinz Guderian, Army Chief of Staff and commander of the Eastern Front, was not exempt.

By 4 o'clock the anteroom was filled with military and political leaders of the highest rank. A few minutes later the doors to the Fuehrer's office were thrown open and Reichsmarschall Goering led the way inside.

Though the office was spacious, it was sparingly decorated. At one end French windows were draped with gray curtains, and drab carpets covered most of the floor. In the middle of one wall stood Hitler's massive desk; behind it, his black-upholstered chair faced the Chancellery garden. The most senior conferees seated themselves in heavy leather chairs while their aides or lesser members either stood or found straight chairs.

At 4:20 P.M. Adolf Hitler shuffled in. Those who had not seen him for some time were shocked by his appearance. Shoulders stooped, his left arm hanging limply, he was hard to accept as the leader who had given them dozens of military and political victories. Only the pale blue eyes occasionally flashed with the old hypnotic power.

Those without personal knowledge assumed that his useless left arm and general appearance were the result of the July bomb plot. Others knew that it was his right arm which had been injured at Rastenburg and that the condition of his left was a recent phenomenon.

He sat down gingerly and glanced slowly around the room. His gaze took in Goering, whose redness of face seemed to indicate a heavy session with the schnapps bottle in the anteroom. Near Goering sat Feldmarschall Wilhelm Keitel, chief of the OKW, the High Command of the Armed Forces, derisively nicknamed Lakeitel— from *Lakei*, lackey—by his fellow officers. Behind Keitel was his Chief of Operations, Generaloberst Alfred Jodl.

The Deputy Leader of the Party, Martin Bormann, sat alone, silent as always, but Guderian was chatting amiably to his own adjutant, Major Freytag von Loringhoven, and Hitler's, Sturmbannfuehrer Otto Günsche.

Seemingly absorbed in a thickish document and heartily loathed by most of those present, Himmler's liaison officer at the Chancellery, SS-Brigadefuehrer Hermann Fegelein, was feeling the effects of a massive lunch. The younger officers called him Flegelein—after *Flegel*, lout—but only behind his back. Fegelein was married to Gretl Braun, sister of Hitler's mistress, Eva, and was a man quick to take offense.

Outside in the anteroom, the commander of the SS guard for the day checked against his list that all those who were due to arrive were in fact now closeted in the Fuehrer's office. Anyone else wishing to gain entry would have to have a compelling reason or be prepared to wait until the conference was over.

If it could be called a conference at all, he thought. Twenty-odd people, only half a dozen of them of the front rank, hardly constituted a major policy-making meeting.

There was a time when the corridors of the Chancellery had regularly echoed the footsteps of the most powerful men in Germany, perhaps the world. Men like Reichsfuehrer Himmler, recently appointed commander of Army Group Vistula; Ernst Kaltenbrunner, chief of the SD; Artur Axmann, head of the Hitler Youth; Admiral Canaris, former head of the Abwehr, and Admiral Doenitz; SS-Brigadefuehrer Walter Schellenberg, Himmler's chief of espionage; and Albert Speer, Minister of Armament and War Production. Men like Dr. Goebbels, Minister of Propaganda, and Foreign Minister von Ribbentrop. Even Rudolf Hess.

But no more. Hess, of course, had gone mad and defected to the British, and Canaris was in a concentration camp, or dead, for his part in the July plot. But of the remainder, most either had offices in Berlin or were regular visitors to the capital, yet they rarely visited the Chancellery. No doubt the Fuehrer had his reasons for keeping them away. Up to a year ago, Hitler would have trusted most of them with his life—but that was before Von Stauffenberg's treason. Now he watched everyone for signs of betrayal, and who was to say who would be next to play Brutus?

Beyond the closed doors Hitler tapped the desk with a ruler and brought the conference to order. "Begin," he commanded.

Guderian got to his feet. His report was a dismal affair from beginning to end.

Two weeks earlier, on January 12, three million Russians, more than ten times the strength of the armies that had landed in Normandy on D-Day, had attacked a force of three-quarters of a million Germans along a 400-mile front stretching from the Baltic right down the middle of Poland. Supported by artillery and led by seemingly endless columns of T-34 tanks, they punched a massive hole through the unprepared and poorly equipped Germans.

In the extreme north, Marshal Chernyakhovsky's Third White Russian Front (the Soviet equivalent of an

Army Group) pushed for Königsberg in East Prussia. On his left, the Second White Russian Front, led by the mercurial Marshal Rokossovsky, smashed its way into Danzig. On Rokossovsky's left the most talented of them all and the man the Germans feared most, Marshal Zhukov, in command of the First White Russian Front, spearheaded the assault on Posen, which stood in the way of his ultimate goal, Berlin. Finally, on the extreme southern flank, Marshal Ivan Konev's First Ukrainian Front was moving quickest of all. In its path stood the POW camp at Sagan, Stalag Luft III, which held 10,000 Allied airmen.

Within two weeks of the initial Soviet push, Generaloberst Reinhardt's Army Group North, the main target of Chernyakhovsky and Rokossovsky, was overrun, and the Fourth Army under General Hossbach was in full flight. But the main assault in the center, that led by Zhukov, was the one causing the greatest concern to the OKW, especially Guderian. Army Group Vistula had been hastily formed to plug the hole Zhukov had made, and from the beginning Guderian had objected to the order that gave Himmler, whose highest rank prior to the advent of the Nazis was that of sergeant major, the command. Hitler had overruled him and was now living to regret his decision. The Reichsfuehrer-SS had ill-advisedly drawn up his battle lines running east-west, from the Vistula to the River Oder, and Zhukov merely bypassed him. On the morning of January 27 the First White Russian Front was less than one hundred miles from Berlin, with only the Oder as the last major obstacle.

For more than an hour Guderian tried to impress upon the conference the seriousness of the situation in the east, but Hitler seemed more interested in the Stalag Luft III POWs.

"The camp must be evacuated. The Russians must not liberate them. I can't have ten thousand Allied fliers roaming around loose." An adjutant left to relay this order to the camp commandant.

Hitler was also concerned about reports of Russian atrocities against civilians. These were increasing daily. What had started as a trickle was now a flood.

"I have it on no less an authority than Kaltenbrunner," he intoned, "that Stalin has given his troops absolute license to rape and murder. In fact, the political commissars attached to each unit are there partly to ensure that that particular direction is carried out."

"With due respect, Fuehrer, this is neither the time nor the place to discuss such matters." Guderian made a despairing attempt to refocus Hitler's attention on the conduct of the war.

"With due respect to *you*, Herr Generaloberst, I think it is. It is precisely because the Russians are the kind of subhuman race to take full advantage of a license to pillage that I declared war on them in the first place."

Guderian gave up. Hitler was off and running on one of his favorite topics, and Guderian knew that it was useless to try to interrupt him. He also knew that this afternoon's session would be like so many that had gone before, where trivia were given importance and matters of immediate concern relegated to the scrap heap. Hitler was like a man dying of cancer reaching for an aspirin: it would do him no good, but at least it was familiar.

The conference ended at 6:50 P.M. with nothing of value discussed, let alone decided. Guderian's report was virtually ignored, as all he had to offer was bad news. The situation in the west was no better, but nevertheless forty minutes was spent discussing whether Generaloberst Kurt Student should retain command of Army Group H in the Netherlands and whether Oberstgruppenfuehrer Paul Hausser was still up to his job.

After Hitler left, the remaining conferees retired to the anteroom to drink coffee and schnapps and eat the sandwiches prepared by orderlies. Few had any real doubts that the writing was now well and truly on the wall.

Guderian and Freytag von Loringhoven were the first to move out into the cold Berlin night, heading for Zossen, twenty miles due south of the capital. Brigadefuehrer Fegelein followed them soon afterward. His first job was to report the tenor of the meeting to his chief, Himmler. And while neither Goebbels nor Von Ribbentrop nor Kaltenbrunner officially had observers at the conference, each had his unofficial representative in the room and was in full cognizance of what had occurred by 8 o'clock.

It took Grand Admiral Doenitz and some of the others a little longer. Nevertheless, by 9:30 on the evening of January 27, most of the Reich's senior Nazis, both military and political, had verbatim reports of the Chancellery meeting, and an hour later the man to whom Sturmbannfuehrer Bauer had spoken on the telephone, code-named Valkyrie by British Intelligence, had decided to act.

At 11:27 P.M., the senior NCO at the listening post set up by Hauptsturmfuehrer Langendorf was half asleep. Like his fellow watch keepers, who manned the monitoring station in shifts, he was quite convinced that Langendorf was mad. They had been at it for ten weeks now, night and day, without so much as a bleep on the frequency.

But at 11:28 the NCO was wide awake. Someone was sending Morse, and that someone was very close, to judge by the strength of the signals. He was not a trained operator, however; the lack of rhythm and speed in the dots and dashes proved that. Neither did the text make any sense: a series of five-letter groups that were doubtless in code. There was no acknowledgment from the other end.

By 11:45 Langendorf had the message form in front

of him, and while drinking filthy ersatz coffee went over it again and again. Not yet twenty-four years of age, the Hauptsturmfuehrer was rumored to have taken an unhealthy interest in youthful SS troopers, but he was nevertheless feared by most of his subordinates and known to be a devoted follower of Hitler and a relentless pursuer of the Reich's enemies.

Two things struck him immediately about the message. The first was the obvious one: that without the help of a trained cryptographer he was going to get nowhere. Code breakers were in short supply in Berlin at this stage of the war, but he thought he knew someone who might assist him.

The second point was less obvious. Although the NCO had no knowledge of the fake Klaus Bauer or the reason for his watch keeping, he had said that the signals were very strong. On the logical assumption that London was on the receiving end, that meant access to a powerful transmitter, no doubt mobile and therefore impossible to trace by direction-finding equipment. But it did lead to a terrifying conclusion: only someone of considerable rank would be able to commandeer such a transmitter, which meant that this treason—there could be no other word for it—was being committed at the highest level.

The signal was received in England at Bletchley Park, Buckinghamshire. The land on which this mansion stood had once been a Roman encampment and later granted to Bishop Geoffrey by William the Conqueror after the Battle of Hastings. The house itself was a mere sixty years old, and hidden in the farmland surrounding it were webs of radio antennas. It was here that the SOE, the Special Operations Executive, sometimes known as the Baker Street Irregulars, kept open lines of communication between the Allies and Axis/Axis-occupied countries.

Once on a message pad, the signal, still in code, was

handed by an orderly to the Duty Officer. This man, a
one-armed captain in his early twenties, recognized by
the triple-S that it was an "eyes only" communication
and by the prefix whose eyes they were.

He placed the signal in a sealed envelope and summoned a dispatch rider. Forty minutes later, in a house
in London's Mayfair, the envelope was in the hands of
Brigadier Greenleigh, known to most of his com-
municators only by the code name Nemesis.

It took Greenleigh less than three minutes to decipher
the message, which read:

To: NEMESIS   CVX/014/SSS/29000/Z/27.1.45
From: VALKYRIE
      AM READY TO IMPLEMENT OPERATION
      HORSETRADE AS OUTLINED.

In spite of its brevity, Greenleigh spent three-quarters
of an hour studying it and considering its implications.
Finally he picked up the telephone and requested an immediate interview with the Prime Minister. Although it
was by now well into the small hours, Mr. Churchill
would have to be told about this latest development
without delay.

The Prime Minister listened carefully. He was a good
friend of the SOE officer, but this was the first he had
heard of Operation Horsetrade since Valkyrie had
originally communicated with British Intelligence six
months earlier. As far as he was concerned it had not
gone any further, but now he was being told that
Greenleigh had actually made a clandestine visit to Switzerland and met with a German courier in November. It
could well be that the Yalta Conference, only a few days
off, was occupying most of his waking thoughts, but he
was very short with his visitor.

"I should have been kept informed," he rasped in his
peculiar lisping voice. "I should have been told that

matters had progressed this far. This sort of thing is a Cabinet decision at the very least. If it got to Mr. Attlee's ears that the SOE are trying to do a deal with a ranking Nazi, we should all be in trouble. He would never believe that I knew practically nothing about it. Neither, for that matter, would President Roosevelt or Marshal Stalin. Good God, the Marshal is already suspicious of Anglo-American intentions.''

"With the greatest respect, Prime Minister," said Greenleigh, "there was very little more to tell you before an hour ago. The Swiss meeting was merely a feeler, to see what our reactions would be. If the Ardennes push had gone better for the Germans, we should have heard no more about it. This signal is the first to state unreservedly that Valkyrie wants to do business. Besides, I had to check his authenticity. You wouldn't have thanked me if the whole thing had turned out to be a hoax.''

"Undoubtedly not," admitted Churchill. "There's no chance of that, I suppose?"

"None at all, sir. Via his courier, Valkyrie has already given us a mass of information which we were able to verify from independent sources. Now he wants to buy his freedom with more—much more.''

"I'm sure he does. But I'm afraid we're not in the market.''

Greenleigh gritted his teeth and recalled a rather unkind comment Lloyd Goerge was reputed to have made about Churchill. "Winston has half a dozen solutions to every problem and one of them is right. The trouble is he doesn't know which it is." The war would doubtless be over in a few months and with it, possibly, the old man's task. But the business of intelligence went on forever. Yesterday's enemies were tomorrow's friends, and vice versa.

"If I may make an observation, sir . . .''

"Please do.''

"It may well be that Marshal Stalin is suspicious of

Anglo-American intentions, but I think we should be
equally suspicious of his. According to the latest reports
his forward troops are within striking distance of Berlin.
I don't see him giving up any territory he gains, no matter what he says. When this war is over we don't want
the Russians sitting in our back garden. More important
still, we need to know where Stalin considers that back
garden should be. It could be Calais and it could be that
he's willing to fight for it, for all we know. All right, I
admit that's an exaggeration, but hard intelligence on
the Marshal's future plans is something Valkyrie can
give us. And please remember, Prime Minister, that he
also says he can provide us with a comprehensive list of
highly placed German agents in the U.S.S.R., those who
can be turned and who would be willing to work for us
when Germany is defeated. Such a list would be of
inestimable value."

"As no doubt are the location of Germany's hidden
gold reserves, the escape plans of other ranking Nazis,
and countless other matters," grunted Churchill. "Yes,
yes, Greenleigh—you told me all this months ago,
although I still don't fully understand why a German
should know more about Stalin's postwar plans for
Europe than our own intelligence services."

"Because this is not just *any* German, sir. This is a
man who has spent his whole life compiling dossiers of
one kind or another. He probably has a man or two in
the Kremlin itself. If he fails or has overstated his case,
he knows we'll execute him."

"An end I would thoroughly approve of," said
Churchill. "I don't like rats of any description, no
matter what class of ship they're deserting. I especially
don't like this particular rat. I know his record. It is far
from laudable."

Greenleigh sighed inaudibly. The old man wasn't
thinking straight. To hell with escape plans of other
Nazis, gold reserves and the rest of it, it was vital to

learn what Uncle Joe had in mind for Europe.

Churchill pulled at his dewlaps. "I understand your reasoning, Greenleigh; don't think me a fool. To your way of thinking I should even make a pact with Adolf Hitler if it could be of some benefit to this country. But I'm afraid I don't see it like that. The Nazis have caused us endless loss of life and destruction of property, and I intend to see they pay for it, every last one of them, with their lives. Besides, you're making the assumption that Zhukov will be in Berlin before Montgomery. I'm afraid I don't agree. I know President Roosevelt doesn't see the strategic importance of Berlin the way we do, but he has assured me that we shall be there before the Russians. I agree that our armies should push as far east as possible fast and in strength. That is what we are doing. Our 'back garden,' as you choose to put it, will be a long way from Calais, I assure you."

Brigadier Greenleigh was far from convinced, but Mr. Churchill was the final arbiter in such matters and could not be argued with. Nevertheless, when encoding a reply for Berlin he was careful not to shut the door irreversibly.

To: VALKYRIE   CVX/014/SSS/29000/Z/27.1.45
From: NEMESIS

      HORSETRADE NOT YET FEASIBLE. POLITICAL
      CONSIDERATIONS PRECLUDE IMMEDIATE
      DECISION.

      •   •   •   •

On the afternoon of March 30, after receiving a cable from Eisenhower in which the Supreme Commander defended his decision once again and stated firmly that it could not be changed, Churchill sent for the SOE officer. He got straight down to business.

"You've heard what the Americans are up to?"

"I have, sir."

"It seems that you were right and I was wrong."

Greenleigh was much too experienced to allow a trace of a smile to creep in. What had happened was yesterday's news; he was concerned only with tomorrow.

"It could have worked out the other way round. You were not to know that Eisenhower would not push for Berlin."

"I am the Prime Minister," said Churchill haughtily. "It is up to me to divine the intentions of allies and enemy alike. I did not do so."

Greenleigh remained silent. Churchill relit one of his huge cigars and exhaled clouds of smoke.

"Valkyrie," he said. "I assume you've been keeping in touch."

"Regularly, sir. Though his signals are somewhat longer than mine."

"And they say?"

"That his situation is now extremely precarious and that he needs a decision; that if we want to do business we'd better do it quickly. Bear in mind that he doesn't want to come out yet; he merely wants a firm commitment that we'll bring him out when the time comes."

"And you have been replying?"

"More or less that he'll have to wait."

Churchill studied his fingertips. "Tell me again what he has to offer and what he wants."

Seizing the opportunity with both hands, Greenleigh explained in brief, terse sentences.

Valkyrie wanted immunity and anonymity. He also wanted money. In return he would betray the whereabouts of other Nazis and the hidden gold hoards. But the major prize was a complete breakdown of Russian intentions in Europe.

When he had finished, the Prime Minister shook his

head wearily. "He's no fool, that's obvious. He knows my mind. President Roosevelt is not a European and is also a sick man. But my God, if it ever came out . . ."

"There's no reason why it should, sir. All told, fewer than half a dozen people are aware of the operation."

"What about those who go in and fetch him out and fulfill the other conditions?"

"There are ways, Prime Minister."

Churchill nodded. "I expect there are. Would you use SOE operatives?"

"Perhaps one, as a courier. But the state Germany must be in at present almost certainly means using troops. Only a handful, perhaps, but it would probably be wiser for them to be led by someone with extensive combat experience. Getting in might not be so bad, but getting out with Valkyrie in tow will be a bloody sight more difficult. It would have to be done fast, too—a commando-style operation; otherwise any information Valkyrie has will be outdated."

"Have you anyone in mind?"

"Major Lassiter, sir."

"Lassiter, Lassiter?" The Prime Minister recognized the name but could not put a face to it. "You've used him before, haven't you?"

"Frequently."

"Then you'd better warn him to stand by. You'd also better signal Valkyrie. I'll leave you to choose the words."

Mr. Churchill put down his cigar.

"I need time, Greenleigh, time to think this through and time to see if all the persuasive oratory I am apparently famed for cannot change the minds of the President and the Supreme Commander. I must ask you to buy me that time. If we are to do this, we must do it without the knowledge of our allies. But it cannot be done lightly. I am being forced to choose between allowing a Nazi thug to escape the rope he justly de-

serves and a potentially Communist Europe. Do what
you can.''

To: VALKYRIE   CVX/019/SSS/21000/Z/30.3.45
From: NEMESIS
            EXPECT FIRM POLITICAL DECISION SHORTLY.
            CAN VIRTUALLY GUARANTEE IT WILL BE
            FAVORABLE.

*Read the complete Berkley Book, available November 1,
wherever paperbacks are sold.*